Praise for Ann Warner's
Persistence of Dreams

"...another wonderful story from a terrific author...a romance filled with mystery...and the power of love. Once I began reading, I could not stop until I had finished."

~ *Kimberly, Coffee Time Romance*

"Persistence of Dreams is a wonderful title that hints at Charles's nightmares...and Luz's elusive memories. Ann Warner's smooth writing style charms the reader..."

~ *Camellia, The Long and Short of It Reviews*

"...wonderfully compelling. I loved the conflict...the little twists of mystery."

~ *J. Miller, Samhain.*

Look for these titles by
Ann Warner

Now Available:

Dreams for Stones
Persistence of Dreams

Persistence of Dreams

Ann Warner

A Samhain Publishing, Ltd. publication.

Samhain Publishing, Ltd.
577 Mulberry Street, Suite 1520
Macon, GA 31201
www.samhainpublishing.com

Persistence of Dreams
Copyright © 2009 by Ann Warner
Print ISBN: 978-1-60504-403-3
Digital ISBN: 978-1-60504-229-9

Editing by Deborah Nemeth
Cover by Scott Carpenter

First Samhain Publishing, Ltd. electronic publication: November 2008
First Samhain Publishing, Ltd. print publication: September 2009

Dedication

To my husband, my partner in life, my best friend, my love.

And to my critique partner and fellow author, Sharon Cullen, and my editor, Deborah Nemeth. Your thoughtful comments and suggestions challenged me to dig deeper and see more clearly. Thank you!

Prologue

He stood in the doorway—a tall man in a suit and tie with a hopeful expression on his face. Several women stopped eating or talking to look him over, but his attention was focused on one woman, sitting by herself.

Lucky woman, they thought, as the man made his way to her table.

The lucky woman's eyes met his. And the man knew he'd lost.

The temptation to turn around and walk out was overwhelming, but after a brief hesitation, he made his way to the table where Kathy was sitting and slid onto the seat across from her.

Her lips moved in a tentative smile of welcome, but her eyes were solemn. A solemnity in direct contrast to the gaiety of freckles dusted across her nose and the bright copper of her hair.

"Charles. Thank you so much for coming. And thank you for the flowers. They're gorgeous."

"I just wanted to set the record straight." That he was in love with her, even if she wasn't in love with him.

And clearly she wasn't, even though she didn't say the *I'm so sorry* that hovered delicately along the edges of what she was saying.

He had done the right thing, hadn't he? But then, once he'd discovered that Kathy loved someone she was estranged from, he'd had only two choices—stick it out and hope for the best, or cut his losses. Except, given the someone had turned out to be his best friend, he'd had one other option. The option he'd chosen and now regretted.

Kathy lowered her gaze. "Alan came to see me."

"I know. He called me."

"You're good friends, aren't you."

"The best."

She picked up a knife and began fiddling with it. "Then you must have known Meg."

Surprising how much it still hurt to be reminded of Meg, but she'd been his friend as well as Alan's wife. "She was his whole world. When he lost her..."

Kathy sat silently, waiting no doubt for him to continue, but he was finished.

"How...d-do you know how she died?"

No way was he going to be the one to answer that question. "You're taking a hell of a chance, Kathy Jamison."

"I don't understand."

Her eyes, wide and guileless, tipped him into agony. "You'll always be second best with Alan. He doesn't have a free heart. But I do."

Seeing the shock on her face, he realized he'd done an awful thing. But he wasn't sorry, not if it gave him another chance with her.

She laid a hand on his arm. "I am so sorry. It seems I don't have a free heart either."

Flinching from her touch, he struggled to summon the cool persona that stood him in such good stead with juries. "If wishes were horses, beggars would ride, wouldn't they." He stopped, to pull in a breath to expand a chest and throat that were tight with pain. Then he forced the rest of the words out while he was still capable of speaking. "Thank you, for meeting with me. For not leaving me hanging."

"You're a good man, Charles Larimore. Any woman in her right mind would find it so easy to love you."

"Just my luck, you aren't in your right mind." He maintained the light tone and even appended a smile, but it was one of the most difficult things he'd ever done. He picked up her hand and rubbed his thumb gently across her palm. The knowledge it was the last time he would touch her almost did him in.

Looking troubled, she met his gaze. "What about you and Alan?"

"We'll be fine. Might take awhile." Not that he believed it. "You know, I'm really not very hungry all of a sudden." He released her hand and stood. "You and Alan...just be happy, okay?" Without waiting for a response, he turned and walked quickly, blindly, out of the restaurant.

The whole thing was his own damn fault. After all, he was the one who'd helped Kathy and Alan reconcile.

And lost them both.

Chapter One

Luz made it through the funeral in the daze that had descended on her with her step-aunt's phone call. Her parents dead. In an auto accident. So abruptly and inconceivably that she still didn't totally believe it. Except some part of her must be beginning to accept, because the world had turned dark and frightening.

She longed to lock herself in her room, huddle under the covers and give in to the grief that had wrapped around her so tightly she wondered why she was still able to move. When she responded to the words of condolence, her voice sounded odd, as if her words were coming from a deep, hollow place. People hugged her, and their tears wet her cheeks, but she refused to cry.

The only thing forcing a normality she no longer believed in were her brother and sister. Marisol, only six, had some inkling, although she still didn't really understand she was never going to see *Mami* and *Papi* again, but Carlito, still an infant, had no idea what had happened. He still gurgled and smiled when she picked him up.

She made sure he was fed and dry, washed and clothed, hugged and cooed back at, surprised she could manage it.

For Marisol and Carlito's sake, she pretended everything was going to be okay, and she was beginning to hope that might eventually be true when her step-uncle, Martin Blair, stopped by the house two days after the funeral.

With him was a woman with a barracuda smile who wore a tailored suit and carried a designer briefcase. The two settled themselves in the living room.

"We have arrangements to make, Luz," Martin said.

Arrangements? Like they had to make for the funeral? But Martin hadn't even asked her opinion, or she would have told him *Mami* disliked the hymn "On Eagles' Wings" intensely.

"What arrangements?" Dammit, couldn't she manage two words without them wobbling?

"Ms. Ross from Children's Services is here to explain where Carlito and Marisol will be living."

"I don't know what you're talking about. They're going to live here with me."

"Now, Luz, you know that just isn't possible."

No, she didn't *know* that. Spots danced in front of her eyes, and her voice continued to betray her. "Why not? They're my brother and sister. And this is our home."

Ross and Martin's faces wavered, and the edges of Luz's vision darkened. She'd begun to float, when a sharp pressure on her arm and a push on the back of her neck jerked her back to earth.

"Here, keep your head down. Now, take a deep breath." The tucked and tailored Ms. Ross pushed on her neck with more efficiency than sympathy

Luz kept her head down, and gradually the ringing in her ears subsided to be replaced by Martin's voice.

"...parents' names, of course, but the bank owns a big piece of it." He sighed, still trying for sympathy no doubt. "I hate to have to be the one to tell you this, Luz, but there's no money."

Blinking, she sat up and pushed Ms. Ross away. "What do you mean there's no money?"

"Sweetheart, I know this is a lot to take in all at once so soon after losing your parents. But I'm the executor, and I've already accessed all the bank accounts. There's very little in them. And lots of debts. The funeral alone wiped out—"

"No!" Luz didn't believe it. Some people lived on every penny, but not *Mami* and *Papi*. Especially not *Papi*, who had arrived in Scottsbluff with Luz and nothing else. Besides, when they'd discussed where she would go to college, *Papi* had told her his business was doing well, as was *Mami*'s practice. They could afford to send her to Colorado College. Even if she hadn't won the scholarship, he said they'd be able to swing it.

"We'll talk about all that later," Martin said. "What we need to talk about right now are Carlito and Marisol."

"Yes," Ms. Ross added, after Martin nudged her with a look. "We'll try to find them a foster home together, of course, but there are no guarantees."

"Foster home?"

"Of course, dear," Ms. Ross said. "Since you'll be away at school, you won't have to go into foster care yourself. But I know Judge Smale very well, and he would never grant custody for two young children to an underage sibling."

Underage? She was nineteen, dammit. Old enough to get married, have her own children.

Judge Smale had to be an idiot.

She sat with her mouth hanging open as the significance of what they were saying sank in. No money, which she found impossible to believe. And even more impossible, they planned to take Marisol and Carlito away from her and make them live with strangers. She wanted to howl, but she was too stunned.

"So. We need to set a time for me to pick the children up. I'd like them to be ready tomorrow morning. You'll pack their things, of course."

The gall, the insensitivity, the idiocy, the evil. Luz ran out of labels for the outrage she felt. Martin was formidable, and she suspected this Ms. Ross was no pushover either. Highly unlikely she'd be able to change either of their minds.

The only option then was to pretend to go along with it.

She dabbed at her eyes. "Tomorrow morning would be awfully difficult." The tears were ones of rage, not sorrow, but she doubted either Martin or Ms. Ross could tell the difference. "I promised Marisol I'd take her riding tomorrow. This has been so hard on all of us." She continued to mop up tears, her brain going into overdrive as she tried to read how they were responding.

"I can have them ready for you Thursday. Please. I'd like this last chance, to, to—" A sob that was totally genuine cut off her words. Through the tears, she tried to gauge how her request was being viewed. Her step-uncle appeared annoyed, but Ms. Ross was attempting a compassionate look. A definite stretch.

"I'll compromise with you," Ms. Ross said with a quick glance at Martin. "You can go for your ride in the morning. I'll pick the children up at two."

Would Martin buy a quick capitulation, or would he be suspicious?

He looked irritably at his watch, and Luz decided she didn't need to lay it on any thicker. He'd bought her cooperation act, likely because he found it impossible to believe she would cross him.

As soon as Martin and Ms. Ross were gone, Luz put Carlito down for a nap. She came back to the living room and was surprised to find Marisol asleep on the couch. She hoped Marisol hadn't overheard, or if she had, that she hadn't understood what Ms. Ross's visit was about.

While Marisol and Carlito slept, Luz went methodically through the house collecting items and moving them into the trunk of her mother's car. First were the photo albums, but she also took linens, towels, kitchen supplies, a cooler filled with food, all of Marisol and Carlito's clothes and Carlito's stroller and high chair. She ran the dirty clothes through the laundry and added them to the growing pile of things in the trunk, all the activity giving her some relief from the rage and fear Martin had left behind.

As she packed, she thought about where they'd go and what they'd do for money. Then she remembered that *Papi* kept cash in the bottom drawer of his dresser, something she'd discovered while playing dress-up years ago.

With a sigh of relief, she found the black wallet had $320 in it. It wouldn't take them far, but it would get them out of Scottsbluff and give her time to plan.

She also pocketed the credit card she found with the money, then she gathered together *Mami*'s jewelry and went through *Papi*'s desk. Among her finds were the title to *Mami*'s car, Marisol and Carlito's birth certificates, and her own birth certificate and citizenship papers. Running out of time, she piled the remaining files into a couple of boxes.

By the time Carlito and Marisol woke up, she had the car packed. She played quietly with the children until dinnertime, and after dinner, she bathed them and got them dressed in their nightclothes. By then, exhausted, she curled up with

Marisol in their parents' bed and managed to doze until midnight. The alarm woke her, and she drank a cup of instant coffee and forced herself to eat a sandwich.

Carlito didn't awaken when she carried him to the car, and Marisol awoke only briefly. She backed down the driveway, heart thudding, and drove a block before turning on her lights. The gas tank was half-full, so she went to the nearest station and filled it, charging it to the credit card.

She was removing the nozzle from the gas tank when a car pulled in behind her. Her nerves stuttered, but the driver, a tired-looking woman in a waitress uniform, barely glanced at her. Sighing with relief, Luz got back in the car, and then with a burst of inspiration drove to the nearest cash machine and put the credit card in. As a pin, she entered the date *Papi* and *Mami* got married. The number worked, but the machine gave her only two hundred dollars. Still, it was a welcome addition to her tiny stash.

She left town, heading southwest, toward Denver. Maybe this was the wrong thing to do—running away. But she could see no other choice. She *had* to get away from Scottsbluff where Martin was in control.

The glow from the lights of Scottsbluff snuffed out behind her, and in the dark, reaction set in. All the fear and uncertainty she'd ignored since this afternoon began spinning inside her, making her nauseated. Not wanting to pull over and stop, she lowered the window. The cool night wind dried her tears and gradually the nausea abated.

It was still dark when they arrived in Denver. Technically, she supposed, she was now a kidnapper, and since she'd crossed state lines, not only Martin but the Nebraska police and the Feds would likely be looking for her.

She pushed the thought and the terror it brought with it away, focusing instead on the immediate—calming Marisol when she awoke to find herself in a place she didn't recognize, stopping to feed Carlito and change his diaper, searching for an inconspicuous place to have breakfast.

She found an inexpensive motel on the outskirts of Denver, and they stayed there until she sold the car. The silver Lexus was bought by a young executive who was thrilled with his bargain and not inclined to ask many questions.

With the money she got for the car, she had a cushion, but it wasn't going to last long. The steady outflow for rent and food was depleting her resources at a frightening pace.

She moved to a dingy residential hotel near a library and bus line and went to the library every day to read the newspapers. After they'd been in Denver two months, she found the ad for the Draper Arms. Wanted: Married couple to live-in and manage twenty-unit apartment building. In return for rent, said couple would be responsible for minor repairs, the cleaning and painting of units prior to rental, the maintenance of the laundry room, etc.

She took Marisol and Carlito with her to the interview, both to give weight to her claim to be one-half of a married couple, but also because she had no choice.

The elderly man interviewing her smiled with genuine pleasure at both children. "My, my. Seems you've got yourself a handful there." He stuck out a finger for Carlito to grab.

"Oh. Yes. But actually, you see, Marisol will start school as soon as we get settled, and Carlito is such a darling. He's really no trouble. And I'm a very good manager." She snapped her mouth shut, trying to clamp down on the nerves that were making her prattle.

"I'm quite certain you are, my dear. But an old building like this, it always seems like the toilets overflow in the middle of the night."

"I'm a very light sleeper. Well, with a baby, I have to be."

"And sometimes it takes a bit of muscle. Getting too old for that part myself. That's why I thought maybe a resident manager would be good. I'm hoping to find a handyman type."

Luz's heart sank. She didn't want to lie, but it seemed she had no choice. "Oh, the kids' dad is really strong. He'd have come with me today, but he's away on business. He'll help with any heavy lifting, of course. As far as repairs, though, I'm better at that than he is. I worked in my family's landscaping business for years so I learned to do all kinds of things. Plumbing, electricity, small engines, painting. Well, you name it. And I'll be available on-site practically all the time." *Stop it, Luz. You sound desperate. You don't want to sound desperate. It just makes people suspicious.*

She shifted Carlito, who was happily sucking on his fist, and smiled at the old man with what she hoped looked like confidence.

He frowned, looking back at her. The silence stretched until she was afraid she was going to start nattering again. Then he started to nod. "You seem a determined young woman. I like that. And your kids are well-behaved. Neat. Clean." He continued to nod.

She kept her mouth shut and crossed her fingers.

"Okay. I'm willing to give this a trial. Apartment 4D is empty, so you can move in today if you like. It's a two-bedroom. Nothing fancy, you understand."

She sighed with relief. She didn't know what she would have done if he'd insisted on references.

Chapter Two

Charles jammed on the brakes and peered through the windshield at the flashing lights illuminating a chaos of fire trucks, gushing water, emergency workers and onlookers. The center of all the activity? The blackened front of his apartment building.

He stared at the frantic scene, feeling detached, as if he'd turned the wrong corner into someone else's nightmare. But, no, that was *his* apartment, and the flow of water was aimed directly through what was left of *his* windows.

He tried to summon a feeling other than a vast weariness. Couldn't, because compared to the loss of Kathy and Alan, this new loss was merely one more difficulty he'd have to find time to deal with. He rolled his shoulders against a flare of anger and frustration. It wasn't fair, dammit.

Nobody promised you fair.

Yeah. And didn't he know that.

The fire smell seeped into the car, sharp and acrid, making his nose twitch and his eyes water. With quick resolution, he backed into a nearby driveway to turn around, then drove until he located a parking place two blocks away. He jogged back to his block and made his way toward the uniformed officer apparently in charge of crowd control, although the crowd didn't need much controlling. They were huddled well back from the fire line, their haphazard dress—robes, coats, and footwear without socks—labeling them tenants rather than gawkers.

A cameraman pushed by Charles, jockeying for a shot, and following him was a reporter from the Denver television station that claimed to always be first on the scene. Truth in advertising it seemed. The reporter thrust a microphone at the policeman. "Officer, can you describe for our viewers what's happening here?"

The officer leaned away. "It's a fire."

The reporter pushed in closer. "Is anyone trapped?"

"Do I look frigging psychic to you?"

The reporter jerked the microphone away and turned to scan the crowd. Charles, who was acquainted with the reporter and had, on occasion, been irked by the man's lack of attention to the issue of personal space, felt briefly like applauding.

The reporter zeroed in on a gray-haired woman who was watching the fire with a look of eager delight, and Charles walked over to the officer. "Nice camera work."

"We aim to serve."

"Charles Larimore. Deputy District Attorney." He extended his hand. "I live there."

"Lived, you mean." The words, as brusque as the handshake, held a touch of commiseration.

"Did everyone get out?"

"Far as we know. The lady who called it in did a real good job spreading the word." The officer pointed at a woman he'd encountered occasionally while picking up his mail. "We're waiting for a list from the landlord. Already got the info on those evacuated from the building. I better get you added. Charles Larimore, you said? Which apartment?"

"Three-fourteen."

The officer thumbed his radio and reported Charles's information.

"Do you know where the fire started?"

"Had to be the north corner area. That's where the flames were when we got here."

His apartment or damn close to it. And did that mean he was somehow responsible? But no way he could be. He hadn't used the stove this morning, and for sure he hadn't left a candle burning, which he'd read somewhere was a major cause of house fires.

He made his way over to speak to his neighbors. The ones from the apartments on his floor were all there, his next-door neighbor clutching a huge gray cat. Pets were not permitted in the building, and the tenants, mostly middle-aged, had no children. No pets and no kids, two of the major reasons he'd chosen to live there. An additional blessing at a time like this, not having to worry a child or an animal might be trapped. Although, seeing the woman with her cat, it appeared the no-pets rule wasn't necessarily the given he'd thought it was.

The cat scrabbled against the woman's arm and with a loud yowl freed itself. Charles made a quick grab, ending up with a handful of fur and a grip on the cat's tail. The animal snarled and snapped as he shifted to hook a finger in the back of its collar.

"Oh, my. Oh, thank you." The woman bent over to soothe the cat, which continued trying to scratch and bite him, all the while yowling loudly. He fished out his handkerchief, tied it to the collar and handed the end to the woman.

She smiled. "Oh, how clever of you. That should work a treat. Now Fluffy, you're fine. This young man just saved your life, you know."

Charles didn't much care for cats, especially ones with loud, complaining voices, but it would have been cruel not to stop the animal from running away. And the pleasure on the woman's face as she once again cradled the animal was a welcome bright spot in the midst of all the destruction.

The background whoosh of rushing water changed to a higher pitch and then ceased altogether as the hydrant was cranked shut. The firemen began to mop up with brisk efficiency, and he knew nothing more would be gained from standing around. No way was anyone getting into the building until the fire was investigated, and that wouldn't be tonight.

A Red Cross team arrived, and Charles returned to his car. He picked cat hair off his sleeve and then sat drumming his fingers on the steering wheel, struggling to hold back a flood of emotion. A mixture of grief at all his losses, and anger that he was being forced into even more changes he didn't want to make.

With an effort, he focused on the question of where to spend the night. If this had happened a month ago, it would have been easy. He'd have stayed with Alan. But that was no longer an option.

He shook off the image his mind insisted on presenting him: Kathy, in Alan's arms.

Nope. Not going there. A place to stay for the night was all he needed to be thinking about right now.

Okay, okay. Only ten-thirty. Not too late to drop in on another friend for the night. Except it would require rehashing the reason he needed a place to stay, something he didn't feel like doing.

A hotel then. Downtown was convenient but expensive, and clearly, he needed to conserve. He had renter's insurance, but this was still going to cost big time. If the destruction of his apartment was as complete as it appeared, all he had left were his car, what he was wearing, and the suit and five shirts he'd dropped off at the dry cleaners this morning.

With quick decision, he drove to the nearby Walgreens and bought the essentials, then he turned north on Colorado Boulevard and drove until he found an inexpensive motel with a vacancy sign lit.

8

The preliminary investigation of the fire at Charles's apartment building was complete. The finding: fire of suspicious origin. Charles, still stuck in a motel and struggling to cope with the fallout of losing nearly everything he owned, felt a flash of anger as he read the report. Whoever set the fire deserved to have everything he or she owned burned to a crisp and then turned into water-logged charcoal.

He put a realtor to work looking for a place in the same neighborhood, something furnished and ready for immediate occupancy.

"I don't think this is going to work," he said as the realtor shoved a pair of children's skates out of the way with her foot and got out a key.

"I agree it's not the most fashionable address." She opened the door and stepped aside so he could enter. "But you did say you wanted a place convenient to downtown. The only other furnished units I have are in Littleton and Westminster."

With a sigh of resignation, he entered and toured the small apartment. It was drab but adequate, and it would do as a temporary measure, with the emphasis on temporary. Besides, the price was right. And until his insurance claim was settled, it sounded like it was the best he was going to be able to do. Reluctantly, he signed a six-month lease.

കൗ

"Mister, can you help?" The small boy held out a shoe to Charles. A shoe that obviously belonged to the toddler who sat on the floor outside his door, kicking her feet in glee, her remaining shoe close to flying off.

Sighing, he stooped and accepted the tiny jogging shoe, maneuvered it onto the chubby foot and tied the lace. Then he settled the other shoe in place and retied that lace. "Does your mom know you're out here?"

The older child, now mute, chewed his finger and stared at Charles.

"Well, you need to let her know where you are."

Still no response.

Charles went into his apartment, but he left the door open to keep an eye on the two. In a minute, a woman spoke to them. From the tenor of her comments, it was obvious she was the mother, and they were absent without leave. He checked and found the two had been retrieved. Relieved, he shut his door.

കൗ

Drip. Drip. Drip-drip-drip.

Charles glared at the kitchen faucet. If it would just find a steady rhythm and stick with it, he could ignore it. It was the sudden riffs that kept snagging his attention.

He turned back to the papers littering the tabletop—a list he was preparing for the insurance company of everything he'd owned at the time of the fire. He was finding it surprisingly difficult, in spite of his ability to remember details.

23

Items kept floating into his mind, trailing regrets that distracted him—like the T-shirts from his Ironman competitions. They were all in pretty ratty shape, but they were what he'd worn when he went jogging, as a reminder of what he was capable of when he put his mind to it. He hadn't competed for five years, and these days, he'd have a hard time finishing a half Ironman, which made the shirts irreplaceable. Not something he could easily attach a price to for the insurance company.

And it was no easier to attach a dollar figure to the contents of the small clay bowl he'd bought in Santa Fe. He'd kept it by his bed to hold the stones he picked up each time he managed to get out of the city to ride or run in the mountains. It was a way of keeping track, he supposed. They were nothing special, simply ordinary bits of gravel he'd found on the trails, but they'd meant something to him.

Sometimes he'd held the bowl in his hands, feeling the smoothness the potter had worked into the clay. And if it had been a particularly difficult week, he would pour the stones into his hand and remember the pull of muscle and sinew, the labor of lungs and heart they represented.

There had been no stones added since he met Kathy.

He pushed the thought away and gathered his notes into a pile for later. The dripping sound followed him into the bedroom. Six months began to seem like a very long time. He was going to need every bit of it to get ready to move, though, given that so far he'd accomplished zip.

A good thing he didn't have to repair the faucet himself, or it would still be dripping when he moved.

∞

Charles opened his front door at the end of another long day to find the lights on. As he stepped in, a metallic clank and a muffled exclamation issued from the kitchen, where he found a backside sticking out from under his sink.

Not a burglar, but the elusive manager repairing the drippy faucet. The backside wiggled, obviously in a struggle with a wrench. With another angry mutter, he?—she?—backed out from under the cupboard, stood and bent over a book open on the counter.

Okay, he was going with a she.

Tall and rail-thin, the woman had a disheveled dark brown ponytail and was wearing retro clothing, although retro without charm: too-large jeans gathered at her waist by a belt and a plus-size T-shirt blousing over the belt.

She bent back through the opening, and he moved closer to look at the book she'd consulted. It was an illustrated manual of repairs.

He stepped back, wincing at the sudden screech of metal, expecting a geyser of water. Instead, the woman popped up again and turned on the faucet.

After the air in the line cleared and water flowed, she shut off the faucet and stood for a time, apparently waiting to see if it dripped. She didn't yet realize he was there, and he was unsure how to let her know without startling her, something he didn't want to do since she still held the wrench.

He settled on knocking gently against the door frame and clearing his throat. She whirled around, treating him to a front view every bit as unattractive as the back. The T-shirt sported several stains, the origin of which he had no intention of thinking about, and she had a streak of grime on her cheek and more streaks on her hands. Her only attractive feature? A whimsical look enhanced by narrow, rectangular eyeglasses that were slightly canted.

"Good evening, and you are?" he said.

"What, you were expecting Martha Stewart?"

At the irritation in her tone, the impression of whimsy faded. She met his gaze, her eyes dark with weariness.

He liked her voice though. A pleasant contralto with the slight lilt of an accent he couldn't quite place, and none of the little-girl squeak some women seemed unable or unwilling to give up.

"She's blonde, isn't she?"

The woman, girl really, sniffed and glared at him, and he regretted his attempt at humor.

"Mrs. Blair, I presume," he added.

"Ms."

"I expected you to take care of this during the day." He made a question of it with his expression.

She shrugged and rubbed her face on the sleeve of her shirt. "Sorry." She didn't look sorry. "I do as much of the maintenance as I can after the kids go to bed."

Kids. In the plural. But that "Ms." indicated there was probably no husband. Something he'd begun to suspect, since he'd yet to hear a male voice as he stumbled over the toys and tots outside his door. What he *did* hear when he arrived home early enough was child noise. A mix of giggles, door-bangings, and high-pitched little voices calling up and down the stairwell, accompanied now and then by the outraged howl of an infant.

So, how many children did she have? He suspected three, although it sometimes sounded like twice that.

"Why not have your husband do the repairs?" he said, remembering the realtor's sales pitch, that the other advantage of this building besides its being furnished was it had a married couple as resident managers.

She bent over to add the pipe wrench to the carryall of tools lying on the floor. "Maybe he has the mechanical aptitude of a brick."

Her answer was perfectly couched. In court, it was the sort of ambiguity he would hone in on until he obtained a more definitive answer. But in this situation, what was the point?

Ms. Blair picked up the book and toolbox, which made her list to one side. "It should be okay. Let me know if it isn't."

From the set look on her face, he decided he'd best not try to be gallant. He moved to let her pass, and as the apartment door closed behind her, he sighed.

He *really* needed to find another apartment.

Chapter Three

Madre de Dios. Luz leaned back against the door to her apartment. So that was the mysterious Mr. Larimore. Marisol had seen him, but she hadn't, and she'd ignored Marisol's excited descriptions—that he was *muy bonito*. Mari tended to easy enthusiasms.

But this time Marisol had, if anything, understated the case. That had to be one of the most beautiful men she had encountered outside of the movies. Athletic and fit-looking, but lean rather than muscle-bound. Hair a multi-toned gold her college roommate would have killed for. And that face. No question it must turn heads, especially feminine ones.

The wire-rim eyeglasses were the only thing saving him from unpleasant perfection. That and the weariness in those blue-gray eyes.

Or maybe they were gray-blue. She shook her head, trying to overcome the tremor of unease Charles Larimore's inspection had set off in the pit of her stomach.

So how long had he watched her? Her face heated at the thought. Glancing at her shirt, she noticed for the first time the olive and tan stains—peas and applesauce from Carlito's supper, or perhaps chicken and broccoli from his lunch. He'd smeared as much on her as he'd eaten.

She left the toolbox by the door and tiptoed into the bedroom to check on the children. The sight of herself in the full-length mirror stopped her in the doorway. The mirror distorted her image, and with only the night-light burning, that distorted image was indistinct. But the light was strong enough to show her why Charles Larimore had had such an odd look on his face when she'd turned around.

¡Sin duda! And to think she used to pride herself on her appearance. Added proof, not that any was needed, of how far she'd left her former life behind.

Now, she barely remembered what it had been like to have time to linger over choosing what to wear, how to fix her hair, or what color to paint her fingernails.

She blew the hair out of her eyes, continuing to stare at her reflection. The jeans had too much good wear in them to discard, although to fill them out, she needed back every one of the fifteen pounds she'd lost. *Mami* would fuss at how skinny she was.

Mami. No es justo.

A sob started its inevitable roll from the pit of her stomach to her throat. She clamped her lips shut and hugged herself to hold it in. She couldn't give in to tears, not when she was tired. So tired, she'd even told the new tenant she was Ms. not Mrs. Blair.

Besides, if she began crying it might wake Marisol and Carlito, and if they saw her crying, they'd start. It was just that today had been a really bad one. Three toddlers in addition to Carlito, and the visit to Marisol's school on top. It had pushed the new tenant and his faucet repair near the end of the list.

And she wasn't finished yet. She needed to do a load of laundry and clean the kitchen floor, which was inevitably sticky by the end of the day. Then maybe she could spend a few minutes on herself.

She stared back at the shadowy image and pushed at her hair. It needed a trim and conditioner, but she didn't dare spend money on anything she didn't absolutely have to have.

The new tenant didn't look like he had any money problems. His tie and charcoal suit didn't come from a discount outlet, if she was any judge. And he drove a Porsche. It was old, but still, it was a Porsche. *Ciertamente*, not the typical Droopy Arms resident. Well, that was what Marisol called it.

So how had Charles Larimore ended up here? Maybe he wasn't as well-off as he seemed. Not that it mattered as long as he paid his rent on time.

She sighed. Break over. There was laundry to do and the

kitchen floor wasn't going to clean itself, although tomorrow she'd have to start over with the same round.

She squared her shoulders. *Luz Cristina, moping is not mopping. Get on with it, chica.*

℘

Charles, on his way to court, recognized the quick tip tap of heels behind him. He slowed his pace to let Joanna Casey de Maldonado catch up.

"Hey, Shorty." Joanna pulled alongside and grinned up at him. "Heard you were wrapping today. Thought I'd sit in. See if I can pick up any pointers."

When Joanna first joined the DA's office, she'd amused him with her irreverent humor. After he witnessed her solid performance in court, respect and friendship followed. And when she made it obvious she considered him her mentor, he'd responded by taking her under his wing, a place where Joanna, at five foot nothing, fit perfectly.

"Save your time. Doubt this will be one of my best efforts."

She grabbed his arm to stop him, giving him a sharp look, which rapidly turned quizzical as her gaze traveled from the top of his head down, taking inventory. "Haven't I seen you wear that tie a lot lately?"

"Yep. Every day."

"*¿Qué pasa?*" Since marrying Eduardo Maldonado, she had begun peppering her speech with Spanish.

"I've got a few minutes. Buy you a cup of coffee?"

"Tea. And it looks like you could use the sympathy."

Yeah, he could. But it wasn't something he was in the habit of admitting. They went across the street to the coffee shop, snagged a table, and he told her about the fire.

Joanna patted his arm and made sympathetic noises. "Maybe you should request a continuance." She blew on her tea.

He shook his head. "I need to finish up so I can get started shopping." He'd been putting it off, but when co-workers started noticing that he was wearing the same tie day after day, it was time.

"What do you have coming up?" Joanna asked.

"Mahoney and Merrit look like they'll plead out, but Griffin's going to trial, week after next." Griffin was accused of molesting his fifteen-year-old daughter.

Joanna nibbled on a soda cracker. "How's that shaping up?"

"He claims the girl is lying, trying to get back at him for making her help around the house. I'm going to bury him." It was the type of case he'd become a prosecutor for.

Joanna bit her lip. "Poor kid. What will happen to her?"

Her tone was more musing than questioning. Besides, she knew the answer. The girl would go into foster care, and unless she was one of the lucky ones, she might never get over it.

"Sometimes..." Joanna looked away, crumpling the wrapper from her crackers and blinking rapidly. "I hate this job. Or maybe I hate that it's needed." She glanced at him. "Don't you?"

Her emotion reminded him of the impotent anger he felt when a case like Griffin didn't go well. He pushed the thought away, and spoke in a careless tone. "Yeah, it can suck, but it sure beats working for a living." To soften it he patted her arm. "It helps not to think about it too much."

"That work for you?"

"Yeah." Sometimes it was the only thing that did work.

ဆ

On quick breaks between court appearances and appointments, Charles had managed to do most of the errands associated with his move, but he had one notification left to take care of.

He dialed, then sighed in guilty relief when he got his mother's answering machine. Whenever they talked directly, he and his mother were like two acquaintances who'd run into each other and, after exhausting their store of small talk, were now desperately searching for a way to terminate the encounter.

"Mom, I'm calling to let you know I moved—"

"Oh. Charles. I'm here." The phone banged. "Sorry. I just came in. You were saying?"

Damn. Two minutes earlier he would have missed her. "I moved. I just wanted to give you my new address."

"Oh. Of course. Let me get a pen." She set the phone down, and he heard the sounds of her opening a drawer and shuffling through its contents.

"Okay. Go ahead."

He recited the new address.

"Is everything all right?" She spoke in the slightly breathy way she had whether she'd been rushing around or not.

"Yes. Fine. And you?" He didn't plan to mention the fire. It would only lead to a series of questions accompanied by expressions of false concern.

"I'm good."

Like him, she never shared what was really happening in her life.

"I...ah...I'm taking a course," she said. "At Pueblo State. I thought I'd try it out. See if I like it."

"Hey, that's great. I'm sure you will."

"Well, I know how busy you are. But thank you for calling."

"Sure. Good luck with the class."

He hung up feeling the familiar edginess that accompanied any conversation with his mother. Hell, he talked to dozens of people every day, in court and out, from the highly educated to the barely literate, and he managed all those interactions without one atom of the angst generated by a two-minute exchange with his mother.

∝

"Larimore, Casey, I hope you two don't have any plans you can't change." Lou Spinell, Chief District Attorney for Denver County, ignoring, or forgetting, Joanna's recent marriage and name change, rubbed his hands in obvious delight. "You both hit grand slams on your last cases. Showed you're ready for the big time. I want you on Maxwell. Larimore, you're lead chair."

"The man or the woman?"

"Both."

All right!

It was a horrific case, but he along with everyone else had been angling for it since the story broke. The Maxwells were foster parents of a four-year-old autistic boy whose body had been found buried under a sandbox in their backyard. Before that discovery, the mother had faked a seizure at the playground in City Park. An ambulance was called, and when she "recovered" consciousness, she claimed her foster child had been with her. A search ensued, but no trace of the boy had been found until the focus shifted from the park and environs to the Maxwells' residence.

The case had triggered a massive investigation into the foster care system, and the trials would be high profile. Unlikely, given public sentiment, that plea bargains would be in the offing.

His cup of tea precisely and Joanna's, too. He glanced over expecting to find her looking eager. Instead she looked uncomfortable. *What the hell?*

"I...that is, I need to clear out some things," Joanna said. "Before...b-but I am flattered you would trust m-me—that is, us with this." Her words stuttered to a stop.

Charles, not understanding her reluctance, but knowing how Spinell would react, jumped in. "We both need time to clear our schedules, put ourselves in the picture on this. Make sure we're set to give it our best shot." He winced inwardly at the clichés rolling from his mouth, but that was the most efficient way to communicate with Spinell. "I have a case coming to trial tomorrow, and Joanna and I need to go over the prelims on the Maxwells. Then we can meet, make sure we're all on the same page."

Spinell rubbed his chin, a sometimes ominous sign.

"Why don't we plan on...is Monday okay with everyone?" Charles looked from Joanna to Spinell.

Spinell, with a thoughtful look, nodded, and Charles stood and got Joanna out of there.

"You want to tell me what that was all about?" he said as

they waited for the elevator.

"I don't know if I can do it."

"What?" She had to do it. You didn't turn down a plum like this and live to talk about it.

"It's about a kid, Larimore. I don't do kids."

"Since when?"

"Since, now. Since I'm going to have one."

"You're pregnant?"

"What, you're not telling me it didn't cross your mind? Me always nibbling on soda crackers?"

Well, of course it had. He'd just hoped he was wrong. He didn't want someone as bright and talented as Joanna short-changing her career. "I thought you were on some weird diet."

She shook her head. "Men."

The elevator door opened, and half-a-dozen people stood staring at them. He took Joanna's arm and walked her away from the elevator, to an alcove where they had some privacy.

"Look, I know why Spinell's put the two of us on this."

She sighed. "Yeah, me, too. Female defendant, female defense attorney. He doesn't want to screw up with the jury on the gender angle."

"I was going to say, he did it because we're a good team."

"Yeah, there is that. I'm sorry to let you down."

"You're not letting me down. You're taking the case. You want me to tell you why?"

"I'm not taking it."

From the expression on her face, he knew how far he'd get if he told her she was committing career suicide. But there were always less obvious approaches. "That little boy. Davey. When he was alive, nobody stood up for him. Someone at these trials needs to be his voice. To make sure he's heard. It can make a difference, Jo. You know it. You also know you're the best one to do it."

"Not fair, Larimore, using an emotional argument on a pregnant woman. It's like using a Glock to kill a gnat."

He flipped a hand back and forth. "Whatever works."

She worried her lip between her teeth. "What if I lose it in court?"

He knew he'd won, and he breathed a sigh of relief. "What if? Say, isn't it about time for some more soda crackers? You look a little peaked."

"I'll get you for this, Larimore."

It worried him that she didn't smile, even a little, as she said that. But she'd be fine. She just needed to stop thinking and get started on the case.

₠

The first time Charles went downstairs to do laundry at the Draper Arms, he found both washers full of clean, wet clothes. Annoyed, he turned to leave when a notice caught his eye:

If washers have completed their cycles, clothes may be removed and placed in the blue hampers. L. Blair, Mgr.

So the woman might look like a train wreck but at least she had some common sense. He quickly transferred one load, mostly baby things, from the nearest washer to a hamper and started his own wash. When he returned a half-hour later, he found *Ms.* Blair emptying the contents of the blue hamper into a dryer.

Her appearance had improved considerably since he encountered her under his kitchen sink. Tonight, her face was clean, her glasses on straight and her ponytail smooth, although she still wore the baggy jeans. Her shirt also still had splotches on it, but it did fit better, verifying his first impression—she was as flat as a boy.

"I hope you don't mind." He pointed at the clothes. "I took those out."

"Of course not." She nodded at the notice. "I put that up. Mrs. Bayley sometimes does a load and leaves it for a day or so. She doesn't mean to. She just forgets."

He pulled his things from the washer, remembering the hatted and gloved elderly woman he'd encountered last Sunday, fussing with her key. He'd helped her open her door. Was she Mrs. Bayley?

"So what does the *L* stand for?"

She glanced at him before pushing in the coin and twisting the start button on the dryer. "Luz."

"I want to thank you. For fixing the faucet."

"That's what I'm here for." She put the blue hamper back under the table. When he turned around, he found her gone.

Her appearance may have improved, marginally, but her personality was still the pits.

ༀ

"Ladies and Gentlemen of the jury. Only a few days ago, Mr. Griffin's attorney and I presented our opening statements." Charles kept his tone easy and friendly, something juries liked. "He told you it was all a terrible mistake. His client never touched his daughter, never forced her to have sex with him or to have an abortion. That Janine's boyfriend was responsible." He paused, to look at each member of the jury in turn. "What a crock."

One or two heads nodded in silent agreement. If it wasn't such a disgusting case, their response would have made him smile. He was going to win this one, and it felt damn good. The only question was how long it would take the jury to fill out the guilty forms.

Janine Griffin had been such a compelling and dignified witness, his job had been easy, while Roger Griffin's defense attorney had had little to work with defending such a dreg.

A few hours later, at the reading of the Griffin verdict, Charles found his instincts had been correct. The jury convicted on every count.

It was cases like this that reaffirmed his faith in the legal system.

Chapter Four

It's a helluva chance you're taking, Kathy Jamison, Charles had said. And then he said the part that still caused her to awaken at night shaking. *You'll always be second best.*

If Charles had spoken in anger, or been trying to hurt her, she would have been able to ignore what he said. But he'd spoken in pain and out of friendship with Alan. A friendship she was responsible for ending.

"Kathy?"

Charles's image receded as she looked across the table at Alan's sister, Elaine.

"Are you okay?" Elaine asked.

"Of course." How could she not be okay? She had her heart's desire. A wonderful man she loved deeply, who loved her in return. She should be over the moon, but somehow she wasn't. Not with Charles's words weighing her down more and more as time passed, rather than less. "Actually, I've been thinking it might be better if Alan and I elope."

"Oh, no! Please. Don't do that." Elaine pulled in a deep breath. "Sorry. You took me by surprise there. But why?"

"It'll be easier for Alan."

"Did he say so?"

"I didn't ask him. It's just...really hard." Kathy loved Alan, and he loved her, but remembering the price they had both paid for their love, sometimes she couldn't stand it. She suspected Alan felt the same way, although they never talked about it.

"It won't be easy for any of us," Elaine said. "We'll probably all cry, but they'll be happy tears." Elaine stopped speaking until Kathy finally looked up. "Please. We all need this wedding. Perhaps Alan most of all."

Kathy pleated her napkin, and Elaine laid a hand on her arm. "Alan loves you so much, Kathy. I can see it in his face every time he looks at you. It's not a competition, you know."

"I know. But sometimes I can't help feeling..."

"What? What do you feel?"

"It's just..." She closed her eyes and took a shaky breath. "I...love him so much, it scares me."

"Good."

Her eyes flew open.

Elaine was smiling a sad smile. "If you weren't scared, it would mean you didn't understand what he's going through. Without that, you wouldn't be the right woman for him." Her eyes brimmed with tears. "The happiness you and Alan share. It will be all the sweeter for the difficulties you've faced."

Difficulties. Such a simple word holding within its syllables so much life...and death—Alan forced to watch his wife drown, unable to save her. And herself, loving Alan, but striking out in pain when he rejected her, pushing him even further away. An estrangement cast in stone. Until Charles.

God, loving hurt. But *not* loving hurt more.

"Will you help me?" she asked Elaine. "Make sure I don't pick the same colors or flowers or something."

"Of course I will. Have I ever told you how thrilled I am we're going to be sisters?"

"Oh, I think maybe you have. Once or twice."

∞

You have to be patient. Give him time.

Alan could easily imagine Elaine telling Kathy that. Which just showed that Elaine didn't understand the situation. Not that he had any plans to enlighten her.

He leaned on the corral fence next to Elaine, watching their father show Kathy how to halter-train a foal and wondering how much time would need to pass before he and Charles might try to be friends again.

Likely it was best to let it lie for a while. Give Charles's pain a chance to fade. Time was supposed to be able to heal anything, and maybe it did. After all, he'd been able, finally, to let go of his grief over the loss of Meg, to plan a future with Kathy.

"Have you seen Angela lately?" Elaine asked.

Angela Taylor, his therapist. The only person besides Kathy he'd talked to about Meg. "I was dismissed. Stamped 'cured'."

"Like a ham," Elaine murmured.

"Precisely."

"Kathy thought you two ought to elope." Elaine's tone was bland.

"Well, seems to me we're planning a wedding." Well acquainted with his sibling's conversational gambits, he had no doubt she was getting ready to skewer him.

"She wants to make sure it isn't anything like your wedding to Meg."

"And I suppose it's your extrasensory powers of psychological perception providing you with this information." He was not letting Elaine get to him. It was too beautiful a day.

"It doesn't take a PhD to see what's going on."

He sighed. Woman talk, he supposed. Hell, if Elaine pushed at Kathy with half the force she used on him, no surprise Kathy might have said something. Or maybe she'd said nothing, and Elaine was on a fishing expedition. His sister was, after all, an expert with the dry fly of innuendo.

"You need to reassure her."

Yeah. He knew that.

He slipped into the corral and walked over to Kathy, who turned and, seeing him, got that look that still overwhelmed him with wonder. He dropped a kiss on her nose.

"Both she and the foal are learning real fine." His father looked from Kathy to him with a contented smile. "She's almost good as you at gentling them."

"Has she earned some time off?" He met Kathy's eyes. Those mountain-stream eyes.

"Well, now," Robert said. "Depends on what you have in

mind."

"Siesta and Sonoro could use a workout." He reached out and smoothed his hand over her hair. God, he loved her hair. Red-gold and sleek as a thoroughbred's coat.

Kathy's mouth curved into a smile. "I thought you'd never ask."

As soon as they were in the barn, he pulled her into his arms.

"Did you really want to go for a ride, or were you looking for an excuse to ravish me?" Her breath tickled his cheek.

He nuzzled her neck, breathing in her sweet smell along with the good scent of alfalfa and horse. "Umm. Ravish first, ride after?"

She rubbed her head against his chin. "I have a much better idea. Let's take a blanket with us."

Alan pulled Kathy against him spoon fashion, not yet ready to get dressed and get back on a horse.

"You and Elaine seemed to be having quite a conversation," Kathy said.

He was being asked a question he didn't know how to answer, but maybe Elaine was right. If he hadn't taken her advice and talked to Angela, he wouldn't be here with Kathy now. "She said you were worried about the wedding." An experiment, really, opening that particular can of worms.

"Yeah." It was more breath than word.

"I can take it." Well, he hoped he could.

She pulled out of his arms and turned to face him, and a series of expressions played across her face. He concentrated on meeting her gaze.

She swallowed and focused on his chin. "I know it's hard for you. It's hard for me, too. Elaine said it wasn't a competition, but sometimes..."

He traced the line of her eyebrow with his fingertip, thinking how to respond without letting loose a curse at Elaine, who always poked her nose in where it didn't belong. No surprise she'd decided to do it for a living. "I hear what you're saying, I just don't know what to do about it. Meg was part of my life for a long time. I can't turn it off and never think of her again." He moved his thumb across her forehead, smoothing the crease between her eyes.

"I know. But what about Charles?"

He sucked in a breath, let it out slow. "We didn't mean to, but we hurt him."

Her eyes darkened, and a single tear escaped and made a silver track down her cheek. He focused on that, his thoughts as suspended as the tear was. Then it gathered itself into bright liquid and fell.

Tears. So many tears. And pain. His, Kathy's, Charles's. Enough pain for a lifetime. But it was Charles who once said what good was pain if it brought no chance for happiness.

And with that, the words he needed came. "You fill me with joy, Kath. So much that sometimes I feel like I'm going to burst with it."

He cupped her chin in his hand, the fingers of his other hand tangling in that amazing hair, holding her gently, his eyes meeting hers. "Kathleen Hope Jamison, I thee wed. To be my friend, my companion, my dearest love."

Her hand came up and stroked his face, soft feathering touches. "Alan Michael Francini, I *thee* wed. To be my friend, my companion, my dearest love."

He kissed her, tasting salt on her lips, then held her close, her head pressed against his shoulder. "Now all we have to do is go through that one more time for the state of Colorado. We'll probably have to be dressed though."

She trembled with laughter, and he knew. For once he'd got it exactly right.

Chapter Five

Charles was somewhere hot and dusty. Earth and sky heaved in a dizzy dance and someone was screaming. An abrupt switch to dark and silence jolted him awake.

As he lay breathing carefully, waiting for his heart rate to return to normal, the toilet began to fill. The sharp hiss lasted four or five seconds before it stopped with a click. Eventually he dozed off, only to be reawakened again and again by that intermittent hiss and click.

At five-thirty he gave up trying to sleep and rolled out of bed to go for a ride. His bicycle, which had been stored in the basement at his old place, was the only thing he'd salvaged from there. It was one of his favorite possessions, and he was glad not to have lost it. With it, he'd explored most of Denver's five-hundred miles of interconnected bike trails.

Once outside, he thought about where to ride this morning. He doubted he'd notice the scenery. Something simple then, like the Washington Park loop, where he could focus on the pumping of his legs and the rasp of his lungs. Two miles per lap, but he could keep circling until the repetitive motion and fatigue calmed him.

It always took a lot of miles to make him feel better after the nightmare.

80

"That's a really cool bike."

Charles had seen the little girl before and was pretty

certain she was a Blair. She had Luz's coloring and wore similar glasses, although hers had one of the bows taped.

She pushed the crooked glasses up her nose and gave him a friendly smile punctuated by a snaggly tooth. "It's good you wear a helmet."

She sounded at least twenty, which made her resemblance to Luz more pronounced, although she couldn't be more than five or six. Not that he knew enough about children to make an accurate guess.

"Ms. Blair, I presume?" He spoke formally, because he found talking to children awkward.

She giggled.

"I'm Charles Larimore. Your new neighbor."

She extended a slightly grubby hand. "Pleased to meet you. I'm Marisol. Aren't you cold?"

"I'm cold now, but while I was riding, I was very warm," he said, amused.

"Do you ride on the street?"

"Mostly I ride in one of the parks."

She sidled closer and reached out to touch the cycle with a finger. "I want to go to City Park, but Luz says I can't. It's too far, even if my friend Maggie comes with me." She wrinkled her nose, looking solemn. "There's lots of traffic, you know. It can be dangerous."

Odd, the way the child referred to her mother by her first name. It must be how children were being raised these days. "Luz is right. Getting to the park can be very dangerous."

Marisol cocked her head and frowned. "Why do you do it then?"

Were children always so literal? "I'm very careful, and I wear my helmet. And once I get to the park it's pretty safe." Usually, his biggest concerns were trying not to mow down any unsuspecting pedestrians or get a ticket for speeding.

Her face lit up. "I'll tell Luz. Maybe she'll let me go."

"Uh, Marisal—"

"Marisol."

"Marisol. Luz is right. You need to be with a grown-up to go to the park."

She gave him a hopeful look. "Maybe you'll take me sometime. When it gets warmer?"

"Marisol!"

He turned to find Luz glaring at the little girl. Luz was pushing a stroller and wearing a heavy coat that looked like it came from army surplus and would better fit a large man. She followed up with a sharp burst of Spanish, which explained the faint accent he'd been unable to place. She spoke so rapidly, he doubted he would have understood even if he knew Spanish, which he didn't.

Marisol scuffed her shoe against the uneven sidewalk, and Luz turned to him with a distracted expression. "I'm sorry Marisol was bothering you."

He nodded in acknowledgement, although it wasn't entirely true that Marisol had bothered him. He was intrigued by the whole interaction, though. After insisting she was *Ms.* Blair, Luz's Spanish accent indicated Blair had to be her married name.

He followed the Blairs inside, took his bike upstairs and parked it inside his front door. Then he pulled off his helmet and ran a hand through his hair. It was matted to his head with sweat.

He'd had a good ride this morning, but he had no idea what to do with the rest of his day off. He hadn't taken one in weeks, and he needed one, but the problem with a break was it gave him empty time to fill with something.

He had plenty of things he might do, of course—laundry, and the apartment needed cleaning, although he didn't have a vacuum yet, or even a dust-cloth. And it sucked he had practically no casual clothes. Not to mention he needed a haircut and groceries. Too bad that, at the moment, none of it appealed to him.

Maybe instead he could do something to make the apartment less drab. He'd disliked the furniture in his old place, which had been chosen by an ex-girlfriend in a fit of what he eventually recognized as nest-building. An uncomfortable mix of chintz and ultra-modern chrome and glass, it had made his apartment look like the victim of a decorator with a multiple-personality disorder. But this monochrome scheme of tan carpet, beige walls, and dark brown furniture was worse somehow.

He turned in a circle looking at the combination living and dining room, trying to decide what would make it more bearable. A couple of plants might help, although paint would be even more effective.

Probably only a woman, and an obsessive one at that, would consider painting a place she planned to live in only a few months. But what the hell. If it made him feel better, what difference did it make if it was weird. He didn't have anything better to do, and it would give him something to focus on besides the parts of his life he had no control over. Still, it wouldn't be worth it if he had to repaint it all beige when he moved out.

He took a quick shower, and before he could talk himself out of it, went next door and knocked. Marisol opened the door and grinned while Luz, coming from the kitchen, frowned.

The Blair apartment, sporting the same furniture and color choices as his, was neater than he expected, given that Luz usually seemed so ungot-together. Carefully squared piles of newspapers, magazines and a dozen library books covered one of the end tables. It, along with the other furniture, was pushed back against the bare walls. No television, but it might be in one of the bedrooms.

The only disorder was a scatter of objects littering the floor: pots and pans, a large cardboard carton and blocks. A toddler, a boy, sat on the floor chewing on a pot handle.

Remembering the two youngsters he'd helped with their sneaker crisis, he wondered if Luz could possibly have four children. But no way was she old enough. She looked barely old enough to be Marisol's mother.

"Do you have another problem?" she asked, cutting off his speculations about her domestic setup.

"Oh. No. Well, the toilet runs, but actually, I need to ask you something. I thought I might do some painting, as long as I don't have to change everything back when I move."

Her frown deepened. "You're here for only six months."

"Yeah. But the apartment's depressing. I have time, and it would be nice to come home to something other than brown walls every night." The unmitigated brown did at least keep dirt from showing, but in his opinion, as a decorating strategy, that ran a close second to the plastic furniture covers he'd grown up with.

"What color are you thinking?"

Marisol leaned against Luz, and Luz gave her a slight push and pointed at the toddler. Marisol flounced over to the sofa, watching Charles over her shoulder.

"I'm not sure. Something light. I need to pick up samples, but only if you tell me I can do it."

Luz tipped her head, looking more fey than usual. "I guess whatever you pick couldn't be any worse. Unless you're thinking purple or orange?"

"Of course not."

She chewed on her lip, obviously trying to decide.

"So it's okay?" he nudged.

She took a breath. "Yeah. Okay. It should be okay."

"You don't sound too sure."

She shrugged, looking distracted. "Well, if you make the place more attractive, that's a good thing, isn't it?"

Marisol came back to lean against Luz. "I can help you pick the colors, Mr. Larimore."

Luz spoke in rapid Spanish, and the light in the little girl's eyes extinguished.

He smiled at Marisol. "I would very much appreciate some help."

Her eyes shone. "Thanks, Mr. Larimore."

He wanted to tell her to call him Charles, but he'd already done enough to undermine Luz's authority. "When I'm ready, I'll let you know," he added.

He wasn't crazy about kids. Actually, he usually avoided them. But although Marisol, with her missing teeth and crooked glasses, had to be one of the homeliest youngsters he'd ever met, she was getting to him in a way he couldn't explain. The opposite of her mother, whom he didn't find the least appealing.

Luz laid a hand on Marisol's shoulder and gave him a questioning look that reminded him to get on with it.

He added paint samples to his list, and when he returned from shopping, Marisol was depositing a bag of trash in the dumpster. "I can help you," she said

"Thanks." He handed her the two lightest bags.

She followed him into his apartment and wandered over to the dining table where he'd dropped the paint strips. Frowning, which made her look like Luz, she laid the paint strips out like a set of cards.

He was putting away the pizzas when she spoke from right behind him. "I like Tony's Pizza the absolute best. Luz says it's too expensive, though."

He paused in the act of adding to the stack in his freezer. "What's your favorite topping?"

"Pepperoni, but Luz likes mushroom."

He shuffled through his pizza selections and pulled out the pepperoni one, then he rummaged in the sack of groceries until he came up with a can of mushrooms. "There. Pepperoni *and* mushrooms."

Marisol beamed, but then her smile evaporated, and she put her hands behind her back, refusing to accept the pizza. "Luz says we shouldn't take handouts like we're poor, because we're not. We're just temporarily economically challenged."

Her tongue tripped over the last bit, and he fought the urge to smile. "Economically challenged, huh? Well this isn't a handout. It's a thank-you. For helping me carry the groceries upstairs. That's an entirely different thing."

Marisol sucked in her lip and swayed back and forth a moment before grinning at him and reaching for the box. When he finished putting away his purchases, he found her rearranging the paint colors, although she'd shifted her base of operations to the sofa.

"Have you picked a color?"

"It's really, really hard." Her forehead puckered in concentration. "Everything goes with brown. Sorta." She spread the strips out. "It's like a tree trunk, so I guess...green. Maybe this one?"

She pointed at a strip of greens that varied from a pale mint to a deep teal. He picked it up, thinking about it. Maybe he could use the deep color on one wall and a pale tint for the rest.

"Okay. I like it." He pointed to the two colors and explained how he thought he'd use them. "If Luz gives you any lip about the pizza, you tell her you earned it. For helping with my groceries *and* as my color consultant."

Marisol giggled.

After she left, the apartment seemed drearier than before, but a guy had to be pretty hard up to miss the companionship of a six-year-old girl.

Charles was standing on the coffee table, doing the careful work of extending the teal color to the ceiling, when Marisol returned. Before starting to paint, he'd opened the door, telling himself it was to air out the paint fumes since it was too chilly to open the windows. If he was honest though, he would have to admit the paint had little smell, and the real reason for the open door was to encourage Marisol to keep him company, not an urge he could readily explain.

She grinned at him before disappearing. Then she was back, and Luz was with her.

"See. I told you. I said green would be best, and Mr. Larimore agreed."

Luz frowned. "I thought you were going to use light colors."

Her obvious annoyance ticked him off. Did she even know how to smile, for Pete's sake. "I'm not finished." Dammit, she said he could paint, and she hadn't said anything about color except the purple-orange thing, and no way would he do something that tasteless. He continued to dab on paint, ignoring Luz and trying, without success, to avoid getting the green on the ceiling.

"He's painting the other walls light green," Marisol said. She skipped over to the couch and picked up the paint strip to show Luz.

Luz glanced from the paint strip to Marisol to him, then she shooed Marisol toward the door. "Go check the laundry, *niña*."

"It's only been five—"

"Mar-i-sol." At Luz's sharp tone, Marisol, looking deeply offended, stomped out.

Luz turned back to him. "I've told her she's not to bother you."

"She's not bothering me."

"Well, it bothers me when she disappears and I don't know where she is."

He gave up trying to paint and stepped off the dropcloth-shrouded coffee table. He set the brush on the lid of the paint can and scrubbed at the paint on his fingers with a paper towel.

"If you're not going to use masking tape, you could at least use a putty knife to keep the paint off the ceiling," she said.

He raised his eyebrows, glancing at her. "More hints from the *Dummy's Guide to Household Repairs*?"

Luz's face reddened, and her eyes snapped. "You're only a dummy if you refuse to learn."

It was the sort of misstep he rarely made, and the best fallback position was immediate and sincere contrition. "Sorry. Cheap shot." Besides, he'd been wrong.

"Look. Marisol is...well, she's too friendly sometimes, and she tends to...and, I just don't want—"

"I get it," he said. "Hell, I'm a district attorney. You think I don't know what kind of perverts are out there?"

"Then you understand why I prefer—"

"I know you don't know me from Adam, but I can't hurt Marisol's feelings and tell her to get lost if I run into her." He had no idea why he was so upset. He didn't even like kids. Kids got in the way. They were a pain. So why not agree with Luz that between the two of them they needed to discourage Marisol from being his friend?

"Just leave her alone." Luz spoke with a clenched jaw.

Although he understood Luz's concern, it still annoyed him. "Okay. Got it. Now if you'll excuse me." He climbed back onto the coffee table and continued his painstaking effort to finish off the edge.

She left, but quickly returned. With a long-suffering look, she held out a wide putty knife. "Here."

He took it from her, trying to figure out what he was supposed to do with it.

"You set it in the crack of the ceiling and paint up against it," she said. "Just make sure you don't have too much paint on your brush." She sounded like she was giving instructions to the last person on the planet who didn't know how to use a putty knife. But after all, it was called a putty, not a paint knife.

"Thanks."

"You're welcome."

She left, pulling his door closed with a sharp snap that added to his annoyance.

It took a couple of tries to work out how to use Luz's suggestion, especially about keeping the amount of paint on the brush to a minimum, but once he got the hang of it he quickly finished the edges. They still weren't perfect, but if he'd had to go back to buy the masking tape he'd forgotten, he might never get started again. He also found the putty knife technique worked to keep paint off the woodwork, and it gave him a clean edge between the two colors. It was a clever approach; quicker and more effective than wiping smudges, as he'd been doing.

By evening, he had a green living room and a yellow kitchen. He cleaned up, pulled the furniture back into position and examined his handiwork.

In the early autumn dusk, the teal took on a jewel-like tone and the contrasting pale green made the room seem lighter and larger. The yellow walls in the kitchen glowed like sunlight.

Leaving his door open, he went next door to return the putty knife to Luz. "Thanks. It did make it easier," he said by way of additional apology as he handed it to her.

Marisol danced up, carrying the toddler from the morning. "Oh, can we see how it looks?"

Luz rolled her eyes.

"Why don't you all come?"

Marisol went ahead, and when he and Luz arrived, she was standing in the middle of the room, her eyes shining.

"It's cool, isn't it, Luz."

"It's very nice." Luz's voice sounded stiff. She took the toddler from Marisol and buried her face in his neck, hiding her expression. The toddler, sucking noisily on his thumb, turned his head to stare at Charles.

"Maybe we can paint our place, too," Marisol said.

"Maybe."

From the flat, cool tone, he suspected Marisol was about to get another economics lecture. "I've got paint left over," he said. "If you like the colors, you can have it. Seems a shame to throw it out." And exactly when did he get worried about throwing out a little paint?

"Thanks, but I don't have time to paint right now."

That's right. She was, after all, the woman who rarely combed her hair or changed her shirt.

Despite that, he had a sudden inexplicable urge to invite Luz and Marisol to have dinner with him. Strictly as a neighborly gesture, of course. If Luz got to know him, maybe she wouldn't be so concerned about him talking to Marisol.

But meeting the unblinking stare of the toddler, he stifled the impulse. Children who were potty-trained and able to carry on a conversation were one thing. Infants and toddlers were a whole other animal. One he'd just as soon keep at a distance.

Chapter Six

Charles Larimore was a district attorney? The only thing worse would be if he were a cop.

Since that discovery this afternoon, Luz had managed not to think about the implications. But with both children in bed and nothing to distract her, it hit full force, making her hands shake and her teeth chatter.

Madre de Dios. The man asked questions for a living.

ɞ

The Tami and Gary Maxwell cases, fueled by public servant angst and citizen anger, were progressing at warp speed.

After Davey's body was found, Gary and Tami quickly changed their stories to say he'd gone to bed with what they thought was a cold, and they found him dead the next morning. They'd panicked, buried the body and concocted the lost-in-the-park story in order to explain his disappearance.

"So what's our narrative going to be?" Joanna asked when they finished reviewing the evidence.

"The autopsy makes it pretty clear, Jo."

She winced, looking away. "I couldn't look at the pictures."

"But you read it, right? 'Small for age male, evidence of dehydration and severe malnutrition.' That didn't happen overnight." Charles pushed away the pictures of the shrunken corpse. It hardly seemed human.

"So why didn't someone notice?"

They never did.

"Let's run a timeline," he said.

They made notes from the various witness accounts organizing their findings on the dry-erase board. He finished writing, sat next to Joanna and they both stared at the board, examining the information.

He enjoyed this part of a case. The pushing and pulling into place of all the pieces, trivial along with major. Then the standing back to see whether he had enough to articulate a logical explanation for something inherently chaotic and inexplicable. He always waited and looked for it even in cases where explanations had already partially or fully emerged during the police investigation. Sometimes those early surmises were correct, and sometimes they were completely at odds with what this final sifting of the evidence revealed.

When he found that order, he had the fulcrum on which to rest his case.

This time, it was right there, staring them in the face, emerging out of the confusion of conflicting stories that had circulated in the media, and strengthening the hypothesis that one officer had written into his report. He waited to see if its inevitability would hit Joanna as it had him.

"Okay. Here's what we have so far." Joanna spoke in a thoughtful tone. "Five days before they claimed Davey wandered away in the park, the Maxwells spent the weekend in Black Hawk, gambling. They said they took Davey along, but nobody at the hotel remembers seeing a child with them, and the waitress who served them several times said it was just the two of them at meals, and they never asked for any food to go."

Joanna stopped speaking, still staring at the board. "They *did* leave him behind, didn't they."

Bingo. Give the lady a prize. "Keep going."

"They were gone two days. Do you think they left him food and water, or...house was a pigsty. One of the closets—" She stopped abruptly, an appalled look on her face.

One of the closets had been smeared with feces and stank of urine.

"I can't do this," she whispered. She stood and rushed from the office, a hand held over her mouth.

Maybe he'd been wrong to push her. But then, he hadn't expected it to be this bad.

Joanna came back ten minutes later, looking white and shaky She sank back in the chair and turned to him with wide eyes. "They left him. In that closet, didn't they."

"Yeah. Looks like it." Then went off to gamble, leaving the child to die in the dark. Alone.

They sat for a time in silence.

"I'll go to Spinell with you," he offered.

"What for?"

"For moral support when you tell him you're withdrawing from the case."

"I'm not withdrawing." With a stubborn look, Joanna challenged him to say something. He didn't.

"They're monsters, Charles. And we're going to put them away for a long, long, long time."

༄

Charles was shaving when the shower began to drip. If he stayed at the Draper Arms long enough, likely he'd awaken one morning to find the whole apartment underwater.

He knocked on Luz's door on his way out to report the problem, and Marisol opened the door. Behind her, four toddlers played on the floor with pans and blocks.

"Luz, it's Mr. Larimore," Marisol sang out before returning to the table to finish her breakfast. Her coat and a small book bag were draped on the second chair.

Luz walked into the living room, pulling her hair back. "Oh. It's you." Her tone was flat, or maybe that was his imagination. Still, she didn't look pleased to see him.

"And a good morning to you, too." He gestured at the children. "So how many of these are yours?" It was only a random comment, as he was pretty sure Luz had only two children.

"This is Carlito's play group." Her words and her slightly jerky delivery tickled his suspicions. Why was Luz nervous about him walking in on a play group?

"Is there something I can help you with?" Her expression had smoothed, and her composure was re-established.

"The shower started to drip."

She muttered under her breath, "Darn drippy arms," then she gave him a look as if to say, "So what else is new, Mr. Larimore?"

She didn't think he invented these drips in order to see her, did she? Because, if so, she needed to take an inventory of that prickly personality of hers. He shook his head, trying to push away the unpleasant thought. She obviously had her hands full. And clearly, his temper wasn't in any better shape than hers.

"I'll try to get to it today." She gave him the bright, insincere smile he disliked more than the annoyed look.

Suddenly, he'd had enough of her thinly veiled dislike, and he wanted to take a poke at that insincerity. "You or Mr. Blair."

The jibe was much more successful than he expected. Her eyes filled with panic, but so fleeting anyone else would likely have thought they'd imagined it. Charles, used to watching and waiting for such responses, had no such doubt.

"You're lucky I'll be fixing it." She recovered her balance as quickly as she'd lost it. "He's got the mechanical aptitude of—"

"I know. A brick."

From her startled look it was obvious she'd forgotten she'd used the line on him before.

"Well, at any rate, he's away. He travels a lot. On business." She fiddled with her hair, loosening it from the elastic, scraping it back, and re-securing it. That didn't fool him either.

He was now certain Mr. Blair existed only in Luz's imagination. What he couldn't understand was what purpose the deception served.

ॐ

Luz opened the door to find Cora Hartzel from 2B. A relief after the visit from Charles Larimore this morning. He'd stood there with one eyebrow slightly cocked as if he didn't believe a word she said. It had unsettled her, making her not only feel guilty, but look it.

Mrs. Hartzel, whom she suspected of putting on a hat and gloves to take out the garbage, was, for her, casually attired in a navy blue dress with white collar and cuffs. As always, her gray hair was perfectly styled, her face rouged, lipsticked and powdered, and she smelled faintly of lavender. She was clutching several books.

"Is there a problem?" Luz asked.

"Oh no, dear, no problem. I see you have a full house today." Mrs. Hartzel beamed at the group of children playing in Luz's living room. "You're going to think I'm batty."

"Of course not."

"The thing is, I used to be a librarian. And I thought perhaps I might read to the children. If that's okay? I miss it so much. I brought some books. The ones the children always liked the best."

Mrs. Hartzel's fluttery speech reminded Luz of a sparrow, hopping along the sidewalk looking for crumbs. "I thought it might give you a break as well."

"Why, it's a terrific idea. How sweet of you. They love being read to." Luz didn't know if it would give her a break, but she thought refusing Mrs. Hartzel would be cruel.

"Please, call me Cora. You know, dear, reading is so good for them."

Luz ushered Cora in, and within minutes her neighbor was sitting on the sofa, with children on either side of her and another on her lap listening as she read *One Fish, Two Fish.*

The elderly woman was good with them. She read in funny voices, and she was patient and gentle. When the story ended, she let one of the children choose a second book.

Cora stayed until it was time for Luz to put everyone down for their afternoon naps. The next afternoon, she appeared again, and after that, she came most days.

Cora's reading was a huge help, and it did give Luz a break to take care of quick chores. She felt guilty at times, thinking she ought to offer to pay Cora, but she simply couldn't afford it. The small amount of money she made from babysitting was already stretched to the limit taking care of Marisol and Carlito's needs. Instead, she invited Cora to dinner a couple of times a week.

"Do you have any children?" Marisol asked Cora at one of their first dinners.

"Oh, no, dear. You see, my fiancé was killed in the war."

Luz wondered how long it took to be able to say something like that so matter-of-factly.

"That's sad," Marisol said.

"Yes, it was. I was very sad for a long time. Now, I think of him as watching over me."

"Do you think *Mami* and *Papi* are watching over us, Luz?" Marisol asked later as Luz tucked her into bed.

She lifted the glasses off Marisol's nose and placed them on the table she'd found at Goodwill, then smoothed her hand across Marisol's forehead, swallowing the lump in her throat. "Of course I do. They're right here, we just can't see them."

"Luz?"

"What is it, *niña?*"

"I'm glad we're all together. I didn't like that lady who came."

Luz's gut clenched in memory of her terror when her step-uncle had shown up with the woman from Children's Services. She'd hoped Marisol had forgotten by now, but Marisol was too bright for that. Thank goodness Carlito was too young to understand or remember any of it.

"Luz, can Mrs. Hartzel be my pretend grandma?"

"You can ask her. I think she'd be honored." She leaned over and snuggled with Marisol, breathing in the sweet soap and powder smell of freshly-bathed little girl. "*Te amo, nena.* God bless."

Marisol chuckled softly, already half asleep. "I love you, too, Luz. A gazillion."

For a moment the memory of all their losses was so overwhelming, it was unbearable.

∞

"*No sirve.*" Joanna pushed back from the table piled with the files and documents from the Maxwells' cases.

Charles sifted through his tiny store of Spanish vocabulary. "What's not working?"

"I'm not pulling my weight."

"What's not to pull?"

She bit her lip. "You know what I'm talking about. The potty break every hour and the nap break in the afternoon." She blinked rapidly. "Not to mention I leave every night at six while you're here until seven or eight."

Now was definitely not the time to say he sometimes worked until ten. The Maxwells' cases being high profile hadn't meant he could offload the rest of his cases. He just had to juggle faster than usual.

"So, what's your point?" He pushed back from the table and rolled his shoulders to stretch them out—something he did every time Joanna took one of her infamous breaks. And a good thing, or he'd be too stiff by the end of the day to move.

"It's just going to get worse. I didn't realize it would hit me like this. And I'm barely showing."

"Seems to me, I should be the one to decide about the weight-pulling thing. And as far as I'm concerned, I don't have any complaints."

She cocked her head and narrowed her eyes. "You lie good, Larimore. So how's the shopping going?"

"Good."

"I'll bet. And the social life?"

"Shopping takes all my free time. And right now that's working for me." Since they were not only colleagues but friends, he'd been unable to hide for long the fact he wasn't seeing anyone.

She stared at him, shaking her head. "Yeah. Right. It works for me, too. But I'm married *and* pregnant. If word got out you were available, we'd have more clerks buzzing around here than a beehive with a super queen."

"And here I had no idea you knew anything about bees." He tried a grin, and she grinned in return, patting her stomach.

"*Estoy encinta.*"

And getting pregnant was the only misstep she'd made since joining the DA's office.

"So you tell me." He breathed a sigh of relief, glad he'd managed to deflect her, something she was too sharp to let him get away with often.

Maybe pregnancy *was* slowing her down. But whether she was completely pulling her weight or not, he preferred working with Joanna to her likely replacement, a DA named Fritchie who was nicknamed Twitchy for a very good reason.

Chapter Seven

"And Charles is coming for Thanksgiving, of course." Stella Francini spoke briskly as she stirred a pot on the stove.

Alan tensed. "I doubt he'll make it this year, Mom. He's been pretty busy."

Stella frowned, and Kathy held her breath. "Well, you just tell him he's expected, and that's that."

"Besides, it's his turn to do the Christmas puzzle," Elaine said, walking into the kitchen carrying her infant son.

"Christmas puzzle?" Kathy was relieved at the change of subject and that Alan's reaction had gone unnoticed.

"You haven't told her about that? Shame on you, Alan." Elaine gave her brother an arch look. "It started when Alan and Charles took an English class together, and the professor gave them an assignment to demonstrate the pliability of the English language. Instead of writing essays like the rest of the class, the two of them brought in puzzles. Charles's was a bare tree, a small one of course, with a cartridge hanging in it. He got an A plus, didn't he?"

"He did," Alan said.

"A cartridge in a bare tree?"

"A partridge in a pear tree." Elaine grinned.

Kathy, delighted by the wordplay, was also glad to see that Alan no longer looked tense.

"Alan got an A minus," Elaine continued.

"What did you do?" Kathy asked, playing her part.

Alan raised his eyebrows, ceding the storytelling to Elaine.

"He cut out a picture of peas, glued it to a stick, and stuck it in a flower pot."

"Peas on earth?" Kathy guessed.

"See. His was easier, so he got a lower grade. And you fit right in." Elaine chuckled. "Anyway, after that, they decided to take turns delivering a puzzle to each other every Thanksgiving. This year it's Charles's turn."

Kathy didn't think Charles would be doing a puzzle this year, but it wasn't her place to say so. It bothered her that Alan hadn't yet told his family he and Charles were having difficulties. She knew Alan was hoping they would work things out before anyone noticed, but lately she worried it wasn't going to happen unless someone gave it a push.

That thought was still with her the next morning. She decided to drive over to Charles's apartment to waylay him before he left for work, but when she did, she discovered his building partially gutted by fire and boarded up.

Oh my God. Oh no. He has to be okay. Please.

The next thing she knew, she was out of the car, standing on the sidewalk, staring at the devastated building.

An elderly woman came toward her walking a small terrier. The dog sniffed at Kathy's legs before wandering over to water a tree. The woman stopped and peered at her. "Are you okay?"

"This building. I have a friend who lived there. Do you know what happened?"

"Well, as you can see, there was a bad fire. But everyone got out safely. Your friend is fine."

Thank God. "Thank you. Thank you so much. I thought..." She smiled at the woman, only realizing once her panic abated that if Charles had been injured, it would have been in the news.

"Glad to help." The woman pulled on the leash, and she and her dog continued down the street.

But even if Charles hadn't been injured by the fire, he'd had a near miss, and she knew she couldn't let any more time go by without trying to set things right between him and Alan.

She called and pried Charles's new address from his receptionist by pretending to be a florist with an urgent delivery. The next morning she was at his new place at six-thirty. She discovered that, although it was located near his old apartment, it was a world apart in terms of amenities. Looking at the tired brick façade, she had difficulty picturing Charles here. But his name was on the mailbox for 4C.

Since the front door was ajar, she went in and took the ancient elevator to the fourth floor. Getting off, she squeezed around a young woman carrying a laundry basket.

"Can I help you?"

"I'm here to see Charles Larimore."

The expression on the young woman's face altered abruptly from helpful to guarded. She pursed her lips toward the door on the left. "That's his apartment, but he's out jogging."

She must be keeping a close eye on Charles to know where he was. Not that Kathy blamed her. Charles did tend to have that effect on women.

"I'll wait, if that's all right. Maybe he'll be back soon."

"Suit yourself." The woman, girl really, got on the elevator, and Kathy took a seat on the stairs, wondering if the neighbor's reaction meant she had a crush on Charles, and if so, what he thought about it. But, then, it was none of her business.

She pulled out an envelope containing a manuscript submitted to Calico Cat Books and began reading. She was on page seven when Charles's neighbor came back upstairs. At page fifteen, she heard rapidly ascending footsteps. She looked over the banister to see Charles's head bobbing up from the floor below. A moment later, he reached the landing below her and stopped abruptly.

Blinking rapidly, perhaps hoping she'd disappear between one blink and the next—which now that she was facing him was her choice as well—he ran a hand through his hair, making it stick up.

"I brought rolls." She held up the brown paper bag trying to appear casual, although her heart was pounding. "Homemade cinnamon." She was glad she'd thought to bring them. An icebreaker of sorts.

His shoulders slumped, and he came up the last of the steps slowly, pulling a key out of the pocket of his jogging pants.

Given the obvious age and condition of the building, she

was surprised by his apartment. True, the furniture was ugly, but colorful pillows on the couch acted as both camouflage for its lack of style and as a pleasant contrast to the green walls. It was in sum much homier and more attractive than his old place. And did he decorate it himself this time, or had he had assistance? Perhaps the young woman with the laundry and the worried look had helped.

"Coffee?" He walked ahead of her into the kitchen.

"Please."

He poured a cup and handed it to her. "Give me a minute, will you." He disappeared into the bedroom, and shortly afterward the shower started.

She took a deep breath, trying for calm. Okay, she'd known this would be difficult, but she hadn't known seeing him would make her so nervous. She unclenched her hands from the cup and set it down in order to put the bag of rolls in the microwave. After warming them briefly, she transferred them to a plate and poured him orange juice and coffee. Then she sat, sipping her own coffee, breathing in the warm cinnamon smell, and willing her heart to slow down.

Charles came out of the bedroom dressed for work. He looked at the food sitting on the table and, with a sigh, sat across from her. "So why are you here, Kathy Jamison?"

Now that the moment had arrived, words failed her. She bit her lip, trying to decide how to begin. Charles drank the juice, picked up a roll and began to eat.

"I was sorry to see your apartment burned."

"Yeah. Hell of a thing. I did need to redecorate, though."

"Pretty extreme approach, don't you think?"

His lips twitched, and although it was fleeting, she took it as a good sign.

"You and Alan." Her mouth went abruptly dry. She took a sip of coffee, but it didn't help. "He misses you."

"Yeah?" Charles finished the roll without looking at her.

"He's waiting for you to say it's okay. To be friends again."

Charles picked up a second roll.

"You said the two of you would be okay, but you're not. He needs you to... Call him. Please." The one thing she was not going to say was, "Do it for me." No telling how Charles might react if she did.

He took a bite of roll without looking at her.

"It's your turn to do the Christmas puzzle." It was her last shot.

He gave her a quick, hard glance before putting the roll down, picking up the mug of coffee and hiding behind it.

Desperate, she said the first thing that popped into her head. "Did you have a decorator this time?"

He glanced around as if he was assessing the apartment for the first time. His lips curved. "Sure did. Marisol. She's six."

It was Kathy's turn to be surprised. "Well she did a great job." And perhaps it was best to leave it at that. "Thanks for the coffee."

He gestured at the cinnamon rolls. "You ever want to drop off any more of these, feel free."

She pulled her coat on, gathered her things and left him starting on his third roll.

&

Luz had begun to wonder if Charles Larimore might be gay. After all, what self-respecting heterosexual male spent a weekend painting an apartment he intended to live in only six months? And pale green no less.

But then a woman came to see him. Luz had left her door slightly open, so she'd seen Charles's face when he first spotted the woman. It was most definitely the reaction of a man to someone he was attracted to.

Not that Luz was much of an expert on men. A non-expert, actually, given her lack of success to date. *Mami* always said she had beautiful bones and, as soon as she stopped growing and caught up to herself, men would be stumbling all over themselves to ask her out.

That wasn't exactly what she wanted, but it might be nice if occasionally a man like Charles realized she was a woman. Instead, the best she seemed able to elicit from him were quick glances or an assessing look that reminded her she sure didn't need a district attorney wondering about her.

But even if she did happen to interest a man, no way would she be able to manage the casual liaisons most of her contemporaries talked about. Better then if men viewed her with disinterest. Actually, it had distinct advantages. No worries about pregnancy or nasty diseases.

Probably most people would consider her views weird, so when she'd got together with the other women in the dorm to chat about boyfriends, sex, herpes, and the latest lit assignment, she'd offered comments only on the lit assignment.

Now, struggling to keep her family together, she didn't have time to consider dating. Well, not to mention there wasn't anyone for her to date. The Draper Arms was mostly populated by single women, with and without kids, and couples on the downside of fifty.

Charles Larimore was the only anomaly. A temporary one at that. Apparently single. Reasonably young, although probably still too old for her. Usually so formally dressed, she'd begun thinking of him as Cora Hartzel's secret son.

In college, he had to have been one of those jock types who swaggered around campus, so assured of his devastating good looks he only talked to and dated the most gorgeous women. A group she hadn't even belonged on the fringes of, in spite of her beautiful bones.

But now, feeling her heart sink at the memory of the expression on his face when he saw the woman waiting for him on the stairs, she realized. She had begun to develop hopes about Charles.

Hopes that were at best useless, at worst, dangerous.

୪

Charles was expecting it to be a good day. The high point would be the sentencing hearing for Roger Griffin, the man who had forced his daughter to live as his wife for five years.

The court settled into place, and the judge read through the charges, assigning a sentence to each one. Charles, adding up the years as the judge read them out, was pleased with the total. Roger Griffin wasn't going to be eligible for parole until he was ninety.

"Furthermore, it is the decision of the court that the sentences run concurrently."

Charles was certain he had misheard. If the sentences ran concurrently, Roger Griffin would serve, at the most, five years. Roughly a year for every year of hell he'd put his daughter through.

Griffin's attorney leaned over and whispered in his client's ear, and Griffin began to grin.

Sometimes it didn't pay to get up in the morning.

&

Charles pulled off his glasses and rubbed his eyes. Joanna had left for the day an hour ago, after making him promise to leave soon himself. They'd been working on their strategies for the hearing Monday. As expected, because of the overwhelming media attention, both Tami and Gary Maxwell's public defenders had petitioned for changes of venue.

Charles was planning to argue that the Maxwells had invited all the attention by falsely reporting Davey missing in City Park. In fact, they'd positively courted it with several tearful pleas for Davey's safe return. He also planned to argue it wouldn't be known if an impartial jury could or could not be seated until they tried it. That the best test of a juror's willingness to judge the case on what would be presented in court was to ask the potential juror.

The judge they'd drawn rarely granted changes of venue, so he wasn't worried the ruling would go against them. Still, it paid to be prepared and have his arguments lined up.

He leaned back, stretching, staring at the piles of paper on the conference table. *A veritable blizzard, burying the intrepid man of jurisprudence and hiding the barn where he will find warmth and safety.*

Okay, okay bad analogy, because if it was one thing he avoided it was a barn and, more specifically, the animals it housed.

Odd then, that he and Alan Francini had managed to be such good friends, since barns and the large, dangerous animals living in them were Alan's passion. In turn, Alan had little interest in triathlons or vintage Porsches which, outside of work, were his interests. What he and Alan *had* shared were Rockies baseball, holidays, regular lunches, a love of reading and memories of Meg.

And now Kathy.

Lord, it had been a shock, finding Kathy on his stairs the other morning. Seeing her without warning had shaken him profoundly.

Taken separately, none of her features was particularly striking, except for her hair, which was the rich red-gold of fresh copper. But when Kathy focused her attention on him, something magical happened.

Used to happen.

Nope. Still happened.

He sighed.

It would all work out eventually, he supposed, given the depth of friendship he and Alan shared. More than most men did, and possibly more than many married couples.

Besides, marriage wasn't for him, especially the part to do with kids. Although he had begun to rethink all that after he fell in love with Kathy. Before her, he would have said he'd been in love a half-dozen times, but she showed him he'd been only attracted. His libido involved, not his heart.

So would he have passed on meeting Kathy if he'd known how it would all turn out?

Well, he had learned something of value, he supposed. Highly unlikely that he'd mistake lust and love again. Maybe it was why so many people divorced. They'd confused the two. But what if there was only one person for him to love, and she was now out of reach. What then?

He cut off the thought. It didn't do a bit of good. If he planned to go down that road, he might as well pack it in. But such a course was as impossible to consider as stopping halfway through a competition because of the exhaustion creeping through his body making it heavy and numb.

It was the reason he used to compete, and why he still

pushed himself hard on workouts and on the job. Because when he was tired enough, everything went numb, including his emotions.

℘

The ruling came down on Gary Maxwell's request for a change of venue. As Charles had expected, the judge denied the request and set a trial date for early in the new year.

With the ruling on Gary out of the way, Charles didn't expect any difficulty with Tami Maxwell's change-of-venue request, since it would be heard by the same judge. Joanna would handle it, using the same arguments.

It meant he was again able to turn his attention to the rest of his caseload. It was the one constant in this job, the heavy workload. Still, it kept him from boredom and gave him the perfect excuse to limit his social life when he wanted to, and lately that was what he'd wanted.

But a week after Kathy's visit, he finally got tired of feeling guilty. He called Alan and invited him to lunch at an Indian restaurant. Personally, he preferred Italian; but if one intended to reconcile, one should be willing to go all out.

At the Tandoor, Alan perused the menu. Charles didn't know why Alan bothered since he always ordered the same thing. "So how's life treating you?" A stupid question. All Charles had to do was look at Alan's face to know the answer. Unlike other lunches since Meg's death, when Alan had refused to meet his eyes and had looked tired and strained, today his expression was calm and happy, and Charles was the one averting his gaze.

"I'm writing again," Alan said.

"That's good. Real good. I'm glad to hear it."

Alan had stopped writing after Meg's death and had been unable to start again even to secure tenure. So writing again was huge, further proof Alan had finally dealt with the memories that had trapped him for so long. Although Charles already knew that had to be the case, given the reconciliation with Kathy.

The waiter took their orders, and Charles glanced over at Alan to find his friend regarding him with a worried expression.

"The new case must be a doozy. You look exhausted."

"Thanks." He resisted the urge to rub away the odd dislocation of Alan worrying about him, after he'd spent years worrying about Alan. Okay, and now he understood why Alan had hated it. "Actually, I'm worn out from shopping. My old place burned."

"What? When did that happen?"

So Kathy hadn't shared that she'd come to see him. Not that he'd expected her to, given her mission. "In early September. I'm now living at a place called the Draper Arms. Actually, it would be more appropriate to call it the Dreadful Arms. Still it's better than living in my car and cheaper than a Holiday Inn."

"I'm sorry about that." Alan glanced away, obviously uncomfortable. "Mom wants me to invite you for Thanksgiving."

Charles shook his head. He knew from Alan's tone he expected a refusal and wouldn't push.

"I wanted to be able to tell her I asked."

"Yeah. And if she suggests it again for Christmas you can just reference this conversation." Christ, he sounded bitter. He wasn't, not really. He just hurt like hell. "Sorry. The Maxwell cases are getting to me. Damned if I wouldn't ask for the death penalty if I could."

Alan let him get away with the change of subject, and they stuck with generalities while they ate, then Alan pushed his empty plate away and spoke quickly. "We've set a date for the wedding."

Charles realized he'd still been hanging onto a thread, a cobweb of hope—the slim possibility Kathy and Alan might not get married. After all, Alan had so much baggage, it would take a considerable amount of time to unpack it, and during that unpacking, Kathy might change her mind about marrying him. But if they'd set a date, it made that possibility infinitely fainter.

"Congratulations." He followed the word with a swallow of iced tea so Alan wouldn't expect him to say anything more.

"Yes. Well." Alan cleared his throat and shifted slightly.

For a moment, Charles, still raw over the loss of Kathy, was pleased at Alan's discomfort.

"I want my best friend there. As my best man."

He hadn't seen it coming. He blew out a breath and made himself sit still. "I ahh..." *I can't.* How did a red-blooded American male who'd finished several Ironman competitions admit something like that?

Answer: He didn't.

"When is it?" He had an overpowering urge to run a finger around his neck to loosen his collar. He picked up his iced tea as a distraction, hoping his brain would kick in with a halfway rational excuse to save him from something with all the potential joy of an execution.

"In May. Right before Mom's birthday."

Okay. There it was. Birthday. Always possible to come up with a wonderful excuse if a family celebration was involved.

"What day have you picked?"

"The twentieth."

"Let me check." He pulled out his pocket calendar and pretended to find his May schedule, running through possible scenarios. "Nope. Can't do it. It's my grandmother's seventy-fifth. We're all gathering in..." *What was far enough away it would preclude making a quickie trip back to Denver? Ah yes...* "Nova Scotia to celebrate."

"Nova Scotia? Your family lives in Pueblo, and besides you never go see them."

That was the problem with good friends. They knew all your secrets. "This is special. Grannie came from Nova Scotia." With that, his voice settled into its usual rhythms and more ideas started to flow. "She always wanted to go back, but never made it. Finally, she decided, she wasn't getting any younger. I've been commanded to be present."

"I was hoping we'd figure it out."

Alan's tone put a stop to his mental search for more embellishments, and he was a half-second too slow. "Figure what out?"

"How to be friends again. None of us was trying to hurt the other, but we've done a damn fine job of it."

Charles stiffened. "Low blow, Francini."

"It would mean the world to Kathy. She's feeling guilty as hell about the mess we're in."

"Even lower."

Alan's eyebrows went up. "No lower than you used on me a time or two."

"Well, I don't see how I can fly back from Nova Scotia for the day. Isn't it enough to wish you well? I'll send a big splashy present. You explain it all to Kathy."

"Kathy has an even finer bullshit detector than you or I do, Larimore. Suck it up and say, 'yes, Alan, of course I'll be there, Alan, how high, Alan'?"

"Screw you, Francini."

"Good. I'm glad that's settled." Alan motioned for the check.

Charles had told Kathy he and Alan would be fine, and he was relieved to discover it was the truth. Or it would be eventually, although he still didn't know how he'd get through the actual wedding. Thank God he had seven months to work on it.

He'd manage it somehow. Clearly, his nonexistent Grannie's seventy-fifth notwithstanding, he had no choice.

ೞ

Luz rang the doorbell of apartment 2B. A click was followed by the recorded sound of frenzied barking, which usually made her smile. "It's okay, Cora. It's Luz."

With a click, the barking stopped abruptly, and was followed by the snicking of bolts and sliding of chains. The door opened a crack, and Cora Hartzel peered out.

"Can I come in?" Luz held out a plate. "I brought you chocolate chip cookies."

"Of course, dear. How lovely. Why don't I make us a cup of tea."

"I can't stay long, but I need to tell you something. The landlord said your rent check bounced this month." This was the part of the manager's job she hated. Hated with a passion.

A panicked expression flitted through Cora's eyes, and her

hand covered her mouth. "Oh. Oh, dear. Well, I can't imagine why that would be."

"I told him there had to be a mistake. You're one of our best tenants."

Cora's hand dropped, leaving behind a stricken expression, then she walked over to her desk. She sifted through the contents of a drawer for a moment before turning back to Luz, her hands empty. "The truth is, dear. I don't have the money right now. You see, I did something very silly."

When Cora finished explaining, Luz was as upset as her elderly neighbor. "I need to get back upstairs. I left Mari with Carlito, and he'll be waking soon. Why don't you come up in a few minutes, and we'll talk some more about this."

Luz went thoughtfully upstairs. She was familiar with the Turner financial scandal from reading the *Denver Post*. Poor Cora, losing everything. Although thousands of others had also been scammed, likely that wasn't much consolation when you were left with only an inadequate social security check to live on.

Luz knew how it felt to scrabble from day to day, trying to feed and clothe, hoping and praying nobody needed a doctor, because it would tip them right over. And knowing what it was like, she couldn't possibly turn Cora onto the street. Besides, Cora was Mari's honorary grandmother, and Luz wasn't about to turn her back on family. She didn't have all that much left.

By the time Cora knocked timidly, Luz had a plan. Since Cora's apartment was a studio, moving the elderly woman to their second bedroom would be easy. And if they put off Cora's actual move for a day or so, Luz would even have time to fix up the room with the leftover paint Charles had insisted on giving them.

Chapter Eight

Working on the Maxwell case was making Charles hypersensitive to the issue of nutrition. He found the best way to erase the image of Davey's emaciation was to see others eating heartily. Joanna wasn't helping his obsession. She nibbled at food and complained the smell of meat or anything fried nauseated her.

He also found himself eyeing his Draper Arms neighbors. Most of the women and their kids were, if anything, overweight. Except for Luz and Marisol. They were thin and sallow, and to his newly-awakened perception, they looked like they weren't getting enough to eat. The thought began to gnaw at him whenever he opened his refrigerator.

He occasionally shopped at a warehouse store for paper products and cleaning supplies, but the food items were packaged in large portions, making them impractical for a person living alone. It occurred to him he might buy some items and ask Luz to help out by taking half. Although, given Marisol's hesitation in accepting the pizza, he would need to find a way to convince Luz sharing would be doing him a favor, and not the other way around.

He stopped at the store on Wednesday evening and put his plan into action. The large family-sized trays of lasagna came in a two-pack, as did the pot roasts. Pizzas were in packages of six. *Yeah. Definitely a plan.* No way would all this fit in his freezer. He added bags of onions and potatoes, a large package of strawberries and a box of apples to ensure the refrigerator would be full as well.

Satisfied, he drove home, his trunk bulging. He placed half the frozen dinners in his freezer and left the remainder sitting on his table. The apples, strawberries, onions, and potatoes he divided into two batches. Then he went to talk to Luz.

She answered the door, frowning as she always did when she saw it was him.

"I'm in desperate need of your help."

Her shoulders drooped slightly, and she gave him a resigned look. "What's leaking now?"

"Nothing. Come see. You don't need your toolbox, and it'll take only a minute."

Marisol came out of the bedroom dressed in a flannel nightgown. "Oh hi, Mr. Larimore. It's nice to see you again."

"It's nice to see you, too, Marisol."

"Mari, I need to check something next door. You keep an eye on Carlito, okay?" Luz's words cut off what he was certain would have been Marisol's request to come too.

He led Luz into his kitchen, opened his freezer and then pointed at the table. "The thing is, I got carried away tonight. I forgot how small this freezer is, and now I've got a problem, because it doesn't all fit. I thought, well, maybe..."

Luz folded her arms and stared at him.

He pushed on. "I figure with kids to feed, you can use this. I'd hate to have to throw it out."

"You can put it in the refrigerator."

He swept open the door. "Nope, thought of that." Granted, he'd stuffed things in the back that didn't strictly need to be there, but Luz wouldn't figure that out unless she looked closely. He was counting on her not fighting too hard, but he was glad he'd though to also fill the refrigerator.

"Please. You've got to help me out. I hate to waste stuff." Which fit in with what he'd told her earlier when he talked her into taking the paint.

She gave him a withering look.

"See, the truth is," he steeled himself and continued, "I love this vegetable lasagna, and the pot roast. I get hungry for them, but since I can't buy smaller sizes, I don't get them very often. You'd do me an enormous favor if you'd take half."

"Potatoes and onions don't need to be refrigerated."

He shrugged. "They were so cheap, I bought without

73

thinking. By the time I get half of them eaten, they'll be going bad."

Luz stood, her lips folded in, obviously trying to find something wrong with his argument. "O...kay."

"Great." He gathered up an armful of groceries and started back to her apartment.

Marisol's eyes got huge at the sight of the pizza boxes.

"We're helping Mr. Larimore out," Luz told her. "He doesn't have enough room in his freezer."

He made a second trip to deliver the last of the fruit. As he turned to leave, Luz stopped him. "This is really nice of you, to share like this. I'd like to do something to thank you. Maybe you could come to dinner. Saturday?"

Well, if that's what he had to do to get her to accept a handout, he would suffer through it. "I'd like that."

"Six?"

Earlier than he usually ate, but when you had kids, likely you didn't eat at ten at night. "Terrific. I'll see you then." He hadn't fooled her. But then he hadn't expected to. All he'd been hoping for was to find a way for her to accept the food without feeling like a charity case. He was pleased he'd succeeded.

Luz closed the freezer with a thump. She hated, *hated*, that Charles Larimore had decided to take her on as a project. First paint and pizza, now lasagna and strawberries.

She struggled to hold onto her irritation, but it was hard to do with her mouth watering. The strawberries were firm and red, and she couldn't remember the last time she'd eaten one. She picked three off the top of the container, washed them and dipped them in sugar. Then she took a bite and licked at the juice running over her hand. *Damn the man.* He was making it that much harder to go back to eating whatever was on sale.

She hesitated over a fourth berry before deciding she needed to save them for Saturday in order to serve strawberry shortcake for dessert.

Speaking of which, what on earth had she been thinking? *Madre de Dios*, asking a district attorney to dinner. Although, how else could she thank him? Still, she didn't like one bit the way those sharp, interested eyes always took inventory. And she especially didn't like it when he asked about the extra kids or her imaginary husband.

She didn't dare take any chances. Not yet. Not until her twenty-first birthday, and maybe not then. After all, she'd broken a few laws along the way. Like taking the kids across state lines and selling *Mami's* car. And pretending she was *Mami* again to enroll Marisol in school.

If Charles got suspicious and started asking questions, he might bring the whole thing crashing down. Unfortunately, it would now be more suspicious to uninvite him than to simply go through with it. She could do it. After all, for nearly a year she'd managed to convince the owner of the building that her husband had just stepped out to go shopping or was away on a business trip.

She could manage Charles.

And at least with his food delivery, menu planning for Saturday was easy. The more difficult task was planning safe topics to talk about, and what to wear. Not that anything she wore would change the condescending expression Charles got whenever he looked at her. But Marisol and Cora would want to dress up. After all, Cora had worn heels just to go downstairs to play bridge with the Bayleys tonight. No question, they'd both nag until she dressed up too.

She didn't have many wardrobe choices, though. The blue dress. Or...the blue dress. The one *Papi* had said made her look as pretty as a bluebell.

Her eyes filled with tears. Swiping at them, she wandered into the bedroom to check on the children. Mari was asleep, lying on her side, a book caught beneath her cheek, and Carlito had his thumb in his mouth and his fat little bottom stuck in the air.

Smiling, she freed the book. Then she glanced at the mirror. That took care of the smile. She loosened her hair from the elastic, grabbed a brush, and tried to smooth it.

She looked like she'd been dunked.

Maybe Cora would give her a trim. A relief, actually, to remember Cora would be there for dinner. And if she'd accepted another invitation for bridge, she'd just have to cancel it.

It had surprised Luz how easy it had been to incorporate

the elderly woman into their household. They'd never used the second bedroom, and Cora was as tidy as a cat. She loved the children, and they loved her. She had a calming influence on the toddlers Luz cared for, who were going through the terrible twos, and she always pitched in on the cooking and cleaning. Best of all, she stayed with Carlito while Luz went grocery shopping or to the library.

But even better than the help with chores, Cora lifted some of Luz's emotional and financial burdens. Cora's presence made life seem a lot less tenuous.

For the first time in a year, Luz had someone in her life, another adult, who understood what she was going through, one who gave her comfort and support. She was growing to love the elderly woman, who never tried to boss her around or give advice unless asked. And, in turn, Cora was so grateful, it made her want to cry.

∞

At six o'clock, Charles got out the six-pack of root beer he'd chosen because of Marisol and the bunch of grocery-store flowers for Luz and went next door. The elderly woman who answered his knock was the one he'd helped with her key shortly after he moved in. She took in the flowers with a twinkle in her eye. "The girls will be right out, Mr. Larimore."

"Please, call me Charles."

"And I'm Cora Hartzel." She pointed at the flowers. "Do you want me to take those?"

He handed them to her.

For once the furniture was in a more normal configuration, and no pots and pans, cartons or blocks littered the floor. The doors to the two bedrooms were closed.

Cora led the way to the kitchen and put the flowers in a tall glass she took from the cupboard, while he put the root beer in the refrigerator.

They were barely settled on the sofa when one of the bedroom doors opened and Marisol came skipping out. Her glasses had fresh tape on them, and her hair was curled and held in place by a barrette on the top of her head. She wore her usual jeans, but she had on a frilly top, and she was surprisingly pretty.

He stood. "What have you done with my friend Marisol Blair?"

Marisol giggled. "I'm Marisol, and you're silly, Mr. Larimore."

"You're very pretty tonight."

The door opened again, and Luz appeared carrying Carlito. She wore a blue dress that showed off a tiny waist and long legs, and her hair, slightly curled, was dark and shiny.

Marisol had been a surprise, Luz was a grade-ten shock. If he wasn't witnessing it with his own eyes, he'd never believe the woman who walked around the Draper Arms in oversized jeans and stained T-shirts was remotely related to this woman.

"Mrs. Hartzel cut my hair, and she cut Luz's, and she helped us make curls," Marisol said.

With an effort he pulled his eyes away from Luz.

She set Carlito down, and the toddler sat staring at Charles, chewing on his hand. Charles looked warily back.

"Charles brought root beer," Cora said.

"Oh. Thank you, thank you!" Marisol said. "My very, very favorite."

"There's real beer if you'd like one." Luz raised her eyebrows in question.

"Thanks. I would." And what was Cora doing here this evening? Playing chaperon?

He felt a tug on his pant leg and discovered the toddler using it to pull himself upright. Marisol bent over and tickled Carlito, who giggled and let go of the pant leg, leaving behind a wet, wrinkled spot. Charles resisted the impulse to smooth it out.

"He also brought flowers. I put them in water for you, dear," Cora said.

He accepted the beer from Luz, struggling to adjust his thinking about women with glasses, because something about glasses and Luz just went together. For one thing, they emphasized that fey look he found intriguing.

He glanced from Luz to the toddler, who was once again pulling on his pant leg.

"Carlito's learning to walk," Marisol said.

Carlito launched himself across the room toward Cora, staggering for about ten feet before landing on his bottom. He tipped his head at Cora, chuckling.

"He's kind of slow," Marisol continued. "But Luz says that's because he's such a champion crawler."

Charles, who didn't remember ever being in a room with a drunken toddler before, found himself watching with amusement.

By the time they sat down to eat, they were all relaxed and laughing. Including Luz. And Luz laughing was another revelation. She had beautiful teeth and a pretty mouth, something he'd missed, likely because it was usually pursed in irritation.

The food was delicious. Luz had done something to the packaged pot roast that made it taste much more savory than when he reheated it. Or maybe it was eating with other people that made it taste better.

Cora asked him questions about his exercise regimen, and in response he said he ran, cycled or swam at least an hour a day, two if he could manage it.

"I read somewhere too much exercise is bad for you," Luz said with her usual frown.

"Been there, done that," he admitted ruefully. "When I was still competing in triathlons, I ran a hundred miles a week plus the biking and swimming. Then I hit my thirties, and I started having problems. Shin splints, aches and pains. I had to dial it back. But since I did, I've been okay."

"So how far did you dial back?" Luz said.

"Oh, I still manage fifty, sixty miles a week when I'm not too busy." And anytime he dropped below that number, he didn't sleep as well.

Cora grinned. "Well sounds to me like you could use another helping of pot roast."

"Thanks. It's delicious."

"When are we going to City Park?" Marisol asked.

Luz frowned, and Marisol bent her head and gave him a sideways glance. He winked at her, and she giggled.

Throughout the meal, he kept an eye on Carlito who alternated gumming, throwing, and smearing a cookie on his face and the high-chair. It explained why all Luz's T-shirts sported brown-hued stains.

"We already fed him his dinner, because he's way too messy to eat in company, you know," Marisol announced, sounding authoritative and forty. She picked up the cookie Carlito threw at her and handed it back, a mistake in Charles's view.

After dinner, Luz took Carlito off to put him to bed, then Marisol dug out Chinese checkers, and they played several rousing games. Finally, Luz declared it Marisol's bedtime. The little girl gave her a pleading look, but Luz remained adamant. Cora, to his surprise, also said goodnight and went into the second bedroom.

Luz bit her lip and stared at Cora's closed door with a frown.

"Cora lives with you?"

She gave him a distracted look. "Oh. Yes, she does."

He tried to come up with something else to talk about, but when nothing suggested itself, he stood. "Dinner was delicious. Thank you for having me."

Luz appeared relieved that he was leaving. It caused him a niggle of disappointment. He didn't want to care about what she thought of him, but it seemed he did.

"You provided most of it. All I did was cook."

"Well, it was really good." And that was most definitely enough of that.

He made his escape.

Going to dinner at the Blair's had been a major mistake. It was one thing to encounter Luz in the hall or in the laundry room wearing baggy clothes and a tired expression. It was another to see her as a vivid young woman able to juggle both a toddler and a dinner party with aplomb and carry on an intelligent conversation in the bargain.

Chapter Nine

Cora stuck her head out of her bedroom. "Such a nice-looking young man. I think he likes you."

Luz turned from shutting the door behind Charles to grimace at Cora. "We better take you in to have your eyes examined."

"Oh he's trying to hide it. But he's intrigued. I could tell."

"That's why he left as soon as you and Marisol went to bed." Although it had been a relief in a way, his abrupt departure had also made her feel...inadequate.

"Well, I believe you're wrong, dear. You're a very pretty girl, and that boy isn't blind."

But Cora was. Blind in at least a figurative sense, and Charles Larimore was hardly a boy, although he probably did seem young to someone as old as Cora.

It had been a mistake to invite him, not because it led to speculation by Cora, but because it rubbed raw emotions she'd managed to keep locked away for the past year.

Lying awake after Charles left, she was no longer able to deny that his presence had both an unsettling and stimulating effect on her. Although the unsettled feeling was familiar, she'd forgotten what it was like to feel the other—a sense of anticipation and adventure.

ॐ

"It just hit me," Charles said. "Thanksgiving's this Thursday. I'm too busy to go home for it, and I can't see fixing a big meal for one. I thought maybe the four of you might join me."

Cora beamed. "Why, how nice of you."

Luz walked up behind Cora. "There's a bit of a problem. I invited the Bayleys to join us."

He was more disappointed than he wanted to admit. Luz, on the other hand, didn't look or sound a bit disappointed.

"I know what we'll do," Cora said. "I was worrying about how to manage with only one oven, but if Charles joins us, that's solved."

Luz frowned at Cora, who ignored her and gave him a happy look.

And here he thought he and Luz had reached a point of friendly accommodation. Obviously he was mistaken. He ignored Luz and smiled at Cora. "That sounds like a plan. You'll let me know my assignment?"

Cora nodded, her eyes as bright as a child's, and he left it at that and went to work.

That evening, shortly after Charles arrived home, Cora knocked on his door. "I thought we needed to talk about Thursday." She carried a small notebook and pen over to his dining table and sat down. "There are going to be seven of us. Isn't that lucky?"

He smiled at Cora's bustle, but she was too busy opening the book to notice. "Now, if we cook the turkey over here, I can use Luz's oven for the sweet potatoes, green beans, and pies. I'm going to make pecan and pumpkin."

"Pecan is my favorite." He wondered what Luz thought about Cora taking over the holiday planning. Personally, he considered it a hoot.

"Luz said I can spend twenty-five dollars," Cora continued. She gave him an earnest look, which he had no difficulty deciphering.

Hell, twenty-five dollars would barely pay for a bird—it most decidedly wouldn't stretch to pecans. "Actually, I'm glad you brought that up. They're passing out turkeys at work"—not true, but she didn't need to know that—"so I'll contribute that, and I'll be happy to pick up pecans for you." Well, he had been prepared to provide the entire feast, so it was a no-brainer to offer.

Cora patted his arm. "You're a lovely young man. And you don't fool me a bit. We're eating a lot better since you started buying too much food. Although she finds it hard to say, Luz does appreciate it."

He wanted to squirm, although it was more a happy-dog-go-ahead-and-scratch-my-belly squirm than embarrassment. Still, he was relieved when the microwave timer dinged.

"Now I don't want to keep you from your dinner," Cora said, "but there is one more thing. We need to decide where to have this. I thought"—for the first time she seemed uncomfortable—"well, your dining room is a tiny bit bigger and..."

Again, he had no trouble deciphering her meaning. He wouldn't have to do as much cleanup as Luz would. For an instant, he regretted his involvement, then he shrugged. "We can have it here. No problem. That is, if Luz is okay with it."

"Oh, I'm sure she will be."

"I'm not entirely sure she's even okay with my being there," he said.

"Of course she is."

If it hadn't been for the too-bright smile, he would have bought it. But the smile told him it hadn't been his imagination Luz would rather chew rocks than eat Thanksgiving dinner with him. Still, there would be seven at dinner—plenty of people to dilute Luz's negativity and his discomfort. And even if Luz didn't want him there, it would still be better than eating Thanksgiving alone.

"Now you go ahead and have your dinner." Cora stood. "I can see myself out."

He watched with bemusement as the door closed behind Cora. Not only had she finessed him into providing most of the food, she'd managed to move the feast to his apartment. All that was left was for her to nudge Luz into line.

8

Charles did a huge shopping on Wednesday and dropped off pecans along with sweet potatoes, cans of pumpkin and beans, stuffing mix, cake mixes, pie crust, cranberry sauce, and a selection of fresh fruit with Cora.

Thursday morning. when he left to go for his run, the hall already smelled warmly of cinnamon. The smell brought with it memories of all the holidays he'd spent at the ranch with the Francinis, not just Thanksgiving but Christmas as well, and that thought made his heart hurt. He eased the ache with a hard, fast ten miles.

When he returned, Marisol poked her head out of the Blairs' door. "Hi, Mr. Larimore. Happy Thanksgiving." She turned and yelled, "Cora, he's back."

He went into his apartment, leaving the door open, and a few minutes later Cora bustled in carrying a pecan pie.

"Can I store this here, Charles? Carlito is learning to climb."

He nodded, and she set the pie on the counter. It had three small holes on one side that he assumed were Carlito's handiwork.

Marisol came dancing in behind Cora and stopped by the table where he'd placed his materials for the Christmas puzzle. "What's this?"

"It's a puzzle, or will be." He might not be accepting holiday invitations from the Francinis, but after Kathy's reminder, he knew he didn't want to give up the puzzle tradition.

Marisol cocked her head and moved around the table, as if other angles would reveal the meaning of the paper parasol he'd retrieved from a drink, a tiny rose he'd found in a gift wrap display and a kitten figurine.

The remaining two pieces of the puzzle were a globe of the world and a child's alphabet block in the shape of an *R*. He planned to give Luz the rest of the set of blocks for Carlito.

Marisol placed a finger over her pursed lips. "I don't get it."

"It's a play on words," he said.

Cora joined Marisol in examining the items on the table.

"Here, let me show you an example." He grabbed a piece of

paper and sketched a quick picture of a tree with a bullet casing hanging from a branch. "They're based on Christmas carols. This one, a cartridge in a bare tree, represents a partridge in a pear tree."

Marisol was still frowning in incomprehension, but Cora smiled. "What a clever idea. Who gets the puzzles?"

"A friend of mine. We've been doing them for years."

"Hmm." Cora stared at the items on the table.

"It's not quite finished. I still have to put it together."

Cora and Marisol left, but they didn't close his door, and for the rest of the day it seemed like the two of them, with or without food items, were in his apartment as much as they were in their own. Apparently, Luz had lifted her ban on Marisol visiting him, at least for the day.

On one of her visits, Marisol watched him put the final touches on the puzzle. Earlier he'd stabilized the globe to prevent it from rotating, glued the plastic *R* on China and left the glue to set. Now, he glued the rose and kitten on top of the *R* and added the parasol to shade them. He set the finished puzzle on the coffee table, well satisfied with his effort, although he'd spent a fraction of the time on it he usually did.

Later, with Luz's assistance, he moved her table and chairs to his place. He covered the two tables with the large yellow cloth he'd purchased and placed a grocery store arrangement of pink, orange and yellow flowers in the middle. He got out flatware and plates, and the next time Marisol showed up, he sent her home to borrow the additional sets needed. He alternated the white Corel plates from his apartment with Luz's mix of plates, which appeared to be leftovers from several sets.

Cora, who had come over to supervise the removal of the turkey from the oven and the making of the gravy, complimented him on the appearance of the table. He didn't catch Luz's reaction, though, because he was in the kitchen with Cora when Luz and the Bayleys arrived.

Remembering Luz's comment about Mrs. Bayley sometimes forgetting her laundry, he was surprised to discover John and Evie Bayley weren't nearly as old as he was expecting—in their fifties to early sixties, he would guess. They contributed two bottles of wine and French bread to the feast. He took out the four wineglasses he'd bought at Target, and when Luz smiled her refusal, he handed glasses to John, Evie and Cora, keeping the fourth for himself.

Cora choreographed the seating. Standing behind the chair at the end of the table nearest the kitchen, she directed Charles to the other end. That was fine with him until, with quick precision, Cora made her next assignment. "Luz, you sit next to Charles on that side."

Luz turned a quick frown on Cora, who pretended to be oblivious. Well, he wasn't any happier about the seating plan than Luz was, but he had no intention of challenging Cora. Luz would just have to make the best of it, like he intended to.

"Marisol you sit on Charles's other side, and I'll keep Carlito here by me so Luz can eat in peace for once."

John and Evie took the remaining two seats across from each other.

"Well," Cora said, with a puff of satisfaction. "Isn't this nice. Shall we join hands? John, perhaps you would say grace?"

Clearly, Luz wasn't happy about having to hold hands, so as soon as John said the "amen", Charles released hers.

Looking at the group sitting around the table, he was unable to imagine a gathering like this at his old apartment, but somehow it seemed perfectly appropriate for the Draper Arms. Maybe, when he started looking for a new apartment, he might consider one less buttoned up than his old place had been.

The thought surprised and discomfited him a little.

He was further surprised at the wide range of topics discussed during dinner. Luz, Evie and Cora were all old-movie buffs, although strictly speaking, they weren't "old" movies in Cora's case. The three had a spirited time discussing favorites. Luz also held her own in a discussion with John about plays they would both like to see performed, and she pitched in a couple of intelligent comments when John got him going on the issue of drug legalization. Clearly, Luz not only recycled the newspapers and magazines for the Draper Arms, she read them.

Kathy had taught him how much more enjoyable it was to date someone able to carry on an intelligent conversation, but the idea of asking Luz out was a definite non-starter, even without the murkiness of her marital status. Not only was she too young for him, she was a mother. Of two children. Major deal-breaker.

After dinner, everyone examined the Christmas puzzle. Looking at it, Luz murmured to herself. "Three little things, three wee things..."

The women cleaned up, John and Marisol played a game of checkers and Charles kept a wary eye on Carlito, amazed at how quickly the toddler could get from one end of the room to the other.

When Carlito toddled over to the coffee table and reached for the puzzle in what seemed to be one quick motion, he finally understood why Luz kept her apartment bare. John pulled the globe away, and Carlito reached his arms out with a piteous cry. His bottom lip pooched out, and he looked so forlorn, Charles was ready to give him the globe and worry about repairs later.

He was about to pick Carlito up and try to distract him as he'd seen Marisol do, but Luz came from the kitchen and swooped the toddler up. With a wrinkle of her nose, she took Carlito next door to change him.

They came back, and Carlito was smiling. Charles had put the puzzle out of sight and got out the rest of the alphabet blocks. Those occupied the toddler for several minutes but then he was up and away again, exploring another corner of the living room. Charles was impressed that one small human could have so much energy. Since eating, he himself was pleasantly lethargic.

Carlito came over and lifted his arms to Charles who reluctantly picked him up. With a couple of wiggles, the little boy settled down and nuzzled Charles's neck before sticking his finger in his mouth and beginning to doze.

Charles continued to visit with his guests, pleased at Carlito's obvious trust and surprised at how pleasant it was to hold the now sweet-smelling toddler.

When Luz took Carlito next door to put him to bed and Cora and Marisol went as well, some of the brightness left the day, although it helped that John and Evie stuck around to help him finish off the second bottle of wine.

They left an hour later, and he closed the door with a sense of satisfaction. It had been a much more agreeable holiday than he'd been anticipating.

ℬ

On Saturday morning, Charles responded to a knock on his door to find Luz. She gave him a smug look before reciting, "We three kings of Orient are."

The puzzle. And she'd solved it in record time. He was unsure how he felt about that. "Would you like a cup of coffee?"

She hesitated, the smug look fading. "Sure."

He poured two cups and waved her to a seat at the table. "When did you figure it out?"

"It came to me as I was dozing off Thursday night."

Good lord. "So, you're saying five hours?"

She nodded, flipping her hand. "*Más o menos.* About that."

"The fastest anyone has solved one of my puzzles has been fifty-four hours." And he wasn't at all certain he liked the idea of Luz shattering the record. Although, if he was forced to explain why, he doubted he could. "I must be slipping."

Impressed in spite of himself, he took a sip of coffee and examined Luz. She was wearing her usual baggy uniform, although her hair was neatly combed and shiny, and her eyes held a lively intelligence. "So, how did you figure it out?"

Her face contracted in thought. "I started with the letter *R,* figuring it had to be the word *a-r-e.* Then I counted how many things were attached to the *R,* which was three. I had "three" and "are", and all the items were small, or wee. Three wee things, which rhymes with kings, and the R was glued to China. The Orient."

"If he doesn't beat your time, my friend will be green with envy." The thought made Charles feel really good.

"He must be a good friend." Luz appeared wistful, as if she, too, had missing friends.

"Yeah." And for once the prospect of Alan marrying Kathy didn't twist as sharply as it usually did.

₭

Charles sat back and stretched. "How about you teach me some Spanish?"

"How much do you know?" Joanna asked.

"*Buenos días, qué pasa, gracias, adiós, cojones.*"

"That's it?"

"Pretty much."

Joanna rolled her eyes. "*¿Cerveza? ¿Hielo?*"

"Beer." He shrugged at the second word. "Yellow?"

"Ice. Why the sudden interest?"

"The manager of my new apartment is Hispanic. Thought it might help me communicate better." Actually, Luz's English was as good as his, but it might be fun to say something in Spanish to Marisol and be able to understand her answer.

And what was that all about, anyway? He didn't like kids, and yet he got a kick out of Marisol. Of course, it didn't mean his entrenched anti-child position was eroding. No way.

"*Buenos días, Señor Larimore. ¿Cómo está?*" Joanna enunciated the words clearly.

He put aside the kid question for the moment and concentrated on Joanna. "You're doing something different. It doesn't sound right."

"After you fractured *hielo* I figured I'd better slow down."

"Say it the way you would normally."

"*Buen día. ¿Cómo 'stá?*" She grinned at his look of confusion. "It's like using contractions in English."

He took a breath. "*Buen día. ¿Cómo 'stá?*"

"*Bien. Y tú. ¿'stás bien?*"

"*¿Bien?*"

She chuckled. "If you don't know if you're okay, I don't know how you can expect me to."

He kept a list of the words she taught him, and a couple of times a day, they practiced simple dialogues. They both found it a welcome break from the grim issues they faced the rest of the time. She told him his accent was awful, but with concentration a native Spanish speaker might just be able to make out what he was trying to say.

သာ

"You're late," Alan said.

Charles checked his watch.

"I mean with the puzzle. Everyone was disappointed." Alan knew he shouldn't jab at Charles, but Charles *had* used the tactic on him a time or two.

"Sorry. The fire put me behind." Charles didn't sound sorry.

"So what did you do for Thanksgiving?" Alan was glad to see Charles looking better. More rested, maybe.

"Got together with a couple of neighbors. It turned into a bit of a madhouse, but it was more pleasant than I expected."

"Single-women type neighbors?"

Charles looked amused. "Single women at the Draper Arms tend to be over fifty or have a couple of kids."

And Alan knew Charles's aversion to kids. He turned his attention to the globe Charles had brought with him. They always kept track of how long it took to solve the puzzles. To date, the scores tilted in Charles's favor, a mild annoyance, since he, not Charles, was the English professor.

"One of the people at dinner on Thursday solved it by Saturday morning," Charles said.

"Well, there ought to be a penalty of at least twenty-four hours for late delivery of the goods."

Charles shrugged. "You're right."

Alan stared at his friend in surprise. Charles conceding any point without a battle was a brand-new Charles. "They must put Valium in the water supply."

Charles lifted his eyebrows in question.

"Or else you're an alien, and my friend Charles Larimore is being held prisoner."

"Nope. If twenty-four hours is okay with you, I'm good with it."

Alan left after lunch, carrying the puzzle, but puzzling instead over the change in Charles.

Chapter Ten

Charles glanced up from folding clothes to greet Marisol.

"*Buenos días, Señorita Marisol.*"

Marisol looked startled, then she giggled. "*Buenos días, Señor* Larimore. You do laundry almost as much as we do."

"And there are four of you and only one of me." A good thing all around she'd switched back to English. He wasn't certain even Joanna would know the word for laundry.

Marisol shook her head emphatically. "Four? You can't count." She held up her hand, and pulled her fingers down, one after the other. "Me and Luz and Carlito. That's only three. Oh, I know. You mean Mrs. Hartzel. She does her own laundry. And she lets me call her Nana if I want." Marisol transferred clothes from her hamper to the washer. "Carlito is so messy. He wears more clothes in a day than any five people. Luz says I used to be messy, too, but I'm growing up."

With only the slightest twinge of guilt, Charles decided to probe some of the mysteries of his next-door neighbor while the chance presented itself. "How come you call her Luz, instead of Mom?"

"Because she's not my mom, silly."

The simple statement rocked him. Aside from thinking Luz looked entirely too young to be Marisol's mother, it had never crossed his mind she wasn't. He grappled with his surprise as Marisol continued blithely on. "I just pretend she is for school, so social—social something doesn't try to take me away. They tried once, but Luz saved us, me and Carlito. We ran away like Snow White from the evil stepmother. Well actually, we ran from our uncle, but Luz says he's just like an evil stepmother."

She pulled quarters from her pocket, and with a practiced motion put them in the slots and pushed in the slide.

"You never know, Luz says. People can act all shiny and nice on the outside but be all ugly inside."

Marisol left, and he continued to fold his clothes, turning over what she'd told him.

It was one thing to turn a blind eye to a possibly illegal babysitting operation. It was something else entirely to ignore the fact Luz might be hiding Marisol and Carlito from Children's Services. If that was so, as an officer of the court, he had a clear duty to report her.

The thought jarred him. Luz, a possible kidnapper? It didn't fit somehow. Or maybe he didn't want it to fit.

₧

"Mr. Larimore is so funny," Marisol said.

"What do you mean?"

"He thinks you're my mother."

¡Dios mío, no! Luz stared at Marisol. "You didn't tell him I wasn't. Please, Mari, tell me you didn't tell him."

"He's a nice person, Luz. He likes us. He wouldn't hurt us."

Luz, her heart sinking, knew. Marisol had told. She tried to question the little girl further, but Mari clammed up. If he hadn't already, Charles would figure the whole thing out soon.

It meant she needed a plan. But she was too frozen with fear to think of one.

₧

Sunday afternoon, driving back to the apartment, Charles saw Cora Hartzel get off the bus on Colfax. Deciding it gave him the perfect opportunity to find out what she knew about the Blairs, he offered her a ride.

"Why, how nice of you, Charles." She climbed in and settled her handbag on her lap.

"Your moving in with Luz. It seems to be working well for all of you."

"I thank God every day for Luz. That young woman is... Well, I can't even come up with the proper words to describe how wonderful she is. I would have been homeless, if she hadn't taken me in."

"How did that happen?" Well, if he didn't ask, he'd never find out.

"I—well, I imagine you've heard about the Turner Financial Freedom Plan that turned out to be a scam. I'm afraid I was taken in."

Turner was currently under indictment, and his case was being handled by the financial crimes unit. Charles would have liked to ask what in particular sucked Cora in, but right now he needed to keep the focus on Luz.

"I'm sure Luz is happy to have your help with the children."

"Oh, Marisol and Carlito are such darlings."

"I meant the other children."

"Other children?"

"Well, I've often seen other children at Luz's."

"Oh. Yes, of course. You're talking about Carlito's play group. Luz thinks it's so important for his social development, you know."

She gave him such a bland look, he knew she was lying.

"I find it hard to believe Luz could possibly have a daughter as old as Marisol." He tossed the line out, and Cora, the wily old trout, flicked it away with a sniff.

"Luz is an amazing young woman. Much more mature than she appears."

Okay, time to play hardball. "Did you know it's illegal to operate an unlicensed daycare in this state?"

Cora blinked, but she recovered quickly. "And well it should be. Why, I've seen stories of children being left in their own filth, not being given anything to eat but juice that rots their teeth and being hit if they make the slightest noise. The state should do everything in its power to prevent abuses like that."

The words made him queasy, describing, as they did, the

Maxwells' treatment of Davey. But Cora's tone made him want to smile. The old biddy might look fragile, but she was tough as titanium, and she'd warned him off in no uncertain terms.

"Well, here we are. In no time at all. Thank you for the ride, Mr. Larimore." Cora exited the car, shoving the door shut and completing the rout.

He made a mental note to check with Financial Crimes to make sure Cora was on the victim list so she'd have a shot at getting compensation. As to the rest of the conversation, it had only raised additional questions.

Ↄ

Because of Marisol's comment about social services, Charles began his search by checking missing children reports. He typed Marisol and Carlito Blair in the search field and got no matches in Colorado, Wyoming, or Kansas. The Nebraska database gave him a record of a Marisol and Carlos, but the last name listed for the two was Montalvo, not Blair. Since it was the only record that came close, he opened the file.

He examined the first picture. Marisol Joan, age six. The little girl's glasses weren't taped, but it was his Marisol all right. Also listed as missing was Marisol's brother, Carlos Stephen, age four months. Charles squinted at the picture. Babies changed so fast it was difficult to be certain, but Carlos had to be Carlito.

The third picture was of the woman he knew as Luz Blair. Her real name was Luz Cristina Montalvo. Not Marisol and Carlito's mother. Their sister.

All three had been reported missing from their home in Scottsbluff, Nebraska last year. Also missing was a silver Lexus, registered to Mary Blair Montalvo.

Charles next searched the archives of the Scottsbluff newspaper, using a date-frame starting fourteen months ago. He typed in the name Mary Blair Montalvo. It didn't take him long to discover what it was all about.

Ↄ

Now that he knew what the situation was, every day he delayed reporting Luz to the Nebraska authorities, Charles was risking his career. Still, he hesitated to take action without first talking to Luz, because the situation did appear ambiguous.

He hated ambiguity. It was one of the reasons he liked being a district attorney. His role was a simple one—prove the person charged with a crime guilty beyond a reasonable doubt. During trials, he didn't have to worry about shades of guilt or extenuating circumstances. That was the defense's job. For the prosecution, the situation was cut and dried, black and white, exactly as he preferred it.

But Marisol's comment about the evil uncle made him hesitate, because there was an uncle in the picture. Martin Blair. Identified as the brother of Mary Blair Montalvo, the children's mother, he was the person who reported Luz, Marisol and Carlito missing.

Why would Luz, after burying her parents, run away from her uncle, taking her brother and sister with her?

ɛ⌒

Charles, in suit and tie, stood on Luz's doorstep. "We need to talk." The iciness of his tone was matched by the cold look in his eyes. "Here or my place, your call."

Luz's mouth went dry, but the rest of her felt like she was being swept away from land by a huge wave. She shifted her eyes to Charles's mouth. It was carved from the same block of ice as his eyes. She lifted her chin and met his gaze. "And a good evening to you, too." Being a smart-ass wasn't wise, but she was too frightened not to take a swipe at him, although that swipe had all the power of a kitten going up against an elephant.

He simply stared at her, waiting.

Trying to ignore her churning stomach, she stiffened her spine and spoke carefully. "Your place. I need to tell Cora."

"Good."

He left, and she knocked on Cora's bedroom door.

Cora opened the door, wearing a robe, her hair half in curlers. "What is it, dear?"

"Charles wants to talk to me. Can you listen for the kids?"

"Certainly. You go right ahead. I'll leave my door open so I can hear them." Cora patted her hair, giving Luz a meaningful look.

Her world was about to go up in flames, and Cora was worried about hair.

"I'll comb it."

Cora looked at her shirt.

No. "He's already seen me like this. It'll look needy if I change."

Cora patted her arm. "You're so pretty, it doesn't matter what you wear, dear."

Yeah, right. Even if she was as pretty as Cora kept telling her she was, it wouldn't be enough. Not in this circumstance.

She could tell by the expression on Charles's face, and from the tie still firmly knotted around his neck, that this wasn't about the daycare issue. He knew everything, and he was going to turn them in.

She closed her eyes, and panic hit in a black wave. The urge to grab the children and leave, right this minute, was so strong, her body trembled with it. But it was nine at night and she had no car, little money, and nowhere to go. At most, she might get a five-minute head-start before Charles came after them.

And what about Cora? How would she manage without Luz? Or for that matter, Luz was no longer sure how she would manage without Cora. Her only choice was to meet with Charles to see if she could buy more time to plan. Like she'd done with Martin Blair and the woman from Children's Services.

She ran a quick brush through her hair, pulled it back, and grabbed an elastic to hold it in place, then she stood over a sleeping Marisol and Carlito, grappling with a fear so enormous it nauseated her. Breathing carefully, she rested her hand lightly on Carlito's fat little bottom, wordlessly entreating God, the saints, the angels, indeed anyone who might be listening, to help her Eventually her stomach calmed, but standing in front of Charles Larimore's door, her courage failed.

Before she could flee, the door opened. Charles was still wearing his suit, and he still hadn't loosened his tie. He gestured her to a seat on the sofa and sat in the chair across from her.

He had arranged it so the sofa was brightly lit, while he sat in partial shadow. She shifted the lamp to give herself the advantage of the shadow, and faced him. Like her earlier defiance, moving the lamp was a pitiful attempt to appear strong, but at least it gave her enough sense of control to keep the nausea at bay.

He frowned but left the lamp where she'd moved it, regarding her pensively for so long, she had to clench all her muscles to keep from jumping up and running out.

Finally, he sighed and rubbed his head. "I've done some checking. You, Marisol and Carlito are being sought by the Nebraska authorities."

An icy blast of dread left her trembling. Against all reason, she'd still hoped this confrontation might be about something else. But it wasn't. And it was worse than she'd imagined. *Sought by the authorities. Ayúdame, Dios.* What was she going to do?

Denial, Luz Cristina. It's not just a river in Egypt. The thought steadied her, and she had to bite her lip to prevent herself from bursting out in laughter—at herself, at fate, at Charles. But if she started laughing, she might not be able to stop. And behind the urge to laugh, tears gathered in the back of her throat.

"You want to give me a reason not to call them?" Charles said.

What on earth did he mean? Give him a reason not to call. She owned nothing, had no money, and he knew it. And no way was he demanding she sleep with him. Not after he'd made it so crystal clear he didn't find her attractive.

Time. She had to play for time. And the only weapon she had was to go on the offense. She firmed her lips as the possibility of a plan took shape.

Charles expected Luz to be upset. Was even prepared for her to cry and had placed a box of tissues on the table next to the couch for that eventuality. What he wasn't prepared for was fury. Or her continuing silence. But when she finally spoke, he was sorry she had.

"So how do we do this?" she said. "Do you undress me, or would you prefer I do it?"

He blinked in confusion. "Good lord, girl, what are you talking about?"

"You told me to give you a reason not to turn me in. *I* certainly had no difficulty translating that, and I must say, shocked innocence is not your most accomplished role."

He opened his mouth to defend himself, but before he could, Luz pulled off her shirt—one of those ugly extra-large T-shirts that seemed to be a wardrobe staple for her. Underneath, she wore a sleeveless undershirt that made her look as vulnerable and young as Marisol.

His mouth going dry with what he assumed was panic, he reached out to stop her. "Don't. Please. That is *not* what I meant." *Smooth, Larimore. Real smooth.*

For the second time in as many days, a witness had got the better of him. Not only a rare experience, but given Luz's assumptions about his intentions, an acutely uncomfortable one.

She let the shirt fall into an untidy pile in her lap, giving him a steady look while he scrambled mentally to get the conversation back on track.

He'd never done anything to give her the impression he wanted to sleep with her. He knew he hadn't, because he didn't want to. Sleep with her. Ergo, it followed he hadn't given that impression, although that was beside the point. The point he needed to get back to.

Not only was Luz out on a legal limb here, he was out there with her. He'd delayed contacting the authorities, something he could gloss over, no doubt, but the longer he delayed, the more precarious his position became.

"Please. Put your shirt on." While she did, he set about pulling the discussion back where it needed to be. "Tell me why you ran away from your uncle."

"He's not *my* uncle." The tone was fierce.

"But he is your mother's brother?"

Luz shook her head. "My mother died when I was five. *Papi* married Mary Blair when I was nine. She raised me. I was as much hers as Marisol and Carlito, but Martin Blair is no family of mine."

She started wringing her hands, although he doubted she realized it. She looked so forlorn, he had to struggle to remain in lawyer mode.

He leaned forward, pried her hands apart and held them firmly, ignoring his relief at finally having an excuse to touch her. "If you don't tell me what happened, I can't help you."

"How do I know I can trust you?"

"Do you have any choice?"

She stared at him for a time, then shook her head. His heart twisted in pain at the sorrow in her eyes. He bit down on it. "So let's hear it." He released her hands because holding them was making it more difficult for him to remain objective.

Staring at her lap, Luz spoke in a lifeless tone. "Our parents were killed. In an auto accident. After the funeral, Martin came to the house. He had a woman from Children's Services with him who was going to take Marisol and Carlito away. I was supposed to pack and have them ready the next day. Instead, I drove us all to Denver in *Mami's* car."

"So you're saying you ran away to keep the three of you from being separated."

Luz nodded.

"Why didn't you petition the court to give you custody?"

"Martin said there was no money, and we couldn't stay in our house. And the woman from Children's Services said I wouldn't get custody since I was underage."

Her voice trembled with emotion, and again, his desire to comfort her almost overcame his need for the entire story.

"How old were you?"

"Nineteen."

"And did you believe that? About the money?" She'd obviously believed she wouldn't get custody, although he knew she would have, had she chosen to stay and fight.

Luz shook her head. "*Mami* and *Papi* always lived...not frugally, but carefully. *Mami* was a cardiologist, and *Papi* had a landscaping business."

"How have you managed financially?" It was a question he was pretty sure he knew most of the answer to.

"I sold *Mami*'s car."

Something he'd suspected, given it was no longer in evidence.

"And I got a refund of some of my expenses from Colorado College."

That part was a surprise. It hadn't yet occurred to him to wonder what she had been doing when her parents died.

She didn't admit to the babysitting business, but that had to be another income source. He doubted she'd paid any taxes on the money, either.

He added it up: kidnapping, crossing state lines, selling stolen property, running an illegal daycare, possible tax fraud. Luz was a one-woman crime wave, but he understood why she'd done it, why she might believe she had no other choice.

"*Papi* and I...when we came to Scottsbluff, he started a lawn-mowing business. Mary Blair was his first customer. She was a doctor, and she owned a nice house. Martin claimed *Papi* was marrying her for her money and position. She wasn't pretty, you see. He hurt her saying all those awful things. But she was the sweetest and...*Papi* and I...we loved her so much." Luz blinked rapidly, then swiped a wrist across her eyes.

Charles, who'd seen plenty of fake tears, recognized the real thing when he saw it. In the pictures in the newspaper accompanying the Montalvos' obits, the man had been darkly handsome while the woman had the rawboned, homely look of a prairie spinster. But her eyes had been kind.

Luz hugged herself and rocked back and forth, and he was unable to take it any longer. He abandoned the chair, moved next to her and slipped an arm around her. He discovered she was shaking.

Over the past few weeks, as he had gotten to know Luz, his initial negative impression had gradually been replaced, and his respect had grown. Putting together these final pieces of her story, that respect grew further.

Luz continued to shiver. He pulled her onto his lap and wrapped his arms around her. She stiffened slightly, then, with a sigh, leaned into him. She had the same sweet smell as Carlito. Her hair was coming loose. He eased the elastic off and slipped his fingers through satin smoothness to gently massage her scalp. He wasn't certain of the exact moment it happened, but suddenly he wanted to kiss her.

Startled, he lowered his head and let her hair brush across his lips. He had to be feeling this way because it had been so long. The old libido demanding its due, even though the object of that demand was someone he viewed with as much detachment as he would a gangly teenage boy.

But, his libido prodded, *remember how she looked in that blue dress. That was no teenage boy.*

Bad enough he hadn't immediately reported Luz to the authorities. If that was discovered, he might as well kiss his job goodbye, but getting emotionally involved with her would compound his sin. Besides, he needed to keep his wits about him, and whenever libido entered the picture, reason took a breather.

Reluctantly, he eased Luz off his lap, but remained sitting next to her. He still didn't have the whole story, and if he didn't push while she was vulnerable, he might never get it. "Where were you born, Luz?"

Luz gave him a wary look. "I'm not illegal, if that's what you think. *Papi* and I became citizens."

So, at least he wouldn't be responsible for having her deported if he turned her in. He breathed out in relief.

"I was born in Chile. We lived on an estancia, I think. I don't remember really." She shook her head, looking strained. "The only thing from his past *Papi* would talk about were the horses. I think something bad happened. I remember a lot of shouting. Or maybe I dreamed it. Later *Papi* and I were somewhere...I don't know when this was exactly. I asked about *Mami* and he...cried. I was afraid to ask again." She rubbed her head as if the memories were physically painful. "That's it. That's all I know." She gazed directly at him. "You're going to have to report us, aren't you."

He thought about his responsibility, and he thought about Luz. Her gallantry, her generosity, her intelligence. If he let only his lawyer-side choose what to do next, it would harm his soul.

He took a deep breath. "I'm not going to do anything at the moment. I need more time to think about all this."

"But then you'll call them, right? You have to, because that's your job." She sounded resigned.

His heart clenched with a sudden conviction. He turned and gripped Luz by the upper arms, forcing her to meet his gaze. "You are not to run away again, Luz. You hear me? You have to promise me."

She shook her head. "I have to do what I believe is best for Mari and Carlito."

"And I'm telling you, what's best is for you to stay put while I decide what to do."

"Oh. So now this is all your problem. How did that happen?" Her voice shook with anger. "This is *my* family. *My* problem. Not yours."

Of course they weren't his family, and her pointing it out shouldn't be, *wasn't*, a big deal. *Dammit, man, focus.* And actually, if she ran away, it would solve a lot of problems. For him, anyway. Except, he wouldn't be able to get them out of his mind. Would worry whether they had a place to sleep, enough to eat.

"You're right, but does that mean you can't accept help?"

For a moment longer, she remained rigid, then she slumped against his hands. "No. I guess I can use all the help I can get." She bent her head and continued speaking in a strained voice. "I don't want to run anymore, Charles. But I will, if you don't promise me something." She raised her eyes and held his gaze with hers. "If you decide you have to turn us in, promise me you'll give me twenty-four hours' notice."

"I promise, Luz."

At that, the tension drained from them both.

She spoke without looking at him. "I better get back. Cora will be worried."

He let her go, because at the moment, he had no idea what else to do for her. He changed out of his suit and ate a pizza, barely tasting it, mulling over the mess he'd allowed himself to be maneuvered into. He had no idea yet what to do about it.

Follow the money. The phrase popped into his head, as he took the last bite of pizza. Indeed, what *had* happened to all the

Montalvos' Scottsbluff resources? With both parents working and living conservatively it was unlikely the uncle had been telling the truth about the Montalvo finances.

Or was that simply libido getting in its two cents?

Maybe. But it was still worth checking. And until he did, he'd hold off on reporting Luz no matter what the consequences.

Chapter Eleven

Luz returned to her apartment after the talk with Charles to find Cora sitting on the couch, watching the television she'd brought with her as part of what she called her "dowry".

"There you are, dear," Cora said, looking up. "Did he ask about the babysitting?"

"He didn't mention it." And given what she and Charles *had* talked about, the daycare issue no longer seemed the least bit important.

Cora gave her a well-when-you're-ready-to-talk-about-it-I'll-be-here look, before getting up and bidding her good night. Luz took Cora's place on the couch and stared at the television, but she wasn't seeing or hearing it.

Instead, still trembling, she went through what had just happened with Charles. Obscuring everything else was the memory of the moment he pulled her onto his lap and held her. Like *Papi* used to do when she was small and unable to sleep. But she was no longer a small child, and she certainly didn't feel the same way about Charles as she did about *Papi*.

Papi. She needed him now. More than she'd ever needed him when she was little. *She* hugged her knees and the tears she'd been fighting tipped from her eyes and slid down her cheeks.

છ

One of the assistants poked her head around Charles's door. "An officer's here to see you."

His guilty conscience leapt into overdrive, shooting his heart rate up before he realized—no way could it be about Luz.

"A Lieutenant Gray from the arson squad," the assistant added, somewhat belatedly. "He said if you're busy, he'll come back later."

Arson. One of the few things Luz couldn't be accused of. Breathing a sigh of relief, he directed the assistant to show Gray in.

The amenities dispensed with, Gray pulled a paper from his pocket and passed it to Charles, who unfolded it, to find it was a copy of a crudely lettered note.

Don't nobodie try to klip the wings of the Fireflie.

Gray nodded at the paper. "You recognize that?"

"It's the sort of thing William Snodgrass used to do. Called himself the Firefly. One of my first convictions."

"You had any contact with him since the trial?"

Charles shook his head.

"He got out of prison four months ago."

"And you think he set my apartment on fire."

"That's what it looks like. This note makes it an act of revenge. And if that's the case, maybe burning you out once satisfied him, but I sure wouldn't want to count on it." Gray took the note back. "The fire started in the apartment below yours. We found the remains of a can of paint thinner in the front room. All he needed to do was open the can, soak a few rags in the thinner, and leave them sitting near the radiator. Didn't take long for it to spontaneously combust."

"Could the thinner have been left through carelessness?"

"The apartment was being painted, but the painter used latex paint. Besides, in addition to this note, the manager received an odd phone call suggesting an evacuation about the time the fire started."

Gray left, and Charles called his secretary to remind her not to give out his address or phone number. The thought of Snodgrass planning something at the Draper Arms made his mouth go dry. It wouldn't be nearly as easy to evacuate as his other apartment, not with all the children.

His secretary called him later to tell him a woman had

called a month earlier saying she was with a florist. She'd asked for his address, and the receptionist had given it to her.

After a moment, he remembered that was about the time Kathy came to see him. He didn't want to talk to Kathy, but he needed to find out if she'd been the one who called. He phoned her at work to ask how she got his address, and she had the grace to sound embarrassed as she explained she'd used a florist delivery ruse. In his relief, he barely noticed.

But relief was short-lived once he realized how easy it would be for Snodgrass to discover where he'd moved. Snodgrass knew where he worked, so all the man needed to do was hang around and follow him home, although given he kept irregular hours, it was possible Snodgrass hadn't managed it yet.

From here on out, he would take precautions: vary his schedule even more, change which door he left by, where he caught the bus or parked his car.

He also needed to warn Luz about the situation.

Remembering she hadn't panicked when confronted about Marisol and Carlito, he relaxed slightly. He could count on Luz to be his ally in this.

ဆ

Charles put a vegetable lasagna in the microwave, took a quick shower then knocked on Luz's door. With a wary look, she followed him back to his apartment. He seated her at the table and dished up a portion of lasagna for each of them.

"I already had dinner."

"Yeah, hours ago, I bet." Although she was looking better, she was still too thin.

"So, is this my last meal?"

Puzzled, he glanced at her.

"You know. You're going to report me, and this is my twenty-four-hour notice."

"Oh. No. Something came up that I need to talk to you about." Actually, he hadn't thought about reporting her since Officer Gray had given him something much more serious to worry about.

She ate slowly and delicately, and he tried to figure out how to tell her the building might be an arsonist's target. Finally, he just said it.

She stopped eating abruptly. "Is that what happened to your last apartment?"

"That's what the arson investigator thinks."

"Okay. So what do we need to do?"

"Are any apartments empty?"

"Only Cora's old apartment on two."

"I suggest you check it every day to make sure no one's dropped off a can of paint thinner. Gray also suggested sending a fire awareness team here to do an inspection and talk to residents about fire safety. It's probably best not to say there's a specific threat. Tell everyone it's a free program you heard about and thought was a great idea. Make sure you talk to Marisol and Cora about what to do in an emergency. Arrange a rendezvous point for all of you."

"So why does someone hate you enough to burn you out?"

"It's someone I prosecuted."

"Does that happen a lot? People you prosecute try to kill you?"

He shrugged. "Mostly it happens on television. Besides, the guy doesn't want to kill me. Gray thinks he made the anonymous call to the apartment manager before the fire started, so everyone had plenty of time to get out."

He continued to eat, but Luz put her fork down and leaned her chin on her hands, examining him. "If you're the only one he's after, why don't you move?"

Her apparent lack of concern for him was deeply wounding. Not that he'd ever let her know it. "It's probably best if I stay put. I'm taking precautions to make it harder for him to find me, but there's no guarantee he doesn't already know where I live." He turned over the picture Gray had given him and slid it across the table to her.

She frowned at it, shaking her head. "Doesn't look like someone I'd want to rent to."

He finished off his lasagna and offered Luz ice cream, but

she declined.

"I'm going to take a quick look at Cora's old apartment," she said.

"I'll come with you."

"I can manage. Thanks for the lasagna. Let me know when the fire team wants to come."

And that was that. Well, he didn't expect her to fall apart, of course. Part of what he admired about Luz was her courage. That she couldn't be easily spooked. But part of him would have liked the excuse to comfort her.

ॐ

Charles's dance card was filling up. Preparing for Gary Maxwell's trial, looking for a new apartment, shopping for furniture, following up on the inquiries he had set in motion on Luz's behalf, worrying about William Snodgrass. And to top it off, Christmas was only a week away.

The Friday before Christmas, Charles found an envelope under his door. Assuming it was a Christmas card from one of his neighbors, he picked it up but found, instead, a crudely printed note.

I know where you live and I know about the kute naybor with the kute kids who does all that lawndri.

It wasn't signed, but it didn't need to be. He re-read the note with rising panic, although on another level, his brain continued to operate logically, noting the clumsy phonetic spelling, something Snodgrass considered his "signature".

With a final shove, panic replaced logic.

ॐ

Loud knocking jerked Luz from deep sleep and propelled her off the bed before she was fully awake. Shaking with reaction, she made her way to the front door.

She peered through the peephole, and when she saw Charles, she sighed in relief. But that relief was quickly overlaid with dread. What could he be doing here at this time of night, if not to tell her he'd reported her?

She took a breath and, trying to channel annoyance rather than fear, swung the door open. "God, Larimore, give it a rest, will you. Some people actually go to bed before midnight around here."

He reached out and grabbed her arm. "Thank God you're all right."

Blinking, she attempted to sort it out—the frantic look on his face as she opened the door, and now his obvious relief as he continued to grip her arm. How did that fit into the talking-to-the-authorities scenario? Answer—it didn't...did it?

"We need to talk."

"Of course we do." Still going for annoyance, she walked over, plopped on the couch and glared at him.

He sat in the chair, rubbing his head. "I'm sorry I woke you, but I needed to make sure you were okay. There was a note under my door. A threat. It mentioned you."

Midway through a yawn, her mouth snapped shut.

"It was from Snodgrass. It's a new approach for him, but I think we better find you and the kids someplace else to stay for a while."

As if it wasn't enough she was already hiding from her step-uncle and worrying that Charles was going to turn her in. "Right. I'll just call one of my many friends and see if I can't arrange that. Perhaps a week in the Caribbean?"

"Luz, this is serious."

Yeah, she knew that. But what choice, with no car and little money, did she have than to blow it off, pretend it wasn't real. Except, given how frantic Charles had seemed when she answered the door, it had to be real. "There's nowhere for me to go." Abruptly she realized how she was dressed. She pulled on the edges of the T-shirt, trying to cover her thighs.

Charles was staring at a spot over her shoulder and appeared not to notice either her discomfort or her bare legs. Dammit, what would it take for him to *see* her?

"Look, I have an idea," he said, his gaze swinging back to her face. "But we can't do anything about it until morning so I'd better stay here tonight."

It was the last thing she expected him to suggest—well not suggest exactly. The determined look on his face told her she had no choice in the matter. Still, if he didn't stay, and she let herself think about it, she'd be terrified.

Her attempt to appear cool and unfazed was beginning to give way to tremors. "Okay." She took a breath and hugged herself.

"Good. I'll just run next door and get my stuff."

He came back twenty minutes later, dressed in sweats and carrying a pillow and a blanket. By that time, the seriousness of the situation had hit Luz full force. "I—I, d-do you need anything else?"

He dropped the pillow on the sofa, with a frown. "You okay?"

"S-sure."

"You don't need to worry, you know. I called the police. They're going to keep an eye on things tonight."

He plumped the pillow and spread the blanket, not looking at her.

"G-good. That's fine then. I'll just... Good night." She stepped into the bedroom, closed the door and slumped against it. She'd wanted so badly to throw herself in his arms, but he'd made it clear he wouldn't welcome it. One thing to sleep on her sofa apparently, another altogether to get personal about it.

After a moment, she straightened and climbed back in the twin bed next to Marisol's. When they first moved to Denver, Marisol had insisted on them sleeping together, but recently, she'd allowed Luz to push the beds apart.

A good thing. The shakes were getting worse. She rolled over for the third time, trying to find a comfortable position.

She flipped again, getting so tangled in the sheet she had to get up and remake the bed. Before she lay back down, she pulled the blanket over Marisol and checked on Carlito, resting her hand on his head. Standing there, touching that silky baby hair, her breathing finally smoothed out, and the shivers subsided.

She got back in bed and pulled the blanket up and tried to lie still. Her fear had abated, but what now came to keep her company in the dark was the awareness of the man sleeping in the other room. Close enough that she could reach him with a few steps.

She wondered how he would react if she took those steps and asked him to hold her. Would he pull her down to lie next to him, or would he sit up and use words to keep her at a distance? Or maybe something in between? An impersonal hug, like the one he'd given her the other night. Without any meaning to it. Just being nice, because he was a good person, and he was trying to help someone in difficulty.

Eventually she must have slept, because the next thing she knew it was morning, and Carlito was standing in his crib, chewing on his hand and singing his morning song—all of it so wonderfully, amazingly normal after her night terrors.

She changed Carlito and pulled on her jeans before she stuck her head through the doorway. Charles was still fast asleep. She carried Carlito into the living room and stood gazing at Charles, her heart beating with simple happiness. She loved looking at him, but usually she had to do it in quick gulps. An unexpected treat to be able to stare at him without him knowing.

In sleep, with the tension gone from his face, he looked as innocent and beautiful as a sleeping Carlito. For the first time, she noticed how thick and long his lashes were, and seeing the faint golden stubble on his cheeks, she realized she'd never seen him unshaven.

Carlito's gurgles woke Charles up. Awareness came into his eyes, and he sat up, running fingers through his hair and rubbing his cheeks. His eyes came to rest on her face, and he smiled. "What time is it?" Still smiling, he reached out to let Carlito grab his finger. "Hey, buddy."

The smile had been for Carlito, of course.

"Nearly six."

"Look, if I go take a shower, you won't open the door until I get back, will you?"

"That's a joke, right?"

"Luz Cristina."

His tone was the one she frequently used on Marisol, and she disliked Charles using it on her. She bit her lip to keep from snapping at him and shook her head. "I promise, I won't open

111

the door."

He slipped on his shoes and carried the blanket and pillow with him, leaving no sign he'd spent the night. Twenty minutes later, his hair still wet and dressed in jeans and a clean T-shirt, he walked back in carrying a carton of eggs, a loaf of bread and a package of sausages. "How do you like your eggs?"

Although his high-handedness annoyed her, she was hungry enough to overlook it. "Marisol and Carlito eat scrambled, but I like mine over-easy."

Cora walked into the living room giving Luz a puzzled look. "Who are you talking to, dear?"

"Charles is cooking breakfast for us this morning. He's making eggs, scrambled and over-easy. Which do you prefer?"

"Good morning, Charles," Cora said, staring hard at Luz, her expression a mix of *Why is he doing that?* and *See, I knew he liked you.*

Charles stuck his head out of the kitchen and smiled at Cora.

She smiled back. "I do love a nice over-easy egg, if it's no trouble."

"No trouble at all." He ducked back out of sight.

"I'll explain later." Luz spoke softly in Cora's ear, rolling her eyes toward the doorway where Marisol stood, yawning.

After breakfast, Luz sent Marisol to get dressed, and while she was out of earshot, Charles quickly explained to Cora what was happening. "I've arranged for you all to go to TapDancer Ranch for a few days. It's owned by the parents of a friend of mine."

"Well, I don't think I need to go," Cora said.

"It's the only way I can guarantee you'll all be safe."

"But the note only mentioned Luz and the children, right?"

"Technically, yes. But since you live with Luz, you're at risk, too."

"Well, if this person wants to hurt you, he's certainly not going to see me as a way to do it. Luz and the children should go, by all means, but I'm staying. Besides, I have a doctor's appointment on Monday, and I've had to wait three months for it. I *really* don't want to miss it."

"Well, I *really* think you need to go with us," Luz said.

"I'll be fine. You'll see. He's not going to want to be bothered with an old lady, whoever he is. Firefly indeed." Cora snorted. "Too bad woodsheds have gone out of fashion."

"Woodsheds?" Luz said.

"In my day, you misbehaved, you took a trip out back to the woodshed with your dad. Got paddled. Sometimes you weren't able to sit real good for a couple of days."

Charles smiled. "If there'd been a woodshed, I'm afraid Snodgrass would have burned it down."

Cora chuckled.

"Well I'm glad you two are finding this amusing." Luz wasn't a bit happy about Charles's plan, but she had no alternative, and if she had to remove herself, so did Cora. "You have to come. Marisol will worry if you don't."

Cora shook her head. "She'll only worry if you spill the beans."

Luz wasn't sure what that meant exactly, but they were running out of time. Marisol would be back any minute.

As if the thought had been a command, Marisol came skipping into the dining room wearing the frilly top that was supposed to be for dress-up. Not that she had many opportunities to wear it.

Charles started to stand. "I need to go rent a larger car so I can drive you out."

"Why not ask Mr. Bayley if you can borrow his car?" Cora asked.

"Are we going somewhere?" Marisol asked.

"Charl—Mr. Larimore has arranged for us to spend a few days with friends of his," Luz said. "A vacation. Isn't that nice?"

Marisol frowned, pursing her lips. "I suppose so." She sounded uncertain, which was exactly how Luz was feeling.

"Why don't I go talk to the Bayleys?" Cora was out the door before anyone could object. Five minutes later she was back with a set of keys. "I'll help you get ready."

And that was that. Cora pulled together several days' worth of diapers for Carlito, clothes for all of them, and some toys and books. Meanwhile, Luz let the women whose children she took care of know she wouldn't be available next week. There were a few cries of anguish, but Luz, who had never taken any time off, hardened her heart against them. Besides, with Christmas coming on Friday, she'd be away only three work days. At least she hoped they wouldn't be gone longer than that. Otherwise, word might get back to the owner she was away, and if that happened she could end up looking at a permanent absence from the Draper Arms.

Still, this wasn't the time to worry about that. The important thing was to keep Marisol and Carlito safe, and she needed to be safe as well, in order to be there to take care of them.

Charles loaded the plastic bags holding clothes and toys into the Bayleys' trunk while Luz strapped Carlito and Marisol in.

As he drove, Charles told them where they were going. "TapDancer Ranch. The Francinis breed and train horses."

Marisol clapped her hands in excitement. "Maybe we can go riding, Luz. Do you think they might let us, Mr. Larimore?"

"Well, they certainly have plenty of horses."

They topped a rise, to find the ranch spread before them. A huge silvery gray barn, a mix of outbuildings, pastures dotted with horses and, overlooking it all, a wood-and-glass house that seemed to simply grow from the hill. Luz took a deep breath, not realizing she was grinning until Marisol squeezed her hand.

She began to suspect that being threatened by a lunatic might be the best thing to happen to her in a long time.

Chapter Twelve

Charles intended to drop Luz and the kids off at the ranch and return immediately to Denver, but that was foiled when Alan's mother, Stella, insisted he have a cup of coffee first. Feeling guilty about missing Thanksgiving, he agreed.

"You know, we consider Charles our second son," Stella told Luz, giving him a fond look that made him want to squirm. "And it's been awhile since he's been to the ranch."

"Can we see the horses?" Marisol asked.

"Why certainly," Stella said. "Do you like horses?"

Charles smiled at Marisol, pleased she had short-circuited Stella's comments about his sonship and his long absence.

"I used to have a pony." Marisol set her mug of hot chocolate down and licked at the creamy mustache on her lip. "Her name was Miss Springflower, but we called her Missy."

She had to be talking about a stuffed animal.

"Luz told me I have good hands." Marisol sat back and held out her hands for Stella to inspect.

Charles had no idea what that was about, but Stella seemed to understand. "Why, we'll have to introduce you," Stella told her. "We have several Galicenos, which are wonderful with children."

Luz cocked her head. "They're from Mexico, aren't they?"

Stella nodded. "And we have Paso Finos from Puerto Rico."

A shadow crossed Luz's face. "We had a Peruvian Paso."

So maybe Missy was a real horse.

They finished their snack, and Stella led the way to the

barn. Curious to see what would happen next, he went along.

Alan's dad, Rob, was in the corral, working with a horse, and he rode over to greet them. Stella made the introductions, and when she told him Luz and Marisol wanted to ride, he led the way to the barn.

Charles took Carlito from Luz and stood with Stella inside the barn door while Marisol and Luz made their way down the row of stalls. Clearly, both of them were in heaven, their eyes shining with happiness as they reached out to pat inquisitive noses. Rob led a pony out, tethered it, gave Marisol a brush and then led Luz to another stall. Charles didn't think Marisol should be left alone with the pony, but it didn't seem to worry anyone else.

Alan's border collie, Cormac, ambled over to say hello. Carlito leaned toward the dog, and Charles knelt to allow the two to get acquainted.

"Alan said Luz might have to stay several days." Stella's voice held a question.

He stood and bounced Carlito, trying to distract him from his determination to get down and play with Cormac. "We'll try to get things cleared up as quickly as we can. We know who's making the threat. It's simply a matter of finding him."

"Here." Stella gestured for him to hand over Carlito. "What a cutie you are," she cooed, taking the little boy in her arms. Carlito, momentarily charmed, stopped squirming.

"They may have to stay through Christmas, though. I'm real sorry to impose on you like this."

"Don't you worry about that. We have plenty of room, and Elaine will be thrilled we've recruited a playmate for our grandson." Carlito squirmed, and Stella played a quick game of peek-a-boo with him. "You'll be joining us, of course?"

He should have seen the invitation coming and sidestepped it, but somehow he hadn't, and now he had no choice but to accept, unless he was willing to hurt Stella's feelings more than he already had over Thanksgiving. Resigned, he nodded. "You'd better count on one more, as well. Luz has a woman living with her. Her name is Cora. She's Marisol and Carlito's unofficial grandmother."

Stella laughed. "Well, of course, bring her along. The more

the merrier."

Rob helped Marisol saddle the pony, while further down the row Luz, with quick expertise, finished saddling and bridling a larger horse.

Charles took Carlito, who was a big armful, back from Stella, and as Luz led her mount toward them, Carlito reached his arms to Luz, burbling, "Lu lu lu lu."

Luz grinned at the toddler and spoke to him in Spanish. Carlito kicked and straightened, trying to free himself from Charles's arms.

"It's okay, Charles. You can put him down."

He thought that was a bad idea, but Luz was the boss. He set the toddler on his feet, and Luz's horse bent its head and snuffled at the little boy. Carlito sat with a plop, looking surprised, which made everybody laugh, except Charles who had to stifle his alarm at the proximity of horse and toddler.

He moved quickly to pick Carlito back up, and they all went outside. Luz and Marisol mounted and rode around the corral, while Charles held Carlito and tried to calm his nervousness at the sight of Luz and Marisol on horses.

Then it got worse. Luz's mount began to trot, and the pony followed suit. They swept by, going much too fast. What on earth was Luz thinking, letting Marisol ride a large animal all by herself, and then encouraging that animal to run? Swallowing over the lump in his throat, he glanced at Rob and Stella, but they were both smiling and apparently unconcerned.

After several circuits, Luz slowed her horse and leaned over to speak to Marisol, who turned her pony and walked it over to stand near them. Then Luz proceeded to take her mount through a series of maneuvers: quick turns, gait changes, and figure eights.

Although he watched closely, Charles was unable to discern how Luz, sitting straight and still in the saddle, was getting the animal to do what she wanted.

Alan's father turned to him with a wide grin. "Daggone it, Charles. Why didn't you tell us you knew a world class rider?"

And how was he expected to know that?

Rob's tone was reverent. "We're going to have to find out what she's doing this summer. If she's not busy, she's got a riding job."

Luz came over and swung to the ground, smiling. "You have a good little horse here." She patted its neck, and the horse responded by pushing at her, making her laugh.

Charles didn't remember ever hearing Luz laugh so easily, or look so carefree—like the woman she was meant to be.

Marisol wanted to ride some more, so Luz remounted and rode with her. Then Luz rode over and had him hand her Carlito, and she gave the giggling toddler a turn. That made Charles's mouth dry out completely.

They finally dismounted, and he breathed a sigh of relief and took his leave to return the car to the Bayleys.

ಬಿ

Luz had tried not to even think about the horses. When she did, the realization that Martin had probably sold them both made her hands clench in fury. Missy was the first luxury *Papi* had allowed them after his business got established, and Salsalita, the Peruvian Paso, had been *Mami*'s wedding gift to *Papi*. When Luz's legs got too long for Missy, she'd ridden Salsalita, and *Papi* had worked with her, teaching her dressage.

To be around horses again was an unexpected, overwhelming gift.

In addition to her pleasure in the horses, there was the delight of getting to know Rob and Stella, both of whom she took to immediately. After an hour at the ranch, she felt herself opening up, everything inside her loosening.

Although she worked hard to help around the house and the barn, being at the Francinis' felt like a vacation. It was the first time she'd been able to relax since the day she ran away from Scottsbluff. When she wasn't worrying about the arsonist doing something to hurt Charles or Cora, she was giddy with the pleasure of it.

ಬಿ

On the dresser in the bedroom Stella had given them was a photo of Charles and another man with a beautiful young woman. When Luz asked Stella about the picture, a shadow crossed the older woman's face. She took the photo from Luz and stared at it for a moment before she handed it back. "That's Charles, of course, with our son, Alan, and his wife, Meg." She sniffed, her eyes filling. "I thought about putting it away. She died, you see."

"Oh. I'm so sorry," Luz said.

"Six years ago. Now Alan is remarrying. We love Kathy, and we're thrilled Alan found her, but we don't want to forget Meg."

"No. Of course not." She remembered *Mami*'s insistence that she have a picture of her mother for her dresser. Further, *Mami* had insisted that Marisol and Carlito have Spanish as well as English names, and she'd made sure Luz continued to speak Spanish, although there were times at school when Luz, not wanting to be different, pretended she didn't know how.

It had been that generosity of spirit that led the small girl Luz had been to love her stepmother so much, she viewed Mary Blair as her very own *mami*.

She wondered if Kathy would also understand the necessity for not turning completely away from the past.

෨

"Charles sure doesn't seem to like horses very much." Luz and Rob were currying the two youngsters they would be working with that day, and Luz viewed it as a perfect opportunity to learn more about Charles.

Rob shook his head in apparent wonder. "Nope. Boy will get on a bike and ride in Denver traffic, but he considers a horse dangerous."

"Why do you think that is?" She liked being with Rob. He reminded her of *Papi,* with his weathered skin and lean body hardened by years of outdoor work.

"He's never said."

"Do you think he's in any danger right now?" Mostly she tried not to dwell on the reason she was at the ranch, but sometimes it hit her, making it hard for her to breathe.

"Well, a policewoman's living right next door. I expect he's safer in the apartment than riding in traffic."

She frowned. "What policewoman?"

"They've got someone impersonating you, hoping they'll fool the guy into trying to grab her."

Luz blinked. "What about Cora?"

"Oh, you mean the lady who lives with you. Well, I don't rightly know. Charles didn't mention her, but I'm sure she's fine."

Charles called at least once a day to check on them, but he never asked to speak to her. Further proof, not that she needed any, that he didn't consider her an equal.

A thought as painful as knowing he was in danger.

&

"Was Charles ever married?" Although she tried, Luz couldn't seem to stop asking the Francinis questions about Charles.

"Oh my, no." Stella shook her head, clicking her tongue. "He always has a girlfriend, but they never seem to stick."

Her immediate pleasure at the news Charles had never been serious about someone quickly evaporated as Luz realized it was simply additional evidence he wasn't going to fall for her. She vowed to stop asking about him, but her vocal cords refused to get with the program. "That's odd. He seems like such a nice man." Her fingers, also ignoring the vow, crossed.

Stella, chopping onions, paused. "He's one of the finest young men we know, and he deserves to find a special woman who appreciates him and loves him dearly. He's been on my prayer list for years, but it just hasn't happened yet."

Luz thought about all the months Charles had lived at the Draper Arms without bringing a woman home. At least not that she'd seen or heard, and if he'd done it regularly, she was pretty sure she would have known about it. Of course, he did come home late a lot of nights. That could mean he'd been out with a woman. Still, if he did have a girlfriend, it was odd he hadn't spent Thanksgiving with her.

Or maybe he didn't want to bring a woman to the Draper Arms. It wasn't exactly the most romantic place, although since he'd painted and bought the new quilt for his bed, his apartment *was* quite pleasant. And he kept it meticulously neat and clean.

That first time, when she'd gone in to fix his faucet, she'd been surprised to find his kitchen completely free of clutter, without even a dirty coffee cup in the sink. His bathroom was equally neat, and his bed was always made and all his clothes put away. Not that she'd pried or anything, but he did keep complaining about leaks, so it *had* been her job to fix them.

&

Stella knocked on Luz's door to ask if she had any jeans to add to a load of laundry. Luz handed over a pair of Marisol's.

"What about yours?" Stella asked.

Luz grimaced. Her jeans were beginning to show the effects of mucking out and riding. "I don't have another pair. With me," she added quickly, not wanting Stella to feel sorry for her.

Stella gave her a measuring look. "Our daughter, Elaine, left some things here that might fit you." She pointed. "In the closet and the bottom drawer. Take a look. I'm sure she won't mind."

Luz found two pairs of jeans, one light blue from many washings and a black pair that were only slightly faded. They both fit much more snugly than her own pair. Wearing the blue ones, she carried her jeans to the laundry area.

Stella beamed. "See, I was right. Other than being a little short, they fit you perfectly. There were some shirts, too, weren't there?"

"In the closet."

"Well, you feel free to wear whatever you like, dear."

Luz spent a happy thirty minutes trying on clothes. None were fancy, but they were well made, and wearing the bright colors made her feel pretty. She settled on a yellow shirt to go with the pale blue jeans.

At lunch, when she walked in carrying the platter of sandwiches she and Stella had prepared, Rob whistled appreciatively. It was so like something *Papi* would do, her chest tightened, and she found it hard to swallow.

Chapter Thirteen

Alan and Kathy arrived at the ranch for Christmas to find Charles's neighbor riding one of the three-year-olds his father was training.

Alan climbed out of the car and walked over to the corral to watch. Kathy joined him, wincing as the filly executed a quick sideways hop. "Hey. She's good, isn't she."

"Uh huh." He smiled at Kathy and looped his arm around her. "Looks like she knows her way around a horse." And if that wasn't the last thing he was expecting, it was close to it. "When that youngster tried that move on me, I ended up in the dirt."

As the day progressed, Alan saw that Luz and her two children had been absorbed into his family as seamlessly as if they'd been a part of it for years. He was glad of it, and even more pleased that their presence eased his own nervousness about the public aspects of this holiday—the gift giving, the family dinner, the inevitable "do you remember the year that..." Such a relief to have this distraction of new people for whose sake reminiscences would be curtailed, helping to make this first Christmas with Kathy a different kind of celebration, a final step away from his past.

&

Charles missed Luz and Marisol more than he expected to. Odd how knowing there was no chance of running into them made laundry so much more of a chore.

The police moved a decoy into Luz's apartment, and she

was subsequently seen around the apartment house wearing loose jeans and oversize T-shirts carrying either Luz's toolbox or her laundry basket. Charles doubted Snodgrass would be fooled by such a graceless version of his neighbor.

Another police officer, dressed as a painter, came in and worked on Cora's old apartment. Charles suggested colors—if they were going to paint, they might as well make it worthwhile.

As for him, he no longer tried to hide as he went to and from work, and when he went running, he stuck to the surrounding neighborhood, always keeping an eye out for the arsonist. But Snodgrass appeared to be taking the holidays off.

It was frustrating waiting for something to happen. Frustrating as well, trying to decide what to do about his other problem—Luz's legal difficulties.

At times, he felt suspended by events and at others like he was slowly sinking into quicksand. He countered his futility by focusing on Christmas preparations, trying to forget he was going to be forced, because of Luz's situation, to spend the day in close proximity to Kathy and Alan.

"Be sure you come early," Stella told him.

Stomach clenching with tension, he said he would.

ॐ

Kathy had spent weeks trying to decide what to get Alan for Christmas, wanting this, their first one together, to be perfect. Wanting her first gift to him to be one he would always cherish. And then, after weeks of angst, the ideal gift simply presented itself when her children's story was released earlier than expected.

On the dedication page, she wrote,

> *Alan,*
>
> *I thought I knew what love was, but it wasn't until I met you that my heart saw clearly. I ask nothing more of the future than to share it with you.*
>
> *Love, Kathy*

She also purchased a copy of the book she considered her inspiration, *The Little Prince*. In that one she wrote,

> *My Dearest Alan,*
> *Although I didn't know it until I found you,*
> *I've spent my life searching for you.*
> *All my love, Kathy*

Hoping for a private chance to exchange these first gifts with him, she was pleased when everyone went off early to bed on Christmas Eve, leaving her and Alan alone by the fire.

Feeling content, she curled into him. He settled the quilt from the back of the sofa over them, pulling her close.

They kissed until they were both dizzy with desire.

Alan pulled back. "If we don't take it easy, I'm going to have a hard time sleeping tonight." At his parents' they still occupied separate rooms.

She smiled, touching him gently. "Seems to me we're already well past that point."

For a time they gazed at each other. Then the smile lines next to his eyes smoothed, and his mouth firmed. He put a finger across her lips. "You have to promise you'll be quiet." His voice was rough, his eyes dark with desire.

She nodded already reaching to undo his belt both of them too excited to draw it out. Afterwards, she felt like laughing and crying in a mad mix of joy, pleasure and relief. All of it part of the long, difficult journey they had taken to this moment, to each other.

They lay twined together for a time, then they sat up, straightened their clothes and stared at the flames until she remembered her plan. "I want to give you your present tonight."

He shook his head. "Already got my present."

She grinned and punched his arm lightly before going over to the tree. He pointed out a package for her, and she retrieved it along with her gift for him.

"You first," she said.

"Nope. Ladies first."

The box from him was large but mostly filled with tissue paper. Nestled in the middle was a small box and in the box was an old-fashioned diamond ring. A number of tiny stones circled a large center stone that threw off shards of green, blue and red as she turned it.

"Oh. Oh. It's absolutely beautiful." She raised her face, letting her love for him blaze in her eyes. "But we agreed not to spend much."

"It was my grandmother's." He smoothed a finger along the bodice of the vintage dress she was wearing. "The perfect ring for an old-fashioned girl."

He lifted her right hand and slid the ring on. That surprised her as well, but also pleased her. The wide wedding bands they'd chosen wouldn't work with this ring.

"Oh, it fits." She threw her arms around him and kissed him.

He shifted a bit. "We'd better stop before I get in trouble again."

Smiling, she let him go and handed him her gift. "I can't compete with a family heirloom, but, well, here."

He opened the package and lifted out the top book. It was her children's story, *Bobby and Brad*. He turned the page and read what she'd written, and from the look he gave her, she knew her gift had touched his heart.

But when he picked up the second book, he froze. He stared at it for a moment before giving her a smile that didn't reach his eyes, or even come close. Instead, he had the look she dreaded seeing. The one that meant he'd been pulled into the past.

She took the book from him and slipped it behind her back. "Well, I can tell you already have that one. I'll return it and get you something else." The bright, false words spilled out, as she careened along a razor's edge. If she slipped, she would fall into the same dark hole as Alan.

Weeks since the last time it happened. So why did it have to happen now? She didn't want her first Christmas Eve with him to end like this, but she didn't know how to alter it.

The fire, no longer bright and blazing, had subsided

without them noticing. Alan got up and bent over to bank it for the night. She gathered together all the wrapping paper, boxes and the offending book.

He straightened, and she kissed him lightly, saying, "Merry Christmas, Alan. I love you."

"Love you too, Kath." His voice was hoarse, and he was having trouble meeting her eyes. Dammit, why hadn't she thought to talk to Elaine before she bought Alan a book? Christmas...a potential minefield, but she'd gone blithely off, not thinking. It was obviously a book he'd shared with Meg. Stupid, stupid. And after she'd been so careful about the wedding plans.

∞

Kathy didn't expect to sleep, but realized she must have when she was surprised awake by Marisol's happy laughter. She dressed quickly and put on makeup to cover the dark circles under her eyes.

Alan was already in the living room, sitting in one of the chairs. The three children were under the tree surrounded by packages, and, watching them, Alan hadn't yet noticed her. She stood for a moment studying him.

He looked as tired as she felt. Then he saw her and smiled. He motioned her over and pulled her onto his lap, murmuring in her ear as she settled against him, "Merry Christmas. Love you, Kathleen Hope." He took her hand in his and rubbed his finger against the ring he'd given her. She pressed against him, wanting something more, an acknowledgement perhaps, that he understood she was hurting, too. *Dammit, why did it have to be this way?*

Carlito and Mark were more interested in shredding paper than in the toys. "Typical guys," Alan murmured, and she smiled, although the memory of the previous night still hovered, a faint shadow over the day.

Chapter Fourteen

Luz had called to give Charles instructions on where to find the presents. He put them in the Porsche's trunk along with the gifts he'd bought for everyone, and Cora added more packages. Since meeting Luz he'd begun to realize how impractical the Porsche was, although originally that had been its most appealing characteristic. Now, it seemed that sort of thinking was being turned inside out.

He was grateful he had Cora to talk to as they drove to the ranch. It kept him from developing a full-blown case of nervous tension at the thought of spending the day in close proximity to Kathy and having to pretend he was happy she and Alan were together. He was sure he could pull it off, although he did regret not popping a couple more antacids in his pocket.

Luckily, there would be other people around—the senior Francinis, their daughter Elaine and her husband and infant son, Mark, and of course Luz, Marisol, Carlito, and Cora. Plenty of people to buffer any interactions with Kathy.

He distracted himself with thoughts of how Marisol and Carlito would respond to the gifts he'd chosen for them. Actually, he knew how Carlito would. He'd chew on it. He was teething and everything went in his mouth.

Cora had been as easy to shop for as Carlito. A pair of dove gray gloves and a box of embroidered handkerchiefs. He hadn't known such things were for sale until he went looking. The most fun, though, had been choosing the gifts for Luz.

൪

The kids got through their gifts, and Alan eased Kathy off his lap, kissed her and went to the barn to do the mucking out. That was one thing about a ranch—no days off.

He finished, showered and dressed and was almost himself again, except for the nudgy, uncomfortable feeling he'd failed Kathy, again. A feeling that intensified as the family sat around chatting and waiting for Charles and Cora to arrive.

Kathy sat on the floor, resting against his legs, rarely adding to the conversation. He leaned forward and smoothed his hand on her hair, letting it come to rest on her shoulder. She glanced around and gave him a distracted smile, and he knew he had to do something to make things right between them. The only problem? He had no idea what that something should be.

Charles drove up, and Alan went to meet him and the elderly woman with him. Marisol ran over to give Cora and Charles hugs, and Carlito stood and toddled toward Charles, his arms outstretched.

Charles bent over and picked him up, saying, "Hey, Carlito. *¿Qué pasa?*"

Shocked, Alan stared at his friend, who looked exactly like a proud papa greeting his kids after being away.

Alan switched his attention to Luz. He had to admit Luz was looking very pretty today. She was wearing a blue sweater that seemed familiar and black jeans that showed off a trim figure.

She kept glancing at Charles, and Alan could see she was smitten, poor thing. She didn't stand a chance, of course. She might be a terrific cook and wonderful person (his mother's assessment) and a world class horsewoman (his dad's), but she was too young and too encumbered for Charles to give her more than a passing glance. Too bad, because she was probably exactly the sort of woman Charles needed to be attracted to.

Charles glanced quickly around the room. His eyes widened slightly when they reached Luz. Surprise? Or something else? He'd also, in that sweep, located Kathy, and he didn't look in that direction again.

They started opening the rest of the gifts, and the memory of last Christmas made Alan's throat tighten with pain. He'd met Kathy, but he hadn't yet loved her, and grief had still held him fast. But then, last night had shown he still wasn't completely in the clear. And this time, he wasn't the only one who'd been hurt by his memories.

Luz's discomfort with the number of her gifts was obvious. In an aside, his mother had told him Luz had practically no clothes, and the clothes she had looked like they were from the Salvation Army. Well, that would no longer be the case given the two pair of jeans, black slacks, several shirts and sweaters and long wool skirt in a maroon shade that Luz was freeing from their wrappings.

Out of curiosity, he kept an eye on Charles's gifts for Luz and her family. It wasn't difficult. Charles had wrapped all his presents in the same blue and green paper.

For Marisol it was a package of books. *Black Beauty, Misty of Chincoteague*, a large picture book of different horse breeds, and a copy of *Bobby and Brad*. Alan blinked in surprise, as he was well acquainted with Charles's horse phobia. Not to mention his kid phobia. But that he'd included a copy of Kathy's book was the real shock, given that Charles was obviously still pained by the ending of their relationship.

For Carlito, Charles had bought a couple of wooden puzzles and a stuffed bear. Carlito promptly chewed on the puzzle pieces. Charles even had a gift for Cora, and from the way Cora's eyes misted up, it had to be something chosen because he knew her well.

Luz had set the two packages from Charles aside to open last, but she was finally removing the paper from the larger of the two. She lifted the lid off a gold-embossed box and pushed aside tissue paper. Then she sat for a time staring at whatever was inside.

Charles was playing with Carlito, but keeping an eye on Luz as she lifted his gift out of the box. It was a pale pink sweater and a silk scarf in deeper shades of pink and green. She bit her lip, obviously trying not to cry.

She glanced over at Charles, and her lips moved in a silent, *thank you*, as she clasped the sweater to her chest. Charles ducked his head, and Luz refolded the sweater and replaced it in its wrappings before opening her last gift. Slowly she lifted it out of the box with a quizzical expression.

Everyone was looking by then.

"Why it's a Christmas puzzle, isn't it?" Elaine said.

Luz looked over at Charles, who nodded.

The wooden base had four bracelets anchored in place. Two of the bracelets were large enough to fit Luz's wrist, and two were smaller and appeared to be the right size for Marisol. Five pegs rose from the base, and on top of each sat a tiny horse—two were crystal, two were wood and the last pewter. It was the most beautiful of all the puzzles Charles had put together over the years, and clearly, once the puzzle was solved, the bracelets and horse figurines were additional gifts.

"Now there's got to be a story attached to this," Elaine said, walking over to examine the puzzle. She stood with her hand casually resting on Charles's shoulder, and Alan remembered the brief time when he thought Charles might end up not only his best friend but his brother-in-law.

Charles smiled wickedly at Elaine. "She solved this year's Francini-Larimore Christmas puzzle in six hours. She needs something more challenging."

"Hey, you told me it took her a couple of days," he protested.

"That was her official time, but she figured it out before that. Just didn't know she had to report immediately. That reminds me, you guys are slipping. You haven't made a half-way decent guess in days."

"Raindrops on roses and whiskers on kittens," he said.

"So where does the globe fit in?" Charles asked.

"A world of wonder," Elaine said.

Luz blinked and smiled like a cat that had swallowed a goldfish.

Charles shook his head. "So how about it, Francinis? Are you ready to concede defeat to a mere slip of a girl, a neophyte to our grandiose gaming?" He glanced around the room, and when no one objected, he raised his eyebrows at Luz. He picked up the globe sitting on the coffee table and handed it to her.

She pointed to the rose, parasol and kitten. "Wee things and three of them. Wee three things. We three kings. The *R* on China. Of Orient are," she finished.

Alan shook his head in consternation. So easy to see once she said it. Hard to ferret out, though, given Charles's love of misdirection. Not to mention embarrassing to be beat by someone who hadn't had years of experience solving their puzzles.

"So how about this one?" Alan pointed at the horses. "Any thoughts."

Luz shook her head. "Not yet."

Although she was interacting with all of them, Luz's eyes kept drifting back to Charles. No question, she had it bad.

She seemed like a nice youngster. He hoped Charles would let her down gently. Although it was odd Charles would make her a puzzle, admitting her into the tightest ranks of friendship, someplace he'd never admitted a woman before.

But no. Luz had two children, and Charles did not get involved with women who had children.

Although he certainly appeared to be involved with Luz, Marisol and Carlito. At least he was comfortable with them, and that comfort even extended to Elaine's son. Right before dinner, Alan stepped into the living room to find Charles holding both Carlito and Mark while he read to Marisol from one of her new books.

Charles seemed perfectly content, and Alan was both pleased and relieved to see it.

Christmas was very different from what Charles anticipated. The biggest surprise? The sight of Kathy and Alan together didn't seem to be hurting as much as he expected. Of course his attention kept getting diverted—by Marisol and Carlito, Cora and Luz.

The unpleasant surprise of the day was the pang he felt that Luz didn't have a gift for him. Not that he wanted her to spend money on him, but a small token would have meant she at least thought kindly of him, something he wasn't at all certain of.

But then on the way into dinner, she came up to him, detaining him with a touch on the arm. "Thank you for the sweater and the scarf. They're beautiful. And I thought it'd be okay to wear one of the bracelets." She lifted her arm to show him. "I didn't have a gift for you, because I couldn't decide, and then we came here and...I. I just wanted you to know, I didn't forget you."

She looked so worried and serious, he wanted to lean forward and kiss the furrows from her brow. And what exactly was that all about? Luz was...well, what was she exactly? Dressed in the sweater he'd chosen, with her cheeks rosy from nearly a week in the outdoors, she looked nothing like the sallow young woman he first met fixing his leaky faucet, God was it only three and a half months ago?

He laid his hand gently on her shoulder, because suddenly it was impossible not to touch her. "I'm glad you like the sweater. It looks nice on you."

Well, that was certainly eloquent. Nice indeed. She looked delicious, and kissable, and—good lord, this was Luz he was thinking about kissing. That damn libido of his. No discrimination whatsoever. Luz was...impossible. She had two children to raise, for Pete's sake. Granted she wasn't exactly a single mother, but she might as well be. And besides, even more problematic than that were her age and her ambiguous legal status.

He snatched his hand away, and Luz's expression changed to the annoyed look she seemed to reserve especially for him. She turned abruptly and preceded him, back stiff, into the dining room where the last two places, unfortunately, were right across from each other.

Throughout dinner, he avoided looking at Luz. It was even easier, he discovered, to look at Kathy than at Luz, a turn of events he welcomed but also found troubling.

After dinner Carlito and Mark went down for naps, Charles helped Stella do dishes and everyone else went to the barn to take apples and carrots to the horses.

Charles wiped the last pot, then gave Stella a hug from behind and a kiss on the cheek.

She laughed up at him. "What's that for."

"For being nice to Luz."

"She's easy to be nice to."

He shook his head in amusement. Luz, his Luz? The I'm-not-poor-and-I-don't-take-handouts girl? Amazing that she had accepted the gifts this morning without a single tart comment.

"She's a special person," Stella continued. "I'm going to miss her when she leaves. So is Rob. She's wonderful with the horses."

"She needs a job." He was just trying it out. Not because he'd thought it through or anything.

Stella turned and gave him a serious look. "There's more to that story than you're telling us, isn't there."

Well, it served him right for hinting at things. He hugged Stella again. "You'll have to ask Luz about that."

For Luz, Christmas was a day of constantly shifting vignettes as people came together in various combinations. She was thankful for the slightly chaotic quality. It helped keep her grief contained at being here with these people instead of home with *Papi* and *Mami*. But suddenly it was all too much, the gaiety and joy. Sparking memories of another day much like today—and nobody guessing it would be the last time they would celebrate Christmas together. Her eyes filled with tears. Quickly, she left the room before anybody noticed.

She came out of her room to find Charles loitering in the doorway to the living room. He turned at her approach and raised his eyebrows in question, as if he'd seen her distress and was checking on her. Because he was a nice man and because she and the kids were his project. Not because she was special. Something she'd do well not to forget.

But most of the day, she was okay. She listened more than she talked, the multiple overlapping conversations sometimes making her dizzy. Everyone interacting except Charles and Kathy. Luz had been shocked when she recognized Alan's fiancé as the woman who had visited Charles, and their avoiding each other now told Luz something she didn't want to know—that Charles cared more than he should for his best friend's fiancé.

Equally clear, Kathy loved Alan, although Kathy's eyes seemed sad. Impossible for Luz, who barely knew these people, to sort out exactly what was going on.

It was a mystery and likely would have remained one if she and Kathy hadn't ended up alone together the day after Christmas.

They were in the barn grooming the two horses they'd just finished riding, while Alan and his father worked two others. It was an opportunity Luz didn't want to pass up. "You know, Marisol and I read your book last night. We liked it. A lot. I wondered if you'd sign it for her."

Kathy, with a happy look, said she would be pleased to do that, but then the pensive look she'd had since Christmas morning returned. Maybe it was that hint of sadness, or perhaps it was the knowledge Kathy was marrying a widower that gave Luz the sudden urge to tell her what she actually thought about the book.

"Your book. It...well..." She bit her lip as she continued to brush the rough coat of the filly. "I think it's going to help Marisol. And me, too. You see, our parents...they died in an accident. It's been hard, but after we read your story, Marisol asked if *Papi* and *Mami* went into a picture, too. And then we looked through our photos, and she..." She gulped and scrubbed an arm across her eyes. Damn, she thought she could do this.

She didn't realize Kathy had put her brush down and come over to her until she felt the other woman's arms go around her. With a rush, the sobs broke loose.

Such a relief to let go. She'd been holding on tight for so long, trying to keep her grief bottled up so she wouldn't frighten Marisol. Trying to pretend for Marisol's sake that *Papi* and *Mami* were right here with them, watching over them.

The tears came pouring out, and while they did, Kathy held her as if they were dear friends, not two women who'd only just met. Kathy maneuvered them over to a bale of hay, and they sat down. Luz's sobbing eased, and she hiccupped and sniffed. Cormac appeared and nudged her leg, then put a paw on her knee and cocked his head as if asking what he could do to help.

She patted Cormac's head, not looking at Kathy. "Sorry about that. I try not to cry in front of Marisol and Carlito. Guess it got all dammed up."

Withdrawing her arm, Kathy patted Luz's shoulder but continued to sit next to her. After a time, she spoke softly. "I wrote *Bobby and Brad* for Alan. He lost someone infinitely precious to him, and he wasn't able to let her go."

She had to be talking about Meg, perhaps trying to share

something of equal value to the pain Luz had shared.

"It takes a long time to get over a loss like that," Kathy continued. "I don't believe a person ever does, really. Not completely. What's helped Alan are his family, Charles and that story."

Luz, remembering the way Alan's face lit up whenever he looked at this woman, thought she was leaving one major source of his healing unnamed. "And you," she said.

As Kathy raised her eyes, Luz realized the pain she had sensed in the other woman had something to do with what she was saying. That the man she loved and intended to marry had first loved, and lost, someone else.

"Anyone can see how much he loves you." The way Kathy and Alan looked at each other filled Luz with longing. She wanted Charles to look at her that way. Instead, he mainly seemed to view her with either puzzlement or impatience. The ache in her heart demanded she know what Kathy meant to Charles. She cleared her throat, but her voice was still croaky. "You and Charles." She stumbled to a stop, unable to go further.

Kathy, turned her head, surprise widening her eyes.

"When he looks at you..." No, she couldn't do it. Couldn't bear to find out for sure there was something between them. "For such good friends, Charles and Alan seem awkward with each other," she said, instead.

"Last summer, Alan and I were estranged, and Charles and I dated. It was a difficult time, but we never..." Kathy took a breath before going on. "In the end, Alan and I hurt Charles. Although we didn't mean to." Her hands lay clenched in her lap. "They'd been friends for years. I went to see Charles that time, because—"

"He's in love with you," Luz said. Her voice sounded distant and matter-of-fact, but the words had cut her lips and tongue on the way out.

"No. We weren't...no."

For a time, they sat side by side, Luz petting Cormac and Kathy staring at nothing, until Luz found the courage to ask the rest of what she wanted to know. "Stella said Charles has had lots of girlfriends, but none of them stick."

Kathy was silent for a long time before shaking her head. "I don't know why. Charles is a wonderful man. If I hadn't already been in love with Alan...well." She laid a hand on Luz's wrist. "He deserves someone who can love him with a whole heart." She leaned her hands against her thighs and stood, shutting off any more confidences.

Luz went back to the house, and Kathy waited in the barn for Alan, feeling both thoughtful and confused. Luz's grief, and the reason for it, had been a shock. She wondered if Charles knew Luz's story. But he must, given the role he'd assumed as their protector.

"He may not have figured it out yet, but I think Charles is attracted to Luz," Kathy told Alan when he brought in the last of the horses. It was an experiment, really, to find out what he thought.

"She's in love with him, that's pretty clear, but Charles never dates women with children."

She wasn't sure which part of Alan's statement surprised her more—that he'd noticed Luz's feelings for Charles, or the part about Charles not dating women with children. "Why not?"

"He doesn't like kids."

"Well, he sure gave a good imitation of someone who likes them." The subject of children hadn't yet come up when she was dating Charles, but she found Alan's bald statement impossible to believe. "Besides, they're not hers. She's their sister."

"What? What makes you say that?"

"She told me. Their parents died." Remembering Luz's grief, she shivered. "I like her. She's young, but she's exactly the kind of person Charles needs."

"Leave it be." Alan led the colt back to his stall. "You can't fix things for Charles. He has to do it for himself."

He came up behind her and put his arms around her. She snuggled against him, and he rubbed his chin gently against the top of her head. "Speaking of doing things for himself, I owe you an apology."

She shook her head.

"Yeah, I do. It was the surprise, not that it's any excuse. I'm

137

sorry, Kath. It hurts me when I hurt you. Guess it's still going to take awhile."

"I know."

"Sure you still want to stick it out with me?"

"Of course I do." Her voice trembled, thick with tears.

"I wish it didn't have to be this way."

"It's okay, Alan. No beating on yourself allowed."

He turned her, pulled a handkerchief from his pocket and dried her face. "You're really something, Kath. Don't know what I did to deserve you."

"But it must have been something awfully good." She smiled through her tears.

"Yeah." He pulled her back into his arms and held her tight.

And it was all okay again, because he'd been able, finally, to talk about it, at least a little.

Chapter Fifteen

Two days after Christmas, Charles called the ranch to say Snodgrass had been arrested. Luz felt a mix of relief, anger and sorrow at the news—relief that Snodgrass would no longer be a threat to any of the Draper Arms residents, anger that he dared to threaten them in the first place and sorrow that their time at TapDancer was at an end.

She told Marisol they would be going back to Denver in the morning, and the little girl burst into tears. "But why can't we stay, Luz? I like it here. I don't want to go."

Luz wanted to cry herself. The time at TapDancer had reminded her what it was like to be part of an extended family. Although she'd known Rob and Stella only a week, she already loved them. And they seemed to return her affection.

But a person didn't sit on a bed, like Marisol was doing, her arms crossed, with a mutinous expression on her face and tears dripping down it. Although on second thought, Luz wasn't sure why not. It was exactly what she felt like doing.

It wasn't fair. To be given a glimpse of paradise only to have it jerked away. She put her arms around Marisol, but the little girl pushed her away and buried her head in her pillow, sobbing.

In that moment, the full weight of her decision to run off with Carlito and Marisol pressed down on Luz. What if she'd been wrong? Maybe Marisol and Carlito would have been placed with a wonderful family, like the Francinis. Instead, with her, they were barely scraping by, forced to hide from their uncle *and* almost victims of a crazed arsonist.

A tide of terror, huge and black, made Luz double over. She

stumbled into the bathroom and closed the door, glad Marisol was crying too loudly to notice.

She sank to the floor and turned her cheek against the cool wall, her arms tight around herself. For a time the fear she'd been pushing away for a year held sway.

What am I going to do?

Even without the threat of Charles turning them in, they couldn't go on the way they were indefinitely. But the only place she might find the help she needed was Scottsbluff, the one place she didn't dare set foot in.

The door opened, and Marisol, her eyes red and her hair mussed, wandered in.

"Luz? Luz, are you okay?"

With fresh tears, Marisol launched herself into Luz's arms, quivering with fear. Luz was finally able to set aside her own fear as she comforted her sister. "It's okay, Mari. I'm sad we have to leave TapDancer, too. But Cora is waiting for us, and you have to get back to school and everything is going to be fine." Luz held Marisol, rubbing her back and saying the words over and over, until they were both calmed.

Holding Marisol, Luz knew her only choice for the future was the same one it had been for the past year. To simply take this day, do the best with it she was able and not worry about tomorrow.

ꝏ

After Luz and the children returned to Denver on Sunday, Marisol came over to tell Charles they were back. She didn't look happy about it though.

Monday morning, he encountered Luz as he was leaving for work. She was taking out the trash, and didn't look happy either. She greeted him only briefly, before moving past him.

A burst of disappointment, out of all proportion to her action, dampened his mood, and he went to work feeling out of sorts, all the happy Christmas feelings dissipated.

The day went downhill from there.

Joanna called at nine. "I'm so sorry, Charles." Her words

hitched and bumped along. "I just talked to Spinell. Told him I can't. Can't—" A sob cut off the rest.

Charles waited with growing concern as Joanna struggled to speak coherently.

"I had to resign."

"This isn't that pulling-your-weight issue again, is it?" He was trying to jolly her a little, although his heart had plummeted at her words.

"No. Oh, Charles, I almost lost the baby. Christmas Eve. And the doctor says if I don't rest, I will lose her, and I can't. I just can't—"

"It's okay. Take it easy. We'll figure something out."

"No. No, we won't. You don't understand. I've got to stay in bed. And I feel so bad. I'm letting you down. And Spinell and—"

"Hey. Hey. Not true. You're not letting me or Spinell down. The baby has to come first. Spinell and I are big boys. We can take care of ourselves." Charles had no idea where the words were coming from, but they seemed like the right ones to use. On the other hand, telling Joanna he didn't need her might not be the most helpful thing either.

"It'll be tough without you, but I'll manage somehow. The most important thing is that you and the baby are okay." The words felt odd. Not like him at all. More like something he'd heard someone say, maybe in a movie sometime.

"*Gracias por todo.*" Joanna's voice smoothed and softened. "I owe you. Big time. For carrying me."

"Nonsense."

Spinell appeared in the doorway.

"As it is, we've got it mostly wrapped up. It's all over but the shouting."

Joanna giggled, something he would have bet two minutes ago was an impossibility. "Cliché alert, Larimore. Does that mean Spinell has made it downstairs?"

"Yep. That's right."

"I'll let you go then. *Buena suerte.*"

He would have liked more time to think through the ramifications of Joanna's loss from the Maxwell cases.

Unfortunately, he probably wasn't going to get it, although

he did manage to talk Spinell into waiting until after the New Year to decide if a replacement for Joanna should be named.

છ

For Christmas, Cora had given Luz a gift certificate to a beauty salon, along with the promise she'd babysit while Luz took advantage of it.

The owner of Mujer Linda, Priscila Sánchez, was a middle-aged woman with a heavy Spanish accent.

She chuckled in memory of Cora's visit. "She know exactly what she want, that one." Priscila removed the elastic holding Luz's hair back in a utilitarian ponytail. "Oh my, so fine. You're lucky is so much."

"What did she tell you to do?" Luz was beginning to feel uncomfortable.

Priscila cocked her head, "*¿Latina, no?*"

Luz nodded, and Priscila switched to Spanish. "Well she came in, said she wanted to see my work. Sat over there." Priscila raised her chin and pointed with her lips. "Pretty weird, I thought. Old lady like that, no Spanish, checking out a Latina shop. But hey, hair is hair even if it's gray. Figured maybe I'd talk her into a color job. She watched me do three cuts and one makeover before she asked about a gift certificate." Priscila grinned at Luz in the mirror. "Never thought to do something like that. Had to have her write it out, then she paid, and I signed it. I've been wondering who'd show up to use it."

Priscila ran her hands through Luz's hair, letting it drape over her wrists. Peering at Luz's face, she lifted the hair and held it so it covered Luz's ears, but stopped right above her shoulders.

"I'm thinking shorter." She directed Luz's attention to the mirror. "If it's layered, it will give you more fullness. And after that, we'll do makeup. You need to emphasize your eyes more, and with a little color in the cheeks and lips, you'll be a new woman."

But if she wore as much eye makeup as Priscila and made her cheeks and lips as bright, she'd look like a clown. On the other hand, even without the clucking sounds the other woman was making, Luz knew her current look was bland.

Reluctantly, she agreed to a shorter cut. After all, there was little chance she'd end up looking any worse than she already did.

Priscila gave her a shampoo, propped her back up, and combed her hair. Without her glasses, Luz wasn't able to see much. Long hanks of hair fell into her lap and onto the floor as Priscila snipped, all the while chatting in rapid Spanish. Luz consoled herself with the thought hair grew back.

"Now me. I'm *mexicana*. Where are you from?" Priscila said. "Not México, *¿no?*"

Luz shook her head. "Chile. By way of Scottsbluff."

"Scottsbluff?"

"It's in Nebraska."

"Ah, Chile and Nebraska. That explains it."

"Explains what?"

"Your Spanish. It's different. And your English...you sound just like an Anglo."

"Well, I've been here a long time." So long she no longer remembered not knowing both languages.

Priscila rubbed something into Luz's hair and blew it dry. That finished, she stared at Luz for several moments, pursing her lips in thought, then opened a makeup kit large and complex enough to handle the inhabitants of a small country. She hovered over it, squeezing something from a tube into her hand.

Priscila rubbed the something onto Luz's cheeks. "You have beautiful skin, and your bones are very good. If you don't smoke and you're careful with the sun, you'll still be beautiful when you're as old as the lady who sent you here."

Luz didn't try to reply. She was enjoying the touch of Priscila's fingers rubbing her forehead, cheeks and ears. She was completely relaxed until the thought of how Charles might react to her new look sent a shiver of anticipation through her.

"Is it too cold for you, *querida?*"

Luz shook her head, dismissing thoughts of Charles. "It's fine."

Priscila continued to dip into various parts of her kit, explaining as she went along. Finished, she picked up Luz's glasses and handed them to her, then turned the chair so Luz was facing herself in the mirror.

The face looking back at her was both familiar and at the same time completely foreign. Priscila had used softer colors than she used on herself, giving new definition to Luz's eyes and cheeks. The hair framing her face, though shorter, was fuller and shinier than when she walked in.

She blinked, somehow expecting the face in the mirror to disappear, replaced by the way she used to look...more Anglo than most Anglos. Or that's what one of the Latina girls had told her in high school.

"It's...different. I'll have to get used to it, but I like it."

"Wait until your boyfriend sees you." Priscila snapped her fingers. "He is going to say, who is this beautiful woman? Then you realize what Priscila do for you, eh, *¿querida?*"

There was little danger Charles would react to her new look in the way Priscila was hinting. Besides, he wasn't her boyfriend, although now maybe there was a chance he would actually, well, notice her.

She kept taking quick peeks at the strange woman in the mirror as Priscila packaged hair gel, eye shadow, blusher and lip gloss to enable her to replicate the look.

Priscila handed Luz the bag. "All included. That old lady, she think of everything, *¿sí?*"

Luz walked into the apartment, and both Marisol and Cora started clapping.

"Oh, my. My goodness, Luz. You look—"

"She looks cool." Marisol beamed at Luz while Cora wiped a tear from one eye.

"You don't think she overdid it just a bit on the eye shadow?" Luz pulled her glasses off and blinked.

Cora shook her head. "It's perfect, Luz. All of it. You look lovely."

Luz spent the evening hoping she'd run into Charles. She went to the laundry room half a dozen times, on one pretext or another, but his door remained resolutely closed. She finally decided he must be working late.

Disappointed, she eventually gave up on seeing him and got ready for bed, taking one last look at herself before washing her face.

In the morning, if it hadn't been for the shorter hair, she would have thought she'd dreamed the whole visit to Mujer Linda. She toyed briefly with the idea of putting on the makeup, but decided it would just make her look silly. She did rub the hair gel in after she showered, and although she didn't have a hair dryer or the time to use one, when she brushed her hair later, it settled into place, not quite as full, but shiny and curving under like it did after Priscila spent twenty minutes blowing it dry. So at least the makeover experience hadn't been a total waste of Cora's money.

Sighing, Luz pulled her hair into its usual ponytail. Trying to look fashionable while spending the day caring for two-year-olds had to be one definition of insanity.

&

The Wednesday after Christmas, Charles's mail contained copies of the Montalvos' wills, which he'd sent for after that first conversation with Luz about her situation. He set aside his other work in order to read them.

The wills, drafted shortly after Marisol's birth, named Martin Blair as executor and Martin and his wife, Rae, as guardians for the two minor Montalvo children, Luz and Marisol.

In other words, the Montalvos had given Blair control of everything. Although the estate, in the event of both Mary and Esteban's deaths, was to be divided between the girls and any other issue, Blair would maintain control until each child reached the age of twenty-five.

Based on what Luz had told him about Blair, Charles was surprised her parents trusted the man enough to hand over all their worldly possessions, not to mention their beloved children, to him. If he was the man Luz described, he was self-centered and selfish, something that should have been obvious to both Mary and Esteban.

But then, maybe Luz had misinterpreted Blair's actions.

She'd been going through a horrible experience. Maybe she hadn't been thinking clearly. Or worse, was she lying?

With sudden inspiration, he turned to the computer to check on the Montalvos' property. He pulled up a real estate site for Scottsbluff, typed in the address from the wills, and found the Montalvo house sold six months after their deaths for two-hundred fifty-seven thousand dollars. Next he searched for information on Esteban's business, Las Flores. He found the company's website. It carried a picture and obit for Esteban and Mary and a statement that the same great service customers were used to in the past would be provided by the new management team—a group by the name of Prentice Partners, Inc.

He added up what he'd discovered. The family home had sold for a quarter mil, and Esteban's business, Las Flores, and a piece of rural property had sold for a total of three-hundred fifty-one thousand.

So while Luz, Marisol and Carlito eked out an existence in Denver, Martin Blair was sitting on potentially a half-million or more that belonged to them.

Charles next pulled up the Scottsbluff newspaper site and typed in Martin Blair's name with a ten-year time-frame. What he found were two or three articles every year mentioning the man. Blair owned the Ford dealership for Scottsbluff, and the Blairs were active in Scottsbluff society. Martin and Rae golfed, were members of the country club and spent part of each winter in Phoenix.

Charles did similar searches for Esteban Montalvo and Mary Blair Montalvo. Besides their obituaries, he found an announcement of their wedding and three articles. One reported on the addition of a new cardiologist to the practice Mary Blair was part of, and two articles mentioned them as the parents of Luz Montalvo, a National Merit Scholar who subsequently received a scholarship to attend Colorado College.

Charles finished gathering the information, knowing he needed to have another talk with Luz. Maybe he could take her to dinner, because having that conversation in public would be...safer. Besides, it would do Luz good to spend an evening away from the kids. That might be the reason she was always so irritable—one minute a college student with an unlimited future, the next, surrogate mother with two young children dependent on her and few resources to keep them from harm.

The idea of taking Luz to dinner improved his mood, which had been gloomy since Luz walked by him the previous morning, barely speaking. Remembering how prickly she'd been when he first brought home extra food, he decided it could just be a sign of her discomfort with all the Christmas gifts.

He understood it made her feel bad to need help, but it would make him feel worse if he stood by and let them go to bed hungry. Helping had become easier since she'd taken Cora in, because he slipped things to Cora, and she was willing to tell Luz she'd paid for them. It was his and Cora's little conspiracy.

Returning to the idea of asking Luz to dinner, it hit him. Tomorrow was New Year's Eve.

He couldn't remember the last time he'd spent it without a date. Last year it had been Tiffany. Then he'd discovered her New Year's resolution was to get him to marry her and start a family.

Odd, anymore he had difficulty remembering anything about Tiffany, although they'd been together off and on for two years. Maybe she'd been right to call him shallow. After all, he'd barely said goodbye to her before he started seeing Kathy, and four months ago, he'd thought *she* was the love of his life and wouldn't have bet two cents he'd get over her easily. And yet, it seemed he had. Well, not completely, of course. When they were in the same room, the subtle pain of their severed connection was still an ache deep in his gut.

But he didn't seem to have time to think about Kathy much. Since the fire, her face had popped into his awareness with less and less frequency, and the face that had taken its place was Luz's. Although any thought of Luz brought with it equal measures of exasperation and worry.

Taking Luz out for New Year's. The more he thought about it, the better it sounded. He'd have to invite her in the morning, because he wasn't going to make it home early enough to do it tonight. He hadn't forgotten how grouchy she'd been when he awakened her the evening he received the threat from Snodgrass.

God, that situation had taken ten years off him. It still made him shake to realize he'd endangered Luz and her family by simply living next door and having the job he had. A job he was neglecting by not informing the authorities of Luz's whereabouts.

Something he just couldn't seem to bring himself to do.

⁓

Charles knocked on Luz's door the next morning.

"Do you have another plumbing problem?"

And here he thought they'd made it well past the days when the only reason he knocked on her door was to report a problem with his apartment. "Actually, I want to ask you something."

She cocked her head, waiting, her expression more thoughtful than annoyed.

"I wondered if you'd go to dinner with me tonight."

"You mean on a date?"

Hard to decide if her tone meant she was excited about the invitation or appalled by it. He tried to read her expression, seeking to determine how she wanted him to answer. He could go either way. He wasn't exactly sure a "date" was his intention, but going out to dinner did rather sound like a date, come to think of it.

"I need to pick your brain about your family," he said. They could always work the actual *dateness* detail out later.

"Oh. So it's just dinner." The habitual annoyance was back in her eyes, and it made him feel more awkward than he had since junior high, although he had no idea why Luz had that effect on him.

He knew he was attractive to women, and they almost always responded positively to him. Luz's reaction, an anomaly, made him feel damned uncomfortable. So why did he keep putting himself in the position to be the brunt of it? "You can choose the restaurant."

She pushed her glasses back into place and peered at him.

Exasperated, he was ready to say, *Okay, let's sit on your ratty couch or my ratty couch, and leave it at that,* when she pursed her lips. "Chinese."

"Chinese?"

"You did say I could choose the restaurant. I don't know a specific one, but I like Chinese food. What time do you want me to be ready?"

"I'll call for reservations and let you know later."

"Okay."

After a moment, he realized the conversation was over, and he'd been dismissed. He turned away; behind him, the door closed.

At work, Charles pulled out the report he'd started writing the night before outlining for Spinell where he stood with the Maxwell trials. As he revised it, he kept finding himself with pen suspended, musing about Luz and her situation. Not lawyerly thoughts, like what needed to be done next, but libidinous thoughts.

He flipped through his images of Luz: emerging dirty and disheveled from under his sink; young, gawky and too skinny in the blue dress; competent and graceful sitting on a horse; sophisticated and lovely wearing her new Christmas clothes.

With a start, he realized his mind had gone spinning off, and his thoughts were making him miserable. Resolutely, he focused on the work he needed to do. He had to make the report sound like he had everything under control so Spinell wouldn't force a new partner on him.

No more thinking about Luz until tonight.

Chapter Sixteen

Luz wiped off eye makeup for the third time. She tried again, using only a light coating below her eyebrows, leaving her lids untouched. She put her glasses on and checked. Then she took them off and used a brown pencil to make a line along her lower lashes, rubbing it slightly to smudge it, as Priscila had done. She put the glasses back on.

Okay. Only twenty minutes to get her eyes right. At this pace, she should have started getting ready for her dinner with Charles right after he asked her this morning.

She brushed blusher on her cheeks. *Nope. Too much.* She wiped it off, but her cheeks remained red from the rubbing. Sighing, she switched her attention to her hair. Cora had loaned her curlers. Luz removed them and smoothed her hair with the brush before trying the blusher again. She finished off with the addition of rose lip gloss. And there she was, the woman Priscila had first brought to life.

Luz stared at herself, shivering a little, knowing it was silly to be nervous about going out with Charles. No matter what she thought about it, to him she was only a neighbor. Someone he was helping. By his own admission, dinner was about business, even if it was New Year's Eve.

She glanced at her watch, shrugged at the woman in the mirror, and finished dressing.

Cora tapped on the door. "Luz, dear. I thought maybe you'd like to wear this tonight." Cora held a short black shearling jacket. "I'm afraid it's a little old-fashioned."

Luz, felt a wave of gratitude. Her parka would have completely negated her attempt to look sophisticated, but it was too cold tonight to be without a coat. "Oh, no. It's great. That's so nice of you."

Cora helped her slip the jacket on. Although shorter on Luz than it would be on Cora, the jacket fit.

Smiling at Cora, Luz slipped the coat back off and took a deep breath to calm her nerves.

Charles made reservations at the most elegant Chinese restaurant he knew, but it still wasn't a suit and tie kind of place. He settled on the casual sweater and slacks he'd finally gone shopping for, pulled on his coat, picked up a legal pad and went next door to get Luz. He lifted his hand to knock, first taking in a breath to calm a sudden, uncharacteristic flare of nervousness.

Marisol answered the door. Cora was sitting on the sofa watching television, and Carlito was playing on the floor, surrounded by his Christmas gifts. He gurgled at Charles, lifting his arms to be picked up. Charles ditched the tablet and swung Carlito in the air, but quickly set the toddler back amid his toys before he drooled on the sweater.

As he straightened, Luz came out of the bedroom. She was wearing the pink sweater he'd given her and the maroon skirt from the Francinis, and she'd done something different with her hair. It was loose and shiny, swinging against her cheek. And was she wearing...makeup? He blinked, startled. She still had the glasses of course, but they didn't look as funny as usual. Instead they made her appear wise and serious. He had the impulse to lift them off her face and gaze into her eyes, which tonight seemed large and dark, and then...

Whoa. Not going there. Boy, he better find a woman his own age and soon. Celibacy was causing totally inappropriate thoughts. Hell, Luz was practically a client.

He helped her put on a dressy jacket, a surprise to discover she owned such a thing. As she slipped her arm into the sleeve the two bracelets he'd given her chimed with a brief musical note.

Luz kissed Marisol and Carlito good night, and they left Cora in charge, looking proprietary and pleased.

At the restaurant, the waitress handed them each a huge

multi-page menu. Luz perused hers with complete attention, although she looked up long enough to order hot tea. Charles asked for a glass of white wine, and when it arrived, he drank off half of it before he realized what he was doing.

Luz's head remained buried in the menu, but he no longer had any appetite. He sat back examining her, sipping the remainder of his wine. New Year's Eve, and his date wasn't even old enough to drink. The last time that happened, he'd been only twenty himself.

Luz glanced at him, frowning. "Oh, have you decided already?"

"I thought I'd let you pick."

She pursed her mouth in thought. "It's been so long since I've eaten Chinese, it all sounds delicious."

"Pick a couple of appetizers. We'll worry about the rest later."

Her head bent once more, and the shining hair slid forward against her cheek. "Umm...okay. How about potstickers and crab rangoons."

He wanted to reach out, cup her face in his hands, and touch that satin hair. Good thing the waitress showed up and provided a distraction. He placed the order and asked for a refill on his wine, searching for something to say to bridge his discomfort. "I like the new hairdo."

Luz looked uncertain. "It was Cora's Christmas gift. A trip to the hairdresser." She pushed a strand back from her face, still seeming unsure.

"Well, it's nice. It suits you." He'd been abrupt, but he seemed to be unable to help it. He picked up the legal pad from the floor, laid it on the table and pulled out a pen. Luz sipped her tea with a strained look on her face that he tried to ignore.

He glanced through the questions he planned to ask, although he didn't need to. The tablet was simply a prop to give him something to focus on. Something instead of Luz and the buzz of awareness of her as a woman that had settled in and was steadily increasing in volume. "Okay, the first thing you better tell me about is this step-uncle."

The strained look intensified. Gone completely, the happy delight in her eyes as she'd studied the menu. She focused on a point beyond him and began to speak. "Martin knows everyone who's anyone in Scottsbluff. He loves to drop names. You know, my-friend-John-the-president-of-the-bank sort of thing."

As Luz spoke, Charles sipped his second glass of wine.

"And he's one of those hearty types who claps people on the back and always has a deal for them. In restaurants, he always makes a big show of picking up the check, but then he argues with the waiter about the charges. I had a classmate who bussed tables at the country club and he said Martin was a lousy tipper."

Charles, well acquainted with the type, nodded in sympathetic understanding.

"At family dinners, he always made a point of showing off his new car, his new golf clubs, his new whatever, as if trying to make *Papi* feel inadequate. It made me so angry. But *Papi* said it was only because Martin lacked something in his life that he needed to show off."

Luz's father sounded like someone Charles would like. Too bad the good guys always seemed to get zapped while the bad guys sailed on untouched.

"Tell me more about your parents," he said.

Luz went from angry to sad in an instant, but once she started speaking, she seemed better. "*Mami* was a cardiologist. She was on call at night, and she had to work some weekends. *Papi* had a landscape business. He got in with a couple of the big developers, and he did all the landscaping for them. He was busy, but he did a lot of the work around the house, too. Well, both of us pitched in, so *Mami* could relax when she had time off." She paused with a faraway look in her eyes, then continued in a thoughtful tone. "One time Martin told *Mami* she'd married a servant not a husband."

"How did she react to that?"

Luz's lips curved, her eyes still focused on the past. "She was pregnant with Carlito. She gave Martin this contented smile and said, 'You can believe whatever you wish, Martin, but I know I have the most wonderful husband in the world.'" Luz's face tightened with pain.

Charles spoke quickly to distract her. "Your stepmother. How many doctors in her practice?"

153

Luz moved her fingers, obviously counting. "Two pediatric and three adult cardiologists, two cardiac surgeons. Seven altogether. Every year at Christmas, they gave this big party for their staff. Gifts for everybody. Santa came for the kids, and they had a wonderful meal. *Mami* always said, if cardiologists didn't know how to tend to all aspects of the heart, who did."

The appetizers were delivered, and Luz helped herself to a potsticker. "After they got married, *Papi* did the same thing for his staff."

"Were your parents' friends separate from your step-uncle's circle?"

"Definitely. Martin's a golfer, and a country club type. *Mami* and *Papi* weren't interested in that sort of thing. They went out occasionally, and they had people over, but mostly, they liked spending time with each other. And with us."

"So, if they needed to name a guardian for Marisol and Carlito, who would you have expected they'd choose?" Charles ate a potsticker followed by a crab rangoon because the two glasses of wine on an empty stomach were making him lightheaded. When the waitress asked if he needed a refill, he ordered tea.

Luz, eating slowly, waited until the waitress left before answering his question. "I'm not sure. You see, when *Mami* and *Papi* decided to get married, Martin tried to stop it. He told her *Papi* wasn't their kind and tried to talk her into a prenup. So I would have said he wouldn't be *Papi*'s choice. But, after Grammie died, he and Rae were the only relatives, and *Papi* always said family was the most important thing."

She took a sip of tea before continuing in a thoughtful tone, "I didn't understand all that about Martin until Grammie told me about it when I got older."

"Grammie?"

"*Mami* and Martin's mother. At first, she agreed with Martin about the marriage being a bad idea. Later on, she realized how happy *Papi* made *Mami*, and she changed her mind. I think she talked to me about it because she felt guilty, wanted to apologize, maybe."

The waitress returned to take their dinner order, and for a time, Charles let the questions go.

"We'll need only a couple of dishes to share, right?" Luz asked with a brief glance at him. "Because I love mu shu pork, and duck and shrimp and..." Unconsciously, she bit her lip as she turned her attention back to the menu. He watched the play of expression on her face, wishing she would look at him with such obvious delight.

He questioned her about the shrimp and duck dishes to find out which ones appealed to her the most. Based on that information, he ordered the crispy duck, mu shu pork, and a shrimp-and-pine-nut dish. For good measure he added fried rice and a vegetable stir fry.

"Oh, that's going to be way too much."

He shrugged. "There's nothing better than Chinese leftovers." And he ought to be able to convince her to take them with a minimum of fuss, or he was in the wrong line of work.

He snagged the last of the potstickers and dipped it in sauce, then glanced at his questions. Time to get back to the subject at hand. Luz looking the way she did tonight was making it hard for him to concentrate, and he was having trouble, after all, remembering what he needed to ask.

"Did your family seem to have plenty of money?" What he wanted to know was if they spent a lot on expensive toys. It didn't sound like it from what she'd told him so far.

"We always had plenty for everything we needed. But then, as long as he could afford food, shelter and the horses, *Papi* was satisfied."

Charles had forgotten about the horses. Although he didn't like horses and knew practically nothing about them, he did know they were an expensive hobby.

"Where did you keep your horses?"

"*Papi* bought a farm to set up a plant nursery. It has a stable. We used to go there every afternoon. It was our special time together." Her words cut off, and she turned her head away.

With the farm sold, it was likely the horses had also been sold. Something he had no intention of telling Luz, yet. The waitress picked that moment to serve their meal. As she assembled the mu shu pancakes, Charles and Luz sat silently.

Charles kept sneaking glances at Luz over the rim of his tea cup. She was staring fixedly at the waitress's hands expertly wielding the chopsticks. Noting the sadness in Luz's eyes, he decided not to ask any more questions about her family. At least until they finished eating.

The waitress left, and he lifted his tea cup and saluted Luz. "*Buen provecho.*"

Luz seemed surprised, as well she might. It was the first time he'd tried his fledgling Spanish on her. After a brief hesitation, she smiled and said the words back to him.

Her eyes closed in ecstasy as she took her first bite of duck, and Charles's heart caught. He wanted to put a look like that on her face. Just him.

Luz ate slowly, obviously savoring every bite, and watching her, Charles slowed as well. He'd got in a bad habit of eating much too fast. Probably because he'd mostly been eating alone the past several months.

While they ate, he tried to keep the conversation on lighter topics, although it was difficult to ask Luz anything without it being a reminder of sorrow. He learned she had been starting her second year at Colorado College, studying business and fine arts, when her parents were killed; that her father taught her to ride; that she'd loved being at the ranch with the Francinis.

He talked in turn about some of his cases and why he liked being a district attorney.

"So how's the great apartment hunt going?"

"Actually, I've been too busy to bother." And it was a surprise to realize he didn't even care that he might have to stay longer than six months at the Draper Arms.

They laughed together about Carlito and what an imperious little sir he sometimes was. And they talked about Marisol. How she was learning to read, how much she'd enjoyed Christmas.

"So." He pointed his chopsticks at the bracelets encircling her wrist. "Any ideas about the puzzle?"

She grinned. "Sure. I figured it out right away, but I didn't want to hurt your friends' feelings."

"I don't believe it."

"*Sí*, I most certainly did. Although it is a very clever puzzle."

"You can't just say you've solved it. You have to share, or it doesn't count."

"Okay. Bracelets or bangles which rhymes with angels. A herd of horses elevated on posts. I put it together and got 'angels we have heard on high'."

As he dealt with his surprise that Luz had seen through his puzzle so easily, she reached into her purse and pulled out a flat package wrapped in Christmas paper. "I was going to wait for *Tres Reyes,* Three King's, but Cora thought I should give this to you tonight."

He cocked his head in question.

"It's your Christmas gift."

He opened the small package to find a watercolor painting of a tiny tropical island surrounded by turquoise waters. Two palm trees shaded the beach, and offshore, resting on the ocean bottom, was a small rowboat. Charles stared at it a moment before it hit him. It was a puzzle. He glanced across at Luz who met his gaze with a glint of humor in her eyes.

He let the components of the picture flick through his mind. Two palms, island, sea, ocean, one boat, sunken, sunk, sank. A grin slowly stretched across his face, and he nodded in appreciation. "Why you're very welcome."

"It doesn't count to act like you've figured it out." Luz sounded stern. "You have to share."

He shrugged. "One boat sank, two palms. Sank two. Thank you. You're saying thank you. And I repeat, you're welcome."

"You've done so much for us. You...well, I wanted you to know I appreciate it."

He shifted uncomfortably, her words making him aware of what she wasn't saying: *Thank you for not turning me in.* Something he didn't want to think about tonight. He glanced again at the painting, seeking a way out of conversational gridlock. "It's good. Did you paint it?"

Luz shook her head. "Cora did. I told her what I wanted. I thought it would take you longer to figure it out." She sounded disappointed.

"I love it. As a matter of fact, I'm going to frame it."

Luz pointed at the box. "There's another one."

Beneath the island painting was a second one—a picture of

winter bare trees surrounded by untouched snow with a clear sky that was pinking with the first touch of dawn. One tree, a sugar maple, had a tap in place, and hanging from the tap was a small bucket.

Charles stared at the picture, certain the key element was the carefully rendered sugar maple. Syrup, sap, sappy. He searched for the other elements that had to be there, finding them in the clarity of the sky and the untouched snow that delicately lined each branch and snuggled untouched against the bases of the trees.

He glanced across the table at Luz, at the liveliness in her face, the curve of her mouth, and he knew he was going to kiss her tonight, although he also knew he shouldn't. Looking back at the painting, he tried to decide. Did he pretend he had no idea, or did he admit he'd figured it out?

But pretending not to know would be a lie, and he didn't want any lies between them. An odd revelation, given he wasn't in the habit of lying to women, even when he wanted to seduce one. All he knew was, in this moment, facing this choice, he decided to do one thing rather than the other.

He lifted the picture and pointed. "Sap, sappy. Happy. New snow, clear morning. Sappy new clear. Happy New Year." He met her eyes, and for a moment, Luz had a look of yearning that made his heart twist.

He didn't want the evening to end, not yet. It was only nine-thirty, but since it was New Year's Eve, venues with live music would be packed with half-drunk revelers. As he rejected the thought of taking Luz to such a place, he glanced at the snow picture and knew what they should do instead.

Still, he ordered another pot of tea, and they continued to sit and talk. The waitress carried off the platters of food and returned with filled boxes, fortune cookies and the bill.

Luz opened her cookie and read the small strip of paper before handing it over with a lift of her eyebrows but no comment. It said, *Now is the time to try something new.*

His said, *Trust yourself, and anything you do will be right.* Grateful for the vote of approval, he passed it across to Luz, saying, "They sure don't make fortunes the way they used to."

She read his and gazed thoughtfully across at him. Then

she shook herself and put on a bright look. "This has been terrific. Sank two."

"*De nada.*" Although, for him, the evening had been far from "nothing".

He signed the credit card slip and helped Luz with her jacket.

It had snowed the day before. The roads were clear, but snow still blanketed yards and slumped in piles along driveways. Luz sat beside him, not commenting that he seemed to be taking the long way home. A good sign.

The first place he took her was downtown to see the lights on the City and County building across from the Capitol. He'd been seeing them nightly for over a month, but he doubted Luz would have been downtown after dark. He drove in a loop, passing by twice to allow her to look her fill, before he turned onto Fourteenth Avenue and drove east to Cheesman Park. In the park, he circled until he reached the eastern end where he pulled in and parked near the Greek-style pavilion. The cold snap and snow had left the park deserted.

Luz gave him a questioning look.

"I want to show you something."

He helped her out of the car, and she tucked her hand in his arm for the walk to the pavilion. They climbed the half-flight of stairs and walked to the front. Before them, the park stretched out, deserted and silent, the snow looking as fresh as if it had fallen minutes before. Only the dark ribbon of roadway and the clear area around the pavilion were untouched by white. At the far edge of the park, a black line of trees blocked off most of the city's lights except for a couple of tall apartment buildings on the right. Overhead, stars glittered.

He stood waiting, letting Luz look. After a time, she turned to him. "Thank you." The words were soft, as if this quiet scene demanded no less.

Without debating it further, he tipped her face and lowered his head until his lips touched hers. As if she were part of the frozen landscape, Luz was still except for the trembling of her lips against his.

He pulled her close, increasing the pressure. Tentatively, her lips moved in response, sending a pulse of desire through him. As that desire gained momentum, he knew.

It wasn't going to work. He couldn't stand here kissing Luz, knowing he dare take it no further. He wanted her too much.

He broke off the kiss, but continued to hold her. She put her arms around him and stood nestled against him, her face turned away, cradled on his shoulder.

He rubbed his cheek against her hair. "Sappy new clear."

"It's not even ten." Luz's voice was muffled.

"Pretend we're in New York." He should let go of her, but he couldn't seem to bring himself to do it.

Luz took care of that. With a deep breath, she stepped away. "Thank you for showing me this. Can you believe? I didn't even know it was here."

She appeared to be trying for a normal tone, and if that's the way she wanted it, he could do normal. At least he hoped he could. "There's a playground. Over there." He pointed toward the far line of trees. "In the spring, you can bring Marisol and Carlito."

"Yes." Luz took another breath and gave him a tentative smile. "This isn't far, is it."

"No, it's a short walk."

As they continued to exchange meaningless words, Charles ached to pull Luz back into his arms and stop those words with another kiss. Ached to kiss Luz until they were both breathless with it. Except, he already was. His heart pounded, and the shiver of desire had become a flood.

The cold air wasn't having a bit of a damping effect. Luz had awakened something tonight. He stopped the thought, because it wasn't fair. It made it sound like she'd set out to seduce him when nothing was further from the truth. If anything, she'd worked hard to make sure he knew she was indifferent to him.

For an instant it brought an unwelcome memory of Kathy's reticence when they'd been dating. Of course, the whole time they'd dated, Kathy had been estranged from, and still in love with, Alan, so it didn't exactly count.

It made Luz his only failure. A good thing, actually. Because if Luz showed the slightest interest in him, they'd probably end up sleeping together. And that was a really bad idea. Luz was grieving and vulnerable, not to mention painfully young. No way he was taking advantage of any of that.

Luz stepped further away, wrapping her arms around herself. She gave him a tentative smile. "Sorry. It's b-beautiful here, but I'm f-freezing."

"I better get you home."

They walked back to the car, but this time, Luz stayed apart from him, hurrying, her hands tucked in her pockets.

They barely spoke during the few minutes it took to drive to the Draper Arms. He insisted she take the leftovers, and after one brief protest, she agreed.

He waited while she opened her door. A single lamp was lit, and the apartment was quiet, its air heavy and warm with the breath of sleepers. She slipped inside before turning to give him a quick smile that didn't reach her eyes. "Goodnight, Charles. Thank you for dinner."

He nodded, because any words he might say would likely come out wrong.

His own apartment was dark and cool, the heat already lowered for sleeping. He undressed and lay in the dark, feeling tired, sad and wide awake.

He hadn't told Luz about the wills tonight, because it wasn't good news. He'd do it, but after the holiday. Then he pushed away thoughts of her legal difficulties and thought instead about the woman such a short distance away. Separated from him by only a few inches of wall and twelve years.

When he finally slept, he had the nightmare. Along with kissing a woman who was indifferent to him, it was the perfect inauspicious start for the new year.

Chapter Seventeen

Charles, uncomfortable at the thought of seeing Luz, was tempted to manufacture an excuse to skip New Year's Day dinner at the Bayleys'.

He was still debating about going when he realized he'd left it too late. No fair canceling at the last minute because of discomfort. People made plans, cooked a certain amount. The time to have pulled out was first thing this morning. Easy then. He could have told them he wasn't feeling well.

A truth of sorts. After the nightmare, he always felt exhausted and sick. And he was sore as well from kicking himself over the stupidity of, first, asking Luz out and, second, kissing her. That kiss crossed a line he had no intention of crossing again. And the very best way to ensure that was to avoid Luz altogether.

He dragged himself downstairs only to discover Carlito had a cold and Luz was staying home with him. His disappointment was as painful as it was unexpected.

Clearly, he had to do something about his personal life. Letting Luz get to him emotionally was simply unacceptable. Bad enough he had to deal with his professional entanglement with her.

Handle the one and the other would likely be easier to solve. And the easiest to deal with at the moment was the emotional issue. He just needed to ask someone else out. Someone it would be okay to be involved with. And why he hadn't already done it was something he had no interest in examining closely.

Shortly after making that decision, he encountered one of

the court reporters who in the past had made no secret she was interested and available. A good omen. Although she had the rather unpromising name of Harriet Schmidt, she had glossy black hair, good teeth and a nice laugh. He asked her to dinner.

Unfortunately, as a date, she was a dud. Or maybe it was him.

"Do you have any pets?" she asked, precisely cutting a piece of steak. "Personally, I think cats are the only way to go if you have to be away all day like we do. I have two. That way they can keep each other company when I'm not there."

Charles detested cats almost as much as he feared horses. "I live in a no-pets building." He realized he'd slipped a time cog or two and was talking about his old apartment. He knew he was struggling to stay attentive, but this was ridiculous.

"Oh?" Harriet gave him a fixed stare. It was obviously one of her date tests, to ascertain if the man shared her liking for cats.

"Hate them." He wondered what Luz's stand on cats was, then stifled the thought. The whole idea behind taking Harriet to dinner was to stop thinking about Luz.

Harriet appeared startled. "What? Did I miss something?"

"Didn't you ask if I liked cats?"

"No. I most certainly did not."

"Oh. Well, I hate them." They might as well be absolutely clear.

Harriet declined coffee or dessert and pleaded an early court date as a reason to go directly home. Relieved, he dropped her off and returned to the Draper Arms. As he was unlocking his door, it hit him. It was Friday night. There was no court tomorrow. Clearly he'd been as big a hit with Harriet as she'd been with him.

He did envy her briefly, though, for having something animate to greet her. Although he couldn't stand cats, he understood why people liked having animals around. At least they were company.

ॐ

Charles was pulling his clothes from the dryer Sunday morning when the scrape of the door alerted him to the arrival of another person. He turned around to find Luz carrying a hamper and starting to back away.

"Hi, Luz. It's okay. I'll be through in a minute." He turned back to the dryer, ignoring her, but unable to ignore the effect of seeing her. Lord, he was worse than an acne-ridden teenager in the throes of hopeless first love. He struggled to bring up an image of Harriet Schmidt and her boring conversation to counteract it.

Luz dropped her hamper by one of the washers. He turned and began meticulously folding his undershirts. "How've you been?"

"*Bien.*"

So what was it with the Spanish? Her way of warning him off? "I've been meaning to stop by. To update you."

She didn't look up from shaking out the towels she was adding to the washer. "About?"

"Your parents' estate."

After a brief stutter in her movements, she continued to load the washer. "What about it?" Her tone was indifferent, but her body language had become tight and jerky.

"It's going to take some time to explain it all. If you can spare, say an hour, sometime today?"

She added detergent and pulled quarters from her pocket, placed them on the slide and pushed it in. With a rushing sound, the washer began to fill.

"I need to check with Cora." She walked over to the doorway, hesitated. "I'll let you know later." Then she was gone.

So it wasn't his imagination Luz was no more eager to see him than he was to see her. Well, he had his reasons. It appeared hers were the opposite. Whereas kissing her, for him, awakened desire, for Luz it appeared to have quenched it. Not only quenched it, but given rise to its opposite—aversion.

He wished they could find their way back to where they'd been before he kissed her. *And where was that, precisely?* his libido mocked him. Didn't he mean he wanted to go back to a time when he'd had zero interest in Luz? When seeing her under his sink or in her doorway with an irritated look on her face, she'd been no more interesting than that proverbial spotty teenage boy.

But that view was gone forever. Trying to superimpose the too-big jeans on that slender waist, or to remember the hair hanging tangled and unkempt to the middle of her back, was impossible. The only thing remaining the same was the fey quality that always seemed on the edge of tipping into amusement. Except when she looked at him.

He finished folding the last of his clothes and carried them upstairs, determined to go out, if only to the nearest multiplex to sit mindlessly in the dark. Or the other possibility, one he'd been avoiding, was to start the search for another apartment, one considerably less neighborly than the Draper Arms.

In the end, he did neither, because shortly after he came upstairs, Luz knocked on his door and arranged to come over while Carlito took his afternoon nap.

Charles had been avoiding her. Since New Year's he hadn't had a single water leak, nor had he made up any other excuse to see her. Oh, he'd dropped off the extra fruit and vegetables after his weekly shopping trip, but he'd simply set them down, knocked, and was in his own apartment before she opened her door.

Her fault. She'd pushed away from his embrace.

But Charles Larimore couldn't possibly be interested in Luz Cristina Montalvo. She'd just been handy. And clearly, he'd got the message, although likely it had lost something in translation. It wasn't that she didn't want him kissing her. She simply didn't dare let him, not after she realized what kissing him could do to her.

Her lips curved in memory. It had been amazing. Such a simple thing—his head bending and his breath mingling with hers in potent possibility. Then a brushing of lips, followed by a gentle pressure. And because they were Charles's lips, her heart had stuttered with a feeling as effervescent as a cascade of silvery stars.

Cora didn't agree that Charles wasn't interested in her, but there was no future in listening to Cora on the subject. She may have had a fiancé a hundred years ago, but that didn't mean she had any idea what modern men were like. The only reason Charles wanted to see her now was to talk some more about her "case".

In preparation for their meeting, Luz combed her hair, put on a touch of blusher and lip gloss and debated what to wear. Elaine had insisted she take the blouses and sweaters, saying she'd left them at the ranch because they no longer fit.

Luz chose the yellow shirt Mr. Francini had whistled at and her black jeans, then, heart pounding, she knocked on Charles's door.

He opened it and stood looking at her pensively for a moment, as if his thoughts were a long way away, and it was taking awhile for him to rein them in. Finally, he stepped aside and motioned her to come in. "We'll work at the table. Would you like something to drink?"

"A glass of water would be nice."

She stood by the table, fighting the urge to drum her fingers on its top, waiting, while he added ice and water to a glass. He got a beer for himself and motioned her to sit next to him. The table had a pile of papers and the yellow tablet he'd brought with him to their dinner. At the thought of that dinner—and what followed it—Luz's breath hitched.

It was just a kiss, Luz Cristina. Everybody kissed everybody on New Year's. Even strangers kissed. *It's only because you haven't been kissed much, that it seemed special.*

Except, it was special. At least to her. The warmth of Charles's mouth contrasting with the brush of cold night air on her cheek. Encircled by his arms, she had felt both weak and strong, every nerve ending alive, until with a sudden cold dash, reason returned. Not only in the remembered words of her college roommate—*A man will sleep with anybody who lets him*—but from the absolute certainty Charles didn't really see her as special. Not the way she saw him.

Struggling to maintain a calm demeanor, Luz sipped her water. Oblivious to the currents swirling between them, Charles took a gulp of beer and pulled one of the stack of papers closer.

"These are your parents' wills."

"What? How did you get them?" Well she'd known her parents' estate was what he wanted to see her about. She just didn't expect *this.*

"When a will is probated it becomes part of the public record." He paged through the top document and turned a page toward her. "Is this your father's signature?"

There were several signatures on the page, including *Papi*'s. Or at least it appeared to be *Papi*'s. "I-I think so." She clutched her arms trying to suppress a tremor. When she kept busy enough, she was able to curb her memories of *Papi* and *Mami,* although their loss, an amorphous emptiness like a hunger pang that no amount of food would satisfy, was always with her.

But lately, her emotions seemed to have worked their way to the surface of her skin. Now, the smallest memory pricked her. And when Charles touched her, it was as if his touch was magnified and passed from nerve to nerve until it crashed against her heart, the way Aunt Rae's news had so many months ago. Sometimes it hurt to breathe, and sometimes, especially when she was near Charles, each breath seemed so filled with possibility...the possibility stripped from all other aspects of her life.

"You wouldn't happen to have anything he signed, where you know for sure it's his signature, would you?"

It took Luz a moment to remember the two boxes of files she'd brought with her from Scottsbluff and shoved under the bed.

"I do have some of *Papi* and *Mami*'s files. Things I grabbed as we were leaving."

The sudden gleam in Charles's eyes was disconcerting in its intensity. "Can you get them?"

"Sure. Except Carlito's taking a nap, and I don't want to wake him."

"I think you need to take that chance."

She went next door and retrieved the boxes, happily without waking Carlito, and carried them one at a time to Charles. He set them on the floor by the coffee table and, beer forgotten, pulled the contents out and stacked the folders.

"This is great," he muttered, flicking through the pile. "You did good, grabbing these."

He was silent as he paged through several files. "Do you

know what these are?"

She shook her head. "I didn't have much time. I just grabbed. Then I forgot about them."

"Well, what you grabbed looks like it's a gold mine of information. This one, for example, has the financial summaries for Las Flores for the last five years. And here"—he selected another file—"are your parents' tax returns for the past two years."

He pulled out one of the returns and walked over to the table and the wills. He looked from one document to the other, before coming back and sitting next to Luz on the sofa. He pointed to her parents' signatures on the wills and on the tax returns. "I'm no handwriting expert, but it might be worthwhile to ask one to compare these signatures."

Luz leaned over to look. The signatures appeared to match as far as she could tell. Besides, no way could she afford to pay someone to tell her they didn't.

Seeing *Papi*'s strong dark signature, and *Mami*'s lighter, more elegant one, she had a sudden vision. Of *Papi* bowing and handing *Mami* a bouquet of flowers he'd just picked from the garden, and *Mami*'s delighted laugh as she took the bouquet and then leaned in to kiss him.

As a teenager, such demonstrations of affection had embarrassed her. Now she realized how lucky her parents had been.

Charles chose another file. "Okay. This is good. Really good."

Luz picked up her father's will. Whether or not it was *Papi*'s signature at the end, Luz didn't believe what she was reading. How could *Papi* do this to her? Give Martin all this power. And she wouldn't be free to run her own affairs until she was twenty-five? He couldn't have done it. But then she got to the end and saw the date, and her heart sank. When the will was written, she'd been thirteen. Probably *Papi* thought he was doing her a favor ensuring she had someone to watch over her.

But would *Papi* neglect to make another will later? Especially with the expansion of Las Flores and the birth of Carlito? She knew her father to be a prudent man.

"Bingo," Charles said, startling her. "Look what we have

here."

"What is it?"

Charles was scanning a thick document with a happy look on his face. "It's a pair of wills and trust documents." He flipped pages. "All signed and witnessed. As a matter of fact..." His voice trailed off as he reached the final page. "They're dated October twelfth."

She blinked, the implications running through her mind. October twelfth. And on the fourteenth her parents went out for their anniversary and...

"Apparently they were all set to go back to the lawyer who drew them up, but they never got mailed." Charles checked the address label on the envelope, frowning. "That's interesting. They used a Denver law firm."

"What's interesting about that?"

"Most people deal with lawyers located in the same state they are."

"Maybe they picked someone in Denver because it was the nearest big city."

"Maybe."

"So what's the difference between these wills and the other ones?"

He turned back to the first page and began to read. "Well, the biggest differences seem to be that they set up trusts, a law firm is listed as the trustee, and a Jean and Henry Hollis are named guardians for Marisol and Carlito."

It stunned Luz, but as the shock wore off, it all made wonderful sense. "Henry worked for *Papi*, and Jean used to babysit me, before *Papi* and *Mami* married. They're wonderful people. The aunt and uncle I would have picked if I were doing the picking."

"Why didn't you go to them after Blair told you what he was planning for Carlito and Marisol?"

"I didn't believe anybody would be able to protect us from Martin. Henry's a good man, but Martin would have rolled right over him."

Charles looked back at the papers. "This might be sticky, given that Blair's probated the other wills, and he's already disposed of much of the property. But at least we'll have a powerful ally in this law firm."

"What do you mean, disposed of the property?" Luz, relieved at the discovery of the wills, now felt a thick lump of dread accumulating in her stomach.

Charles shifted as if he was uncomfortable. "Your Uncle sold the house, the farm and the business."

"No! Oh, no. He can't do that." She didn't realize she was crying and shaking her head until Charles put his arm around her and pulled her against his chest.

"What about Salsalita and Missy?" She could barely get the words out.

"Those are your horses?"

She nodded.

"I don't know what happened to them. You need to understand, in spite of the new wills, we may not be able to reverse some things. Like the sale of your house."

She pulled out of Charles's arms, although she wanted nothing more than to continue to accept his comfort. "S-so what do we do now?"

Charles straightened the files. "First, I need to go through the rest of these. Get an idea of how well your father's business was doing."

"What difference does that make?"

"It will indicate if your uncle was truthful about the bank accounts being empty and there being nothing but debts." Charles gave her a speculative look. "Was there a witness to that by the way?"

"A woman from social services. Her name was Ross." As if Luz would ever forget that scene. All of it etched in her memory so clearly, she could still picture what the woman had been wearing and exactly word for word what she'd said.

She described the woman, and Charles made notes on a fresh page of his yellow tablet.

"The other thing I need to do is speak with the lawyer who drew up the wills and trusts."

He was doing it again. Assuming he was in charge. "You mean, *I* need to speak to him."

Charles sighed. "I'm not trying to take over, Luz, but you did agree to let me help you. And my advice is that you let me talk to Ryan first. Besides, I expect you'd like to continue to keep your whereabouts a secret from Blair. At least for the time being?" He gave her a steady look until she nodded in agreement.

He tapped the list of names on the envelope. "This is a good firm. They have an excellent reputation. I'm certain they'll be aggressive about sorting everything out."

With a start, Luz remembered what they were actually discussing and why. *Mami* and *Papi* were dead. These new wills were their last wishes. Wishes they should have had to update over a period of years until in the fullness of time they became last wishes.

And now, everything was going to change. Once Charles talked to Ryan, her universe would shift, and nothing would ever be the same again. For one thing, she would no longer carry the responsibility for Carlito and Marisol all alone. Jean and Henry would be there, and Martin would be unable to interfere.

But with that faint stirring of relief, came the realization that all of this would take her inexorably away from Charles. She hugged herself to stop the tremor threatening to become a full-blown case of the shakes. She and Charles, like leaves caught in separate currents, swirling away from each other.

But Charles was going to be out of her life no matter what. Even if nothing changed for her, he would be moving soon, and that would be that. So all in all, better to lose him sooner rather than later, because with every day that passed, she was looking forward to their separation with more dread and sorrow.

Strange how such bright flowers had blossomed amidst the ruin of her life. The joy she felt in Marisol and Carlito, the pleasure of Cora's friendship, the exhilaration of riding that obstreperous filly at the Francinis'. The sweetness of opening a present from Charles to find something he'd chosen specifically for her. The joy of Charles himself and their chance meetings on stair and in doorway.

Since he'd arrived, the Draper Arms seemed less dingy. Less dead-end. Less hopeless.

She shivered again at the thought of a future without him.

He glanced up from making another note on the tablet, his eyes concerned but slightly out of focus behind the lenses of his glasses. "Are you cold? I can turn up the heat."

She shook her head. "Just thinking. Sorry I disturbed you."

He turned back to the documents, his face intent, chewing on the pen, making an occasional quick note as he turned over pages. He'd forgotten she was there. But that was okay. She needed this opportunity. To memorize the line of his jaw, the finely molded nose, the slightly wavy hair that wasn't one color but a mix of shades from light brown to ash. Occasionally his hand came up and rubbed through it, leaving it disordered.

Sitting as close as she was, she could feel the warmth of his body and breathe in his scent. He always smelled fresh, like he'd just showered. She savored his nearness, breathing deeply. Gradually, her eyes grew heavy, and she leaned back and let them drift shut.

The next thing she knew, she was waking up from what felt like the soundest sleep she'd had in months. Usually, she was aware of the noises Marisol and Carlito made at night, always half-awake at their tossings and turnings in case they needed her. Only in these last few minutes had she been able to let go and sink deeply into the void of sleep, and it left her refreshed. As if she'd been dying of thirst and had been given a tall glass of cool water.

The room was growing dim with the onset of winter twilight. Charles was sitting at the table, still going through the files, his hair gleaming under the light of the floor lamp he'd moved over to illuminate his work. Charles himself was indistinct, and as she peered at him, she realized her glasses were missing.

He turned.

She pushed off the blanket now covering her, sat up and ran her fingers through her hair, then she picked up her glasses and put them on. "Sorry about that."

"Nothing to be sorry about."

She glanced at her watch. "*Ay, ciertamente,* you should have awakened me." She'd slept an hour and a half.

"What for?"

"Carlito. I need to make sure Cora is okay."

"Cora's fine. You know, she looks ten years younger since

she moved in with you."

"Cora, *Madre de Dios*, what am I going to do about Cora, if we go back to Scottsbluff?"

"Take her with you."

Luz blinked at him.

"It looks to me like you and the kids are going to be sitting well, financially. Once we wrest it all from Blair's grubby hands, you'll have plenty to buy a house big enough for all of you. Jean and Henry too."

All of you. Already, he was distancing himself from any decisions she might make about the future. She folded the blanket, the refreshment from the nap seeping away.

She balanced the blanket on the arm of the couch. "What happens next?"

"I'll set up a meeting with Richard Ryan as soon as possible. Once we've turned all this over to him, he'll take it from there."

"Maybe now you'll let me pay for the extra food."

"It's been a privilege to help you, Luz. It's why I became a district attorney. So that sometime, somehow I'd get a chance to help right a few wrongs."

Of course. She knew that. The reason he'd helped was because of who he was. Nothing to do with her, specifically.

She stood. "I'd better get back. Thanks for the loan of your couch."

"Anytime."

"I well—" She hesitated, her feet shifting, feeling as young and gawky as Marisol, hoping for...something. "I need to get going."

Charles barely glanced at her.

Catching her lip between her teeth to prevent more meaningless words from tumbling out, she left.

Chapter Eighteen

After all the worry, not only about Luz, but about his own status as co-conspirator in her drama, it all came down to something as simple as a few files stored under a bed. Of course if Snodgrass had succeeded in burning down the building, they would have been lost, and Martin Blair would have been free to do whatever he wanted with the Montalvo estate.

Did everything important in life turn on such a delicate spindle?

Based on his experience, it would seem so. A degree or two to one side or the other, a minute sooner or later, and catastrophe either averted or encountered.

While he was going through the files, Luz fell asleep. He lifted the glasses from her face and saw the dark circles they camouflaged. He covered her carefully, so he wouldn't awaken her, and for a moment, allowed himself to look. As he did, he acknowledged, finally, that she was infinitely dear to him.

Perhaps she wasn't classically beautiful, but she had a whimsical quality that would make her attractive no matter how old she was. He reached out with a finger, wanting to brush the smooth skin of her cheek. Craving the connection touching her would bring, but forcing himself to refrain.

Her life as yet unformed—college, career choices—all ahead of her. Able to dream whatever dream she wished. Marisol and Carlito cared for, loved. Luz free. And still so many years to go before she might catch up with him.

He had no right to ask her to give up any of that growing time just because he'd developed an ill-conceived passion for her.

Although what he felt for Luz was more than physical desire. Gallant. All flags flying. That was his Luz. Loving and gentle with Carlito and Marisol, although she was usually testy with him. But he loved her testiness as much as her gallantry. She was going to be one hell of a woman when she finished growing up, and the only right thing for him to do was step out of the way and let her get on with it.

He'd find someone else, eventually. Someone his age. Someone already fully formed. Someone ready to settle down and have a family.

He gulped at the thought, realizing it had been a long time coming. Starting from when he'd fallen in love with Kathy, he'd begun thinking it might be possible after all, that he could manage to be a father. And now, after spending time with Luz, Marisol and Carlito, he knew it was what he wanted for himself. A wife he loved with all his heart who loved him in return. And children.

He pulled away from staring at Luz and went back to work on the documents. It was all there, everything he needed to help her regain some of what she'd lost. The material part at least.

There was little he could do about the deeper emotional losses.

ℬ

Entering Richard Ryan's office, Charles was accompanied by a growing sense of loss. As if Luz were being pulled rapidly away, her form fading, until he could no longer make out the bright intelligence in her eyes, the quirk of a smile on her lips. He tried to shrug off the bleakness of that thought along with his coat, but an unexpected tightness continued to plague his throat.

Ryan, a well-padded man with manicured hands and thinning hair, sat tapping his fingers together while Charles explained his business. A stutter in that rhythm was the only indication Ryan was surprised by the news Charles brought.

"There are a number of other issues that also need to be addressed," Charles said when he finished explaining about the wills. "The old wills named Martin Blair executor and guardian.

He's the children's uncle. He told the oldest girl, Luz, that her younger siblings would have to go into foster care. To prevent that, Luz ran away, and she and the children have been reported to the authorities as missing."

Ryan raised an eyebrow, but remained silent.

"I have with me a power of attorney from Luz, asking you to represent her in this matter."

"How old is the girl?"

"Twenty. She was nineteen when her parents died. Blair told her she had no chance of being awarded custody. She believed him and panicked."

"That should be easy enough to fix."

Charles hoped Ryan was right. "I also have a question. Why did Montalvo come to you? Why not a firm based in Nebraska?"

"We have a branch in Omaha, and several of us maintain licenses in both states. Many clients find it more convenient to come to Denver. And likely you know the answer to the rest of your question."

Yeah, he did. Martin Blair. No doubt Montalvo had decided against using a local lawyer who might slip and mention something to Blair as they golfed or shared a drink. And professional ethics aside, such things did happen, especially in small towns.

"Blair also told Luz he checked the bank accounts, and there was no money. He said the estate had a lot of debt."

"I very much doubt that," Ryan said. "The Montalvos impressed me as careful managers."

"It may be useful to get a statement from the woman in Children's Services who heard him make the allegation."

Ryan, rubbed a hand over his cheek and chin. "You have only the last name?"

"And a description."

Ryan pursed his lips, obviously thinking about it. "Small town like that. It might tip him off before we're ready. You have a suggestion?"

He did. And as that suggestion crystallized, Charles realized how much he hated simply turning everything over to Ryan and then being relegated to watching from the sidelines.

"Why don't I go to Scottsbluff, talk to Ross, get her to sign an affidavit."

ॐ

It took less than five minutes for Charles to discover that the only Ross working in the Scotts Bluff County Office of Children's Protective Services was a Rhonda Ross. He checked further and found the best, hell the only, way to get to Scottsbluff was to drive. He called Ross's office and made an appointment for the next day, then he cleared his own schedule, something he would find difficult to do once the first Maxwell trial commenced.

He was on the road by five-thirty a.m. As he drove north, the horizon gradually lightened from deep gray to dove to blue, taking on touches of rose along the way. *Red sky in the morning, sailor take warning.* The phrase drifted through his mind, and he wondered if it meant there'd be snow later.

The rose faded quickly, leaving only wisps of cirrus clouds with an occasional contrail stitching above the sere landscape. He'd forgotten how spare, empty, elemental it was out here once the city was left behind.

He stopped in Fort Morgan for a second breakfast then turned north on secondary roads, passing the occasional feedlot, where cows placidly milled in corrals in which mud had been churned to fetlock depth then frozen.

He arrived in Scottsbluff in four hours, two hours ahead of his meeting with Ross, and used the time to get a sense of the place. When he'd explained his mission to Luz, she had drawn him a simple map showing where the farm, Martin Blair's house, and her parents' house were located.

"What's next?" she'd asked as she handed him the map.

"Ryan is contacting the probate judge in Scottsbluff to find out how he wants to handle the situation."

"Will he let me know?"

"Of course. The judge may decide to hold a hearing. If he does, you might have to testify."

Luz shuddered. "But that would mean Martin will know

where we are. And what if the judge doesn't believe us about the new wills? I'm absolutely certain Martin will contest them."

Charles had wanted to take her in his arms and promise her it would all work out. But he didn't dare do either. "You're going to have to take that chance, Luz. It's a gamble, but the odds are stacked in your favor."

The Montalvos' street was lined with huge trees that had to be at least a hundred years old. The Montalvo house, a two-story white clapboard with a deep front porch and a lived-in, welcoming aspect, sat on a corner lot. The front and side yards were beautifully landscaped although they had a slightly unkempt winter look, like someone who had gone too long without a haircut.

He checked the map, following the directions to Martin Blair's house. It was large and showy with a perfectly groomed yard. But although obviously more expensive than the Montalvo house, it had only a fraction of the personality. Or perhaps Charles's view of the owner biased his opinion.

After a slow circuit of the Blairs' block, Charles consulted the map again for directions to the farm. He found it more difficult to locate than the houses, but on his second pass, he spotted the small sign on the mailbox.

He turned into the driveway and drove the short distance to where a house, barn and large greenhouse were keeping each other company. Two white pickups were parked by the house, each with a red rose painted on its side.

In spite of the presence of the vehicles, the place appeared deserted, which made sense, given the time of year. Charles parked and walked over to the barn. The door creaked on opening, and he slipped inside. A quick shuffling sound was followed by a snort, and he found himself being examined by a black horse and a brown pony. Their stalls were clean and food and water was at hand. Although both horses had shaggy winter coats, their manes and tails were neat. As far as he could tell, they appeared to be healthy and well-cared for.

The door to the greenhouse was padlocked, so he had to be content with peering inside. Row after row of small plants beginning to sprout sat on tables that filled about half the space. The remaining space held a variety of small trees and bushes, some with foliage, some without.

Everything looked as neat and well-cared for as the horses.

"Something I can help you with?" The tone was anything but solicitous.

Charles startled, his heart hitting ninety, and turned to find a man standing ten feet away, a pitchfork, not so casually held, by his side. Not Martin Blair. He knew from Luz's description Blair was short, broad and balding, the opposite of this man. Charles decided to take a chance. "Henry Hollis?"

"Yeah?"

Charles pointed at the barn. "Missy and Salsalita, I presume?"

The man's face went from stern to puzzled—he'd be a lousy poker player. Then he narrowed his eyes. "Who are you?"

"Charles Larimore. A friend of Luz's."

"I know Luz's friends. You ain't one."

Charles was trying to decide what would be the quickest way to convince Henry Hollis he *was* Luz's friend, when the back door of the house opened and a woman came out to stand next to the man. She was plump and clearly spent a lot of time smiling, although at the moment she had a worried expression. Still, Charles could imagine her laughing and playing with Carlito, an image that made Luz's return to Scottsbluff seem more real than it had before.

"Says he's a friend of Luz's," Henry muttered to the woman, who had to be Jean Hollis.

She gave Charles a troubled look. "Is that true? Do you know where she is?"

"Are you Jean Hollis?"

The woman nodded.

"Martin Blair," he said, testing.

The distaste on both their faces was immediate and unmistakable. "Bastard," Henry muttered.

"Then yes," Charles said. "I know Luz, and I know where she is. Can we go inside? I have a lot to tell you." Richard Ryan might be furious, but this seemed like the right thing to do.

Jean nodded and turned to lead the way into the house. Glimpsing rooms bare except for a single rump-sprung couch in the living room, Charles realized the house was not the Hollises'

179

home. Only the kitchen was cozy and fragrant with brewing coffee. Two cups sat on the table. Jean dumped them, refilled them with fresh coffee and poured a third cup.

Charles took a sip, trying to decide where to start. Probably, the most important bit first. "Luz, Marisol and Carlito are fine."

"Oh, thank God." Some of the strain smoothed from Jean's face.

"How do we know you ain't lying?" Clearly, Henry needed more assurance before he let go of the tight lump of worry he'd obviously been carrying.

"Luz and her father used to come here every afternoon to go riding," Charles said. "When she was little she rode Missy, and later on she rode Salsalita." Considering his view of horses, it did strike him as odd he'd chosen them to prove who he was. "You used to babysit for Luz, before Esteban and Mary got married," he added, nodding at Jean.

"Okay, maybe you've met Luz, but you still might be somebody trying to take advantage."

The longer he talked to Henry and Jean, the more relieved Charles felt. He no longer worried they might speak out of turn to Martin Blair.

"The Montalvos drew up new wills, shortly before they died. In those wills they named the two of you as guardians for Marisol and Carlito."

Henry's eyes narrowed, again. "How do you know that?"

"When Luz ran away, she grabbed a bunch of files from her father's desk. The will was among those papers."

"Maybe you robbed her."

It would have been amusing if it hadn't been heartbreaking—how hard Henry was working to be certain he didn't make a mistake and hurt Luz. It was a relief to know Luz would have these people, who obviously cared deeply for her, back in her life. But the thought also brought pain. Because if the Hollises were in her life, she'd no longer need him.

Calling on all the self-discipline he'd spent years developing, Charles pulled his mind back to the matter at hand. "Luz showed them to me. I'm a deputy district attorney, in Denver. I can give you the name of someone in my office to call, if you want to verify that."

"I seen that trick. I call and it's someone you got planted."

Charles stifled a smile. Henry had to be a fan of legal and police procedurals. "You can get the number for the DA's office from directory assistance. Ask whoever answers about me. They'll verify my description."

Henry walked over to the old-fashioned wall phone. "What's the Denver area code?"

Charles told him. Henry dialed, asked for the Denver District Attorney's Office number and waited for it to connect. Eyeing Charles, he spoke into the phone. "I'm trying to reach the office of a Charles Larimore. Understand he's a District Attorney." He listened for a moment. "Couldn't happen to tell me what he looks like, could you?" He listened again then thanked the person on the other end, hung up and turned to Charles. "Looks like you're telling the truth."

Jean let out a breath so big she sagged.

"New will doesn't do much good, though. Martin already took the estate through probate." Henry sounded glum.

"Did you know there was a new will?" Charles suspected they had to, given they were named guardians.

"Esteban and Mary talked to us six weeks 'fore they were killed about the guardianship. Wanted to keep it quiet. Didn't want Martin to know. Course we all figured it wouldn't never be an issue." He stopped speaking and took a quick gulp of coffee.

Moisture gathered in his eyes, and it made Charles warm to the man even more than he already had.

"Esteban just couldn't stomach the idea of Martin Blair," Henry continued. "Even though he was family. And Mary finally agreed. But after they died, and nothing was said about new wills, we figured they didn't get it done. And then Luz disappeared."

The explanation answered most of Charles's questions. Only one oddity remained—the wills had no provision for the Hollises taking on the guardianship. They would have court-supervised access to Marisol's and Carlito's inheritance to use in raising the children, but Charles found it hard to believe nothing more had been provided.

"Did it seem strange, they'd have you take the kids, but not leave you anything?"

"Well, we got the insurance."

"Insurance?"

"Esteban had a half-million dollar policy. He done that a couple years ago. Told me it was so Jean and me could keep the business going, anything happened. We used it to buy Las Flores off Martin."

"You're Prentice Partners?"

"How do you know about that?"

"I did a search to determine what happened to the property. The Montalvo house, the business, this farm."

"We tried to buy the house, too." Jean weighed in for the first time. "We wanted it to be there when the children came home."

Charles was suddenly curious about all the ramifications of Luz's decision. "What did you think about Luz running away?"

"Didn't know what to think," Henry said. "Then we talked to Rae. She told us about Martin bringing in the social services."

"We kept hoping Luz would contact us, so's we might help her," Jean said. "The police tried to find her, of course. And we hired an investigator, too. He discovered Mary's car had been sold to a man in Denver, but there was no trace after that. Finally, we figured the only thing we could do was hold as much together as possible, and hope she'd come home one day."

"What about the contents of the house?"

"We got that into storage," Henry said. "Rae helped. She's not so bad when Martin's not around."

"We've been so worried," Jean said, suddenly looking it. "We just couldn't imagine how Luz was managing with the two children all on her own. And now here you are a district attorney. She isn't in trouble is she? "

"That damn Martin tried to accuse her of kidnapping," Henry said.

Charles shifted, suddenly uncomfortable. "That's being handled." At least he hoped it was.

"Could you give us a number?" Jean asked. "So's we can call her. I'm just not going to believe she's okay until I hear her voice."

No doubt Ryan wouldn't like that either, but Charles didn't have the heart to refuse.

Driving to the Health and Human Services offices, Charles thought about how to handle the interview with Rhonda Ross. Finally, he decided it was probably best to play it by ear the way he had with the Hollises.

Ross's office was untidy, but the woman was meticulously groomed, wearing a formal gray suit and white lacy blouse that made her seem more bosomy than likely she was. Fortyish and attractive, with an angular face, wide mouth and large eyes the color of lightly creamed coffee. But the expression on her face effectively negated any appeal. It was a look he'd learned to take for granted and also lately to dislike. Although, it might make things easier, because if she was focused on flirting with him, she might forget to be curious about why a Denver DA had come all this way to ask about the Montalvo family.

She offered coffee. When he refused, she settled herself behind her desk. "You're from the Denver DA's office, you said?"

He nodded. "I do a lot of work with HHS. Sure seem to have their hands full. Imagine you do as well."

"Oh, I'm certain our little town can't touch the caseload in Denver, but we do have our problems. Some of them every bit as complex as a big city's."

Charles shook his head, trying for empathy. "Doesn't seem to matter any more. Big city, small town. We've all got problems." And that was probably enough of that. "Seems we share one particular problem."

"Oh, indeed." She leaned forward, eager and apparently pleased to discover they shared something.

Charles, looking at the toothy smile, tried to imagine her comforting any of the children she dealt with. Couldn't.

"A case from about a year ago. Three minor children. Parents killed in an auto accident." He pulled a notebook from his pocket and flipped pages, pretending to search for the name. "Family's name was Montalvo."

"Oh yes. I remember the case well. We were called in for the two younger children. To arrange foster care."

Charles gave her a questioning look. "There was an uncle,

183

wasn't there? Why didn't he take the children?"

"Yes. His name was Blaine, maybe? His wife was too ill to take care of them."

Now that was a surprise. Luz had made no mention of Rae Blair being ill, and neither had the Hollises. Most likely another of Blair's lies.

He glanced back at his bogus notes. "I have it as Martin Blair. And there's an older girl, right?"

Ross nodded. "Only sixteen. Too young to be their guardian, and nothing for them to live on, you see. She didn't need foster care since she was attending a boarding school."

Sixteen? Boarding school? For a beat it shocked him, but then he realized it couldn't possibly be right. Still it explained something. Why Ross had bought the idea and sold it to Luz that she wouldn't get custody. He left that point for the moment and focused on his original concern. "You mean they were left destitute?"

"Exactly. The uncle was the executor of the estate, and he was certainly clear on the point, I'll tell you."

"And was he the one who told you the older girl was only sixteen?"

Ross frowned in apparent concentration. "Yes, I believe so. He must have been."

"Had you met him before that day?"

She shook her head, the look on her face changing abruptly from eager sharing to one of suspicion. "So what's your connection to the case?"

"I'm afraid I'm not at liberty to discuss the details." He gave her a smile that said, *Of course, you'd be the first one I'd tell, if I could.* "What I need is an affidavit stating what Martin Blair said in your presence about the Montalvo estate."

Her body language closed up, and she sat back. "Well, actually, I know nothing about the Montalvos. The children disappeared, and I had nothing more to do with any of them."

He was losing her. "I understand that, but all I need is for you to attest to what you heard Martin Blair say." He glanced at his watch and braced himself. "It's almost noon. If we can get the statement finished, perhaps you'd let me take you to lunch?"

For a moment, he thought he'd lost his touch. Well, he had been out of training for a while. Then her posture softened slightly, and she took a breath. "Can you help me with it?"

"Be happy to."

She sat at the computer, and he dictated the format for the information, leaving it to her to add Martin Blair's statements about the Montalvos' finances and Luz's age. Then, at his direction, she printed three copies, signed them and had the receptionist notarize them. She handed them to Charles with a coy smile and gathered her purse and coat.

She oohed and aahed over his car before directing him to the Applebee's on the edge of town. "There aren't any really nice places to have lunch in Scottsbluff. Not like Denver."

He did his best to respond to her sallies and be a pleasant host, but it was hard slogging. A relief to return her to her office an hour and a half later. As he pulled to a stop, she fumbled with her purse. "Here, let me give you my home number. Just in case you have any more questions."

He accepted the card she handed him, ignoring the subtext implicit in the gesture. Then he got out and opened her door— she'd made it clear such courtesies were expected. Besides, it got rid of her more quickly.

He drove the first miles back to Denver with the windows open to blow away the smell of her perfume along with her card. Then he rolled the windows back up and took a chance there'd be no state troopers in the area.

He was back in Denver in three hours.

Chapter Nineteen

After Charles took the new wills to Ryan, everything happened so quickly, Luz felt as if the world had suddenly speeded up, like a car whipping through an avenue of trees so fast no one tree stood out. Everything a blur of green and brown.

Ryan submitted the new wills to the court, and the judge required Luz to appear before him to explain why she hadn't turned them over sooner.

Ryan drove her to Scottsbluff for the hearing, spending the time first describing what would likely happen in court and what would be expected of her. Then he questioned her about how she'd managed during her time in Denver.

Luz felt like she was walking a tightrope, wanting to be candid, but not wanting to say something that might put Charles in jeopardy for helping her.

Jean and Henry were waiting at the courthouse. Jean enveloped Luz in a hug while Henry stood by, his eyes tearing up.

"Oh. Oh, Luz, honey," Jean said. "It's so good to see you. We've been so worried. And Marisol and Carlito. Oh, we can hardly wait to see them."

"I haven't told Marisol what's happening yet," Luz admitted. "I'm really scared."

"Oh, sweetie, don't you worry. We're going to be right there praying. It's going to be just fine. You'll see." Jean took Luz's hand, and with her other hand, scrubbed a tissue across her eyes. Then they all walked into court.

Martin was already there. He swiveled around in his seat

and glared. Luz firmed her lips to keep them from trembling, wishing Charles was beside her. But he was tied up in court in Denver, trying the first Maxwell case.

She and Ryan were ushered to seats in front of Martin, and Luz breathed a sigh of relief, but she quickly found imagining that glare aimed at her back was worse than facing it directly.

The judge began the proceedings by asking Richard Ryan to explain the situation.

"Your Honor, if it please the court. Esteban and Mary Montalvo came to me in September a year and a half ago to have me draw up wills for them. Recently, these wills were discovered by the Montalvos' eldest daughter. We ask that the wills previously probated be vacated, and these more recent wills be accepted for probate."

Ryan then responded to questions about the Montalvos' signatures on the wills. "Yes, Your Honor, I have here affidavits from the individuals who signed as witnesses to the execution of these wills."

When the judge finished questioning Ryan, Luz was ushered into the witness chair, and had to once again face the full malevolence of Martin's stare. It turned her words into small rills of turbulence. "N-no, I didn't know about the wills. I had no idea they were mixed in with the papers I took with me. A friend recognized what they were, and he contacted Mr. Ryan t-to ask what to do.

"Yes, I did run away. I didn't know what else t-to do. Martin said Marisol and Carlito had to go into f-foster care. That I was too young to be given custody.

"Yes. I believed him. He also said there was n-no money. And we couldn't stay in our house."

And then it was Martin's turn. On the stand, he dropped the glare and put on an ingratiating expression as he turned toward the judge. "Your Honor, of course I had no idea Mary and Esteban were thinking about making new wills. And, to tell you the truth, I'm not at all convinced these new wills are genuine.

"Of course, Mary and Esteban might have thought about doing this. But there's certainly a doubt in my mind these signatures are theirs.

"Of course, I'm not questioning the honesty of the witnesses. I'm merely questioning whether they actually witnessed these particular signatures on this particular document. Mary and Esteban could have been signing about anything. And besides, some amazing things are being done with computers these days, they tell me.

"Well of course I thought I was doing what was right and proper given the wills I knew about.

"No, Your Honor, you are correct. The foster care situation wasn't ideal of course. But I didn't see how my wife could take on the rearing of an infant and a small child. We're not exactly spring chickens, you know.

"Besides, the girl was in college. I didn't see how she could expect to take care of two children. I was only trying to make it easier for her. Such a tragic thing to lose her parents that way."

When it was over, Luz would have liked more time with Jean and Henry, but she was also relieved that Ryan insisted they start back to Denver right away, since that took her out of the vicinity of Martin Blair.

ॐ

Luz felt as if she'd crammed at least twenty years' worth of experiences into the year since her parents' deaths. She'd learned things about herself she never imagined. That although frightened and grieving, she was tougher and stronger than she thought. That, with few resources, she could hold her family together and be responsible for their safety and well-being. That in spite of being in a perilous situation herself, she could reach out to help someone else.

What had ultimately alleviated some of her grief and fear had been Charles. Such a relief to finally admit she loved him. A relief, but also a sorrow. Because Charles obviously didn't love her. Oh, he respected her, and maybe he liked her, a little. And he might even enjoy making love to her, if the opportunity arose.

He wasn't going to miss her, though. Not the way she was going to miss him.

ಐ

It didn't take long for the judge's decision on the Montalvos' wills. Two weeks after the hearing, he ruled the new wills valid. Martin Blair was ordered to turn over all monies from the property sales and the Montalvo bank accounts to the court, to be placed in a guardianship account for the benefit of Luz, Marisol and Carlito.

As Luz began planning the move back to Scottsbluff, every time she encountered Charles, her heart hurt. So many good things happening, but because of those good things, she and Charles would shortly be separated, and she'd likely never see him again.

As it was, since the hearing, she'd seen him only rarely—additional proof he had managed to get on with his life, once his little neighborhood project had reached a successful conclusion. He hadn't even bothered to keep up the pretense of the extra food after the judge's decision on the wills came down. He now did all his shopping at King Soopers.

She looked out the window and saw him climb out of the Porsche and reach back in for the bags of groceries. She grabbed some clothes and threw them in the laundry basket, walked out of her apartment and stood in the hall awaiting the arrival of the elevator.

"Hi," she said, her throat closing up.

Charles, whose thoughts appeared to be far away, jumped.

"Oh. Hi yourself." He shifted the bags in his arms and smiled at her distractedly before going to his door. He fished out his keys, opened the door and went inside, pushing the door closed behind him.

He couldn't be more clear if he'd had a big sandwich sign hanging from his shoulders with large print saying, *You don't owe me anything.*

How dare he! How dare he walk away, like, like…she didn't matter. Who the hell did he think he was?

She dropped the laundry basket, marched over to his door and lifted her hand to knock. Then she lowered it. Defeated, she went back to her apartment.

After that, whenever she saw Charles, Luz felt like she was in the midst of a game of statues and someone had yelled "Freeze!" Because that's what she did. She froze, croaking out a greeting, trying to remember what she'd been doing when he appeared—going into her apartment, or leaving? She stood there for a time before deciding it no longer mattered.

During those last weeks in Denver, whenever she tried to figure out what came next, her mind stalled. So many decisions to make all of a sudden, and none of them limited any longer by a lack of money. Once again, she was free to consider all the dreams she'd dreamed before the accident choked off her future along with her parents' lives.

But trying to plan brought no anticipation. Instead she found herself stuck, grieving beforehand the loss of her brother and sister from her daily life. At least they would be lost unless she stayed in Scottsbluff. But there was nothing there for her. Jean and Henry had already asked if she planned to return to college. A question she'd been unable to answer.

Ryan had arranged for an allowance, making it no longer necessary for her to babysit, but without that, her days were long and mostly empty. She told Ryan she wanted to stay in Denver a while longer to give Marisol time to get used to the idea of moving, but really it was to give herself more time.

Not willing to wait, Jean and Henry came to Denver for a visit. Luz still wasn't certain Marisol really understood what was going to happen, but she was relieved to see both children responding positively to the Hollises' obvious affection.

Watching Jean with her arm around Marisol, Luz thought her sister would quickly adjust to the new circumstances. And Carlito was young enough to make the change to Jean's loving care with minimal distress. She was the one who felt adrift.

Then one afternoon, when Cora was out, Carlito was napping and Luz was dozing, the phone rang. The caller was Rob Francini, offering her a job at TapDancer. "Thought Alan'd have more time, but seems he's pretty tied up. Wedding to plan and all."

Luz was so taken aback, she didn't realize she hadn't responded until Rob asked if she was still on the line. Then he went on to say she should bring Cora and the children with her. "Imagine this is a bit of a surprise. You'll probably have to give it some thought. But then give me a call back."

"No. That is...it's okay. I want to come. How soon do you want me?"

"You can come tomorrow, you had a mind to."

"Actually, there are some things I need to take care of first." Like seeing Carlito and Marisol settled in Scottsbluff. Something she'd been delaying because she had no idea what came after that. But maybe now she did.

It was a relief, but painful as well. "I can start in two weeks and work at least through the summer. And just so you know, Cora, Marisol and Carlito won't be coming with me." As she said the words, the full weight of what was happening made her knees sag.

"Oh. Has something happened?" At the concerned note in his voice, Luz quickly explained.

"Sure glad to hear it's all working out." He sounded relieved. "We'll be glad to have you, soon as you can come."

She set the phone down, feeling like both crying and smiling. For the first time in days she had something more to look forward to than separations and endings. And going to TapDancer might also help her deal with the imminent loss of Charles.

She'd wanted to find a way to maintain a connection with him, and perhaps now she had. Well, not that she was kidding herself it would do any good, but he'd become tangled up in her life, and trying to pull him out in one swift motion wasn't working. She didn't think she could stand any more sudden, permanent losses.

But working for the parents of Charles's best friend, she might get to see him sometime, and if that happened, maybe she'd be able to figure out how to let him go. Chances were she felt the way she did about him only because he'd shown up at such a low point in her life. She'd over-romanticized him. With time, she'd come to see him as just a nice, ordinary guy. Someone she'd known briefly and would always remember fondly.

But until that happened, the TapDancer job was the perfect solution. And more than that, it was a first step into her new future.

At the realization, her whole body slumped with relief.

"Are you okay?" Cora stood in the kitchen doorway, frowning.

"Yes. I think so. Rob Francini just called. He offered me a job, and I accepted."

Cora cocked her head, beginning to look worried. "But if you go to the ranch, and Marisol and Carlito go to Scottsbluff..." Her words trailed off, and the worried look intensified.

Understanding dawned. Luz spoke firmly. "You're going to Scottsbluff with Marisol and Carlito. They need you."

"I can't help thinking I'm a burden."

Luz went to Cora and put her arms around her. "You're our very own nana." Although Luz had saved Cora, in many ways Cora had returned the favor. "No way, you're a burden." Luz leaned back, put her hands on Cora's shoulders and looked her in the eye. "*Tú eres familia.* And don't you ever forget it."

Cora blinked rapidly. "You know, dear, it may be the best thing that ever happened to me, letting that con man talk me out of my life savings. Just look what I got in return." She pulled a handkerchief from her pocket and dabbed her eyes. It was the one with the embroidered roses Charles gave her for Christmas.

Seeing it, Luz felt like crying herself.

Chapter Twenty

Shortly before they were to leave for Scottsbluff, Luz went next door to tell Charles goodbye. He opened the door and leaned on the jamb, looking at her with a neutral expression.

"I thought, umm..." Not a good start, but being this close to him was making it difficult for her to breathe. "Can I come in please?"

Without any sign of welcome, he stood aside, and she walked past him. Behind her the door closed. She stood in the middle of the living room with her back to Charles, trying to remember what she'd planned to say.

"Are you cold?"

At his question, she realized she was hugging herself. She turned, shaking her head. "Can we sit down?"

He nodded, and when she took a seat on the sofa, he sat in the chair across from her. In spite of his relaxed posture his eyes were both alert and distant.

The combination rattled her. At a minimum she expected courtesy. But was it courteous to make it so obvious he didn't want her here?

"I wanted to thank you. For everything. For helping us."

He lifted a negligent hand and waved her words away.

She put her own hand up to stop him from speaking. "And for not reporting us." He went out of focus, and angrily she blinked at tears. In case this was the last time, she wanted to see him clearly. "I'll never forget any of it. Or you. I just wanted you to know." *I love you.* Those were the words caught in her throat. Those and, *I don't want this, not if it means never seeing you again.*

She wanted to crawl in his lap and have him hold her, but she couldn't just throw herself at him, although, for a moment, she was unable to think why not. But before she could move, Charles stood, and as if he'd read her intention and was countering it, stepped out of reach.

"Would you like something to drink?" His tone, firm and distant, matched his unyielding posture.

It was hopeless. She stood quickly before the pain of that knowledge overwhelmed her. "That was all I wanted to say. Just, thank you." She walked to the door, moving carefully, fighting the urge to run, and let herself out, because Charles didn't come to do it.

Still hanging on by a thread, she grabbed a key to an empty unit and told Cora she needed to check on something. Downstairs, she unlocked the door, slipped inside and sat on the floor next to the radiator. The heat was barely a trickle and the wall was cold. That cold slowly seeped through the fabric of her shirt, chilling her, bringing on a violent bout of shivering. She'd been clamping down on tears from the moment Charles moved away from her, but now that she was free to cry, it seemed the tears had frozen into a hard lump inside her. She sat trembling, until she could once again rely on her self-control, then she returned to her apartment, where Cora was reading to Marisol while Carlito played on the floor.

"Lu lu lu," Carlito crooned. She picked him up and buried her face in his neck, tickling him until he giggled in delight.

From the look Cora gave her, Luz knew she wasn't fooling the elderly woman one bit. Cora knew she was upset. Nothing was said, however, until Marisol and Carlito went to bed. When Luz came back to the living room after reading Marisol her bedtime story, Cora was sitting on the sofa, working a crossword puzzle.

"Do you know who the sixteenth president was, Luz?"

"Wasn't it Lincoln?" Luz sat next to Cora and picked up a book.

"Yes, of course it was." Cora finished writing then closed the puzzle book and pushed her reading glasses up on her head. "There's a story I've been wanting to tell you, dear. I've been waiting for just the right moment, but it never seems to come. Would you mind if I told you now?"

"Sure. Okay." Letting the book fall closed, Luz curled her feet beneath her and turned to face Cora.

"I told you a little white lie. Habit, I suppose. Although nobody's left alive it would matter to in the least." Cora fiddled with the puzzle book. "You see, David was more than my fiancé. We fell in love, and I took him home so he could ask my father for my hand in marriage. My parents were...well, I suppose they didn't want me to be hurt, but the things they said did hurt. We got married, secretly, right before David was sent to San Diego to complete his flight training. I joined him there to be with him as long as possible."

Cora's voice took on a dreamy quality, and her eyes appeared unfocused. "I went by train. It was summer, and the trains were packed. It took five days to get there although it seemed a lot longer. While I was there, David and I spent every minute together we could, but it was no time at all before he shipped out. I came back to Denver, and shortly after that, I realized I was pregnant."

But Cora had told them she had no children. Luz hugged a pillow, wondering what happened to the baby and what the story had to do with anything, but willing to listen anyway.

"Right before our baby was due, I received notification that David's plane was missing. He flew a cargo route over what they called the Hump. The Himalayas. If a plane went down...well, there wasn't much chance of anybody surviving. But a person always hopes, don't they, if they don't know for sure."

Cora's hands stilled, and her voice slowed. "Not long after that our baby was stillborn. A little girl. They wouldn't let me see her. In those days, they thought it was better. That it made it easier. It didn't though."

Luz sat barely breathing.

"It was probably a week later that Margaret, the friend I lived with, woke me to tell me she'd had the most amazing dream. In her dream we were all in David's church. He was a Christian Scientist, you see. Margaret described the church and the service, and all of it was exactly as I remembered. But Margaret had never been in that church, had never attended a service there. Still, her description was exactly right.

"In her dream, when the service ended and we got up to leave, David asked her to stay a moment. He was holding an infant, and he leaned toward Margaret and moved the blanket off the baby's face and said, 'Isn't she beautiful.' He was smiling, Margaret said. David had the most wonderful smile. Then he told Margaret to tell me he wouldn't be with me for a while, but he loved me and was proud of me, and he and Clarissa would be waiting for me." Cora pulled out her handkerchief and wiped her eyes. "That's what I named her. Clarissa."

In the silence that followed, Luz thought about the story, still uncertain why Cora had told it. Feeling confused as well. "But if David wanted you to know he and the baby were together and they were all right, why didn't he appear in your dream instead of Margaret's?"

The old woman nodded. "Yes, I wondered that, too. But then I decided if I'd had the dream, it might have comforted me for a short time, but I would have eventually convinced myself I'd made it all up, and it wasn't real. But by showing Margaret a place she'd never seen, a place she was able to describe in perfect detail in order to convince me she'd seen both it and David... Well, I believe that's why. I still missed David and Clarissa, but I no longer felt such despair."

"It's a wonderful story." Luz wished *Mami* and *Papi* would find a way to let her know they were okay.

"It changed my life." Cora spoke simply. "It proved to me we are being watched over with love and caring, even when things look their darkest."

"That's hard to believe sometimes."

"I know it is, dear." Cora patted her on the arm. "That's why I wanted to tell you about it."

Luz thought of the dark times she'd come through. Right now was harder somehow. Death brought a finality one had to begin at some point to accept. But Charles was alive, closed off from her by his own choice. The pain of that was specific and particular, and it wasn't eased by Cora's story.

Later though, she found the story did help with her grief for her parents, grief the imminent return to Scottsbluff had intensified.

૭૦

When Jean and Henry arrived in Denver to move them to Scottsbluff, Marisol was once again shy. She stood pressed against Luz as Cora and the Hollises talked. Then Carlito toddled over and stretched his arms to Jean. Seeing Carlito being cuddled, Marisol sidled over. Pretty soon, Jean had her arms around both children, and Luz knew everything was going to be fine. For Marisol and Carlito at least.

This return to Scottsbluff felt very different from Luz's previous return to testify at the hearing. For one thing, she wouldn't have to face Martin, and for another, she wouldn't be returning to Denver at the end of the day. It meant Charles was firmly and finally in her past, a part of all her losses.

In spite of the aura of celebration Jean was trying to spin with the balloons on the mailbox, the big "Welcome Home" sign hung across the front door, the bedrooms all ready for Luz and the children and the basement fixed up for Cora, Luz felt bereft.

It was a major struggle to keep a smile on her face as Marisol danced around her room, excited to once again be surrounded by all the toys and furniture, books and pictures she'd had to leave behind when they ran away.

Luz's room looked the same as her old room as well, although her bed and dresser now sat on a pink rather than a blue carpet. But the closet was full of the clothes she'd left behind, and the bookcase was replete with all her books.

The first thing Marisol wanted to do once she'd seen her room was visit the horses. Jean convinced her to eat first, then Henry drove Luz and Marisol to the farm. "They haven't been ridden since you left," Henry told Luz as they stood at the fence watching the horses graze. Luz whistled, and both animals raised their heads. After a momentary inspection, Missy came running, whinnying, followed more sedately by Salsalita.

Luz slipped inside the pasture and hugged first Missy and then Salsalita, who endured it all with a dignity Luz tried and failed to emulate. The horses brought it back more vividly even than being in Scottsbluff. This farm was *Papi*'s place. It was here Luz visualized him most easily and felt his loss most acutely.

Marisol slipped through the fence as well, holding out carrots and chattering first to Missy and then to Salsalita, sense and nonsense, saying some of the things Luz was feeling. "Did you miss me? I missed you sooo much. I'm so happy to see you. Yes, I am. Oh, my you're greedy. Now, Salsalita, Missy gets a carrot too, you know."

Henry gave Luz a leg-up onto Salsalita's back. Then at Luz's urging, the mare flew around the pasture, with Missy following.

They circled the field several times, both because Luz wanted to tire Missy slightly before letting Marisol ride her, and because she needed time to compose her face before Marisol could see what being in this place and riding Salsalita again had made her feel. The recovery of the horses she'd thought lost had made the loss of her parents so much more real, and for a time, she was unable to contain her sorrow.

Finally, Luz turned for the barn where Henry waited to saddle the pony for Marisol. Once Missy was settled, Luz let Marisol ride the pony around the pasture by herself, and she and Henry leaned on the fence, watching.

"Thank you for taking care of them," Luz told Henry.

"Least I could do for Esteban." He shifted from one foot to the other. "Your dad was a good man."

"*Sí.* He was, wasn't he." Marisol and Missy shimmered through a mist of tears.

"You did good," Henry said. "Holding things together with Mari and Carlito. Your mom and dad would be real proud of you." The ragged tone of Henry's voice told Luz he was grieving as much as she was. Awkwardly, Henry patted her arm, and she leaned against him.

They stood that way, without speaking, until Marisol rode the pony back to them.

∽

"When we cleared out your house, we found this in the attic." Jean set a cardboard carton on the floor of Luz's room with a thump. "I'm pretty sure it belonged to your dad."

The box, an unassuming brown cardboard, was the kind you could pick up free at the grocery store. The flaps were tucked over each other and one side was slightly caved in.

"I better get back downstairs before Carlito gets into anything," Jean said, leaving.

Luz moved slowly toward the box, sinking to the floor next to it. She pulled the flaps free and stared at the large framed photograph lying on top. A formal wedding photo. Not her dad and Mary but her dad and her mother, Luisa. Luz lifted the portrait from the box, wondering why *Papi* had never shown it to her. Instead, when Mary had insisted Luz have a picture of her mother, he had produced a small candid photo, which was the only reason Luz recognized her mother now.

The portrait was mounted in a thick old-fashioned frame, which seemed odd, but maybe it had come with her father from Chile.

Luz set aside the picture and turned to look at the box's remaining contents. A clutch of photos, several letters, some still in their envelopes, and a delicate lace christening gown aged to a soft ivory. She examined the gown, to find several areas where it had been repaired. She set it carefully aside and flipped through the photos, finding them damaged, some with missing corners or charred along the edges.

On the back of each was an ornate script as old-fashioned as the frame holding her parents' wedding portrait.

"*Estancia Arellano*" was written on one picture that showed a wide sweep of grasslands bordered by low hills and divided in large squares by fences. Another photo showed a low white house built around a courtyard in which flowers bloomed.

"*Esteban y Salsapicante*" was written on the back of a picture of a boy, almost a young man, in a dark fitted suit, sitting on an equally dark horse with white markings. The horse was obviously a Paso Fino and one of the most beautiful Luz had ever seen. There were several other pictures of Esteban riding Salsapicante. And then came a picture of him with a young woman. Luz turned it over and read, *Esteban y Luisa. El día del compromiso.* She was holding her mother and father's engagement picture.

The next picture was of Esteban and Luisa holding a baby wearing the lace gown. Luz turned it over and read, *Julio Esteban Montalvo y Arellano 1 mes, 1975.*

For a moment she forgot to breathe. She had a brother? But why had *Papi* never mentioned him? And where was Julio? He would be...twenty-five now.

She turned to the final picture. It was of Esteban standing with a hand on Luisa's shoulder. Luisa was holding a baby wearing the lace gown, and a small boy leaned against her knee. Luz turned it over to find it labeled *Esteban, Luisa, Julio y Luz Cristina Montalvo y Arellano 1 mes, 1978.*

She stared at the picture, searching for any faint wisp of memory. How was it possible she'd forgotten so completely? Her mother, her brother, the horses, the estancia. But she had. Her earliest memories were of Scottsbluff, although she and *Papi* had not come to Scottsbluff until she was nearly five. But surely she remembered something from before that.

She fanned the pictures out, and went through them again. Still no memories stirred. Thoughtfully, she put the pictures aside and turned to the letters. The envelopes were postmarked Santiago, Chile and addressed to Steven Monroe at a Denver post-office box. Frowning, Luz opened the oldest one first. The paper was soft and delicate as if it had been handled repeatedly or carried around in a pocket.

Magdalena Cristina Montalvo Arellano was written in a formal gold script across the top and the handwriting that followed was the same as on the pictures. The letter was in Spanish.

March 20, 1984

Dearest Esteban,

We were overjoyed to receive your letter, to know after this long silence you and Lucita are safe.

But the other news your letter brought has made our hearts heavy. Surely you must know how it grieves a mother to hear such things and how difficult it is to believe. Still, your father and I agree. We will respect your wishes.

Frowning, Luz turned to the next page to find an unrelated section.

> *It is not safe for you to come home. S is still in the district and anyone who speaks against him has a mysterious accident shortly afterwards. Unfortunately, he is a young man yet.*
>
> *When your brother asks if we've heard from you, we continue to say we have not. It has become easier to support this lie if we remain away from the estancia, which, at any rate, is too full of tragic memory.*
>
> *We are glad to hear the nena is healthy and happy, and you are doing well. I have hidden the picture you sent, but it warms my heart to have*

That was the last of the pages from the first envelope. Luz set them aside, feeling confused. Clearly, something terrible had happened but what it was, who *S* was, and why *Papi*'s brother couldn't be told where *Papi* was were all mysteries. She pulled the pages from the second envelope.

> *March 20, 1988*
>
> *Dearest Esteban,*
>
> *How wonderful to hear Lucita is doing well in school and has adjusted to life there. And we are pleased to hear of the success of your business. The growing of plants and flowers and the caring for the land is an honorable profession. It is how our family started in this country, tending the land.*
>
> *There are no changes to report. Your brother no longer mentions you. S still struts around, and no one dares challenge him.*
>
> *Your father thinks it best you stay*

Luz turned to the next page, which was dated two years later.

> *March 20, 1990*
>
> *Dearest Esteban,*
>
> *Your father and I cried together with happiness when we read your last letter. How wonderful that you have once again found love. We know your heart must be overflowing. Perhaps one day soon it will be safe for all of us to meet. It is our constant prayer it be so.*
>
> *I am sending you the Arellano christening dress. It is one of the few things we were able to save afterwards. Tomás found it and hid it until he could give it*

Once again, the remainder of the letter was missing. Her frustration increasing, Luz pulled the pages from the third envelope.

> *March 20, 1992*
>
> *Dearest Esteban,*
>
> *Once again, your news made us cry with happiness. A new daughter for you, a granddaughter for us. After all our pain, such joy comes as a wonderful surprise, although we must do our best to hide it. But when we remember we cannot hold this new little one, and tell her stories of her papi when he was a small boy, it is not so difficult to pretend we have not received such wonderful news.*
>
> *We miss our Lucita too, more than we can say. We pray to the Holy Mother and all the saints we will one day be together*

Luz turned the page to find, as before, the following page was from another letter.

March 20, 1997

Dearest Esteban,

Your father has died. I write the words, and yet, I still have difficulty believing them. It was very sudden. A heart attack, the doctor believes. Guillermo was not a young man, of course, and yet, I expected him to always be with me. I do not know if it is possible to die of a broken heart, but if it were, I suppose we all would have died, along with Luisa and Julio.

It is all the harder that you must learn this news in this way. I long to put my arms around you and cry with you at our loss.

Although Guillermo's will named you as his heir, as you requested, it did not say we know you are alive. Only that we do not know. The estancia is yours, my dear Esteban. It hurts my heart to know you are not here, still I must agree at last with your father that it is

That was the last page, and like most of the others, it ended in mid-thought. Luz blinked at tears. When she first began reading the letters, she had been excited to learn she had an older brother. As she read, she hoped the letters would tell her how to find him. Instead, in the space of an hour, she both discovered he existed, and lost him forever. And she'd also found and lost a grandfather.

A sudden memory tugged at her. One night when she was about ten, she'd been unable to sleep and had wandered into the living room. *Papi* was sitting at the table where he worked on his accounts, except there had been no accounts that night. *Papi* had turned, and she saw his eyes were red and tears were tracking down his face. She ran to him, beginning to cry herself, although she had no idea what the problem was. He had taken her on his lap and hugged her. "What is it, Lucita? Why are you crying?"

"Because you are, *Papi*."

"Ahh, it's all right, *niña*. I'm not crying. *Papi* has a terrible cold. See, my nose is all stuffy and my eyes itch something fierce."

She'd made herself believe him, because the alternative was too horrible.

But now she was certain. He had been crying.

℗

"Did *Papi* ever talk about his family or where he lived before he came to Scottsbluff?" Luz asked Henry as they drove to the farm to take care of the horses.

"Well, let's see." Henry spoke in a thoughtful tone. "Don't recall he did. Oh, maybe the odd comment now and again. I knew he was from Chile, of course. Said he come here to give you a better life, away from all the upheaval. Seems to me he said his wife died in childbirth."

"Jean gave me a box today. It had pictures in it and some letters."

"Told me she planned to do that."

"I read the letters. They're about *Papi*'s family in Chile. But they were confusing. And they weren't sent to *Papi* here. They were mailed to a post-office box in Denver."

"Well, that's something I can tell you about, right enough. Your dad made a trip to Denver every April. Reason I recall, it was always about the time taxes were due. He'd get real antsy. Always thought it was the taxes doing it. He'd be gone a couple of days, and when he come back, he was always quiet and sad for a day or two."

He must have gone to collect the letters, all written on the same day, as if they needed to arrive at their destination on a pre-determined schedule.

"The letters were from *Papi*'s mother. Something happened. I'm not sure what, but she told him it wasn't safe for him to come home. And someone she referred to as *S* was the one she was afraid of. And *Papi*'s name is actually Montalvo Arellano."

"Whoa, slow down just a mite." Henry's brow furrowed in obvious concentration. "You're saying maybe something bad happened to your dad back in Chile, but you don't know what it was?"

"Yes. Exactly."

"Hmm. If you want, we could maybe try to find out more."

The gust of fear was sudden and startling. But after all, *Papi* had taken extreme care to remain hidden—even from his brother. "I don't know if I should. In the last letter, his *mami* still seemed to be frightened something might happen to him."

"Your dad's well beyond the reach of anyone trying to hurt him, Luz." Henry stopped speaking, and Luz turned to find him blinking hard, his Adam's apple bobbing. He cleared his throat. "Maybe we ought to ask your trustee about it."

Luz shook her head, still uneasy. "I want to think about it." Luisa and Julio's deaths had to be connected to her *papi* remaining hidden. Since she didn't know otherwise, Luz thought she better assume she, Marisol and Carlito might be in danger as well. The only certainty from the letters was that *Papi* was hiding from *S* and maybe from his own brother as well.

The thought she had family in Chile pushed at her, but over the next several days, anytime she thought about actually taking a concrete step to learn more, dread stopped her.

She wished Charles were there to give her advice. To tell her she was wrong, or maybe right, to be frightened.

She added the framed picture of her parents to the things she planned to take with her to TapDancer, but the letters and the christening dress she left in the box, which she pushed into the back of the closet in her room at Jean and Henry's.

Chapter Twenty-one

On one of her last days in Scottsbluff, Luz was browsing in the produce section of the grocery store, with no other thought but to pick out the items on her list, when a voice cut across the soft sounds of the store's Muzak. "I hope you're satisfied, bitch."

The viciousness froze Luz in the act of reaching for a head of lettuce. She straightened and turned to find Martin Blair standing much too close. She tried to move away, but he pushed his cart at her, backing her against the produce case.

"You don't have any right to Mary's money. Not a cent. You were nothing to her. Nothing! And I intend to make sure you and those mongrels don't get it, if it's the last thing I do."

His face had turned an alarming plum color, and Luz thought it possible he might drop dead right in front of her. Sickened, she pushed away from him, rushed from the store and climbed into the truck, where she sat shaking until she was finally able to drive back to the Hollises'.

When she walked into the house, Jean was getting lunch. "You need some help with those groceries?"

Abruptly, she realized she'd abandoned the partially filled cart and list. "N-no." The trembling hadn't stopped after all.

"What is it, Luz?"

For a time, she was unable to answer, was able only to stand, as Jean held her and patted her back, making comforting noises.

"M-Martin. At the store."

"Oh. You poor girl. Was he awful?"

Luz nodded, beginning to cry. "He said I didn't deserve *Mami*'s money. She wasn't my mother, and he'd make sure I didn't get it." Unbearable to repeat what Martin had said about Marisol and Carlito.

"Your mom loved you with all her heart, Luz. You know that, sweetie, don't you?" Jean had seen right through the issue to the heart of what hurt Luz most. Not anything to do with money, but with the idea Mary Blair wasn't her mother.

"I remember her talking about you when she first married your dad," Jean continued. "Oh, was she crazy about you. Said you and your dad were the best thing ever happened to her."

Luz made an attempt to stop crying, but like the time at Christmas with Kathy, once started, she couldn't stop. It was why she'd had to be so careful about letting go during the months she'd been completely responsible for Marisol and Carlito.

Jean kept on holding her. "Martin's a sad excuse of a man. You don't have to worry, Luz. He can't hurt you ever again."

But Luz did worry. Not about Martin breaking the will, but that he might spew his poison onto Marisol and Carlito. Carlito was still too young to be hurt, but Marisol was in school, and if Martin went around town calling her a mongrel, it wouldn't take long for that to make its way to the schoolyard.

"He needs to be stopped, from saying horrible things. What if he said something to Marisol?"

"Why don't you call Mr. Ryan and ask his advice?"

Luz, remembering the firm way Richard Ryan dealt with Martin, decided it was a good suggestion. As soon as she recovered her composure, she'd call.

ᨒ

After New Year's, Charles and Alan had settled into their old schedule of having lunch together every couple of weeks. Although their relationship wasn't completely back to normal, at least they were interacting once again.

"Dad's got a new assistant. Or he will have soon," Alan said, as they checked their menus.

"Oh?" Actually, there wasn't a single reason Charles could imagine why he'd be interested in that particular topic.

"Yeah. Luz has agreed to come to the ranch and stay through the summer."

His head snapped up, and he found Alan giving him an appraising look. Dammit, he usually managed to keep Luz out of his thoughts. At least he tried. "How'd that happen?" He hoped his tone conveyed only mild interest. Unfortunately, his initial reaction had already revealed that his interest was beyond mild.

"He and Mom weren't sure how it would work out long-term, having all of them at the ranch, but they decided to give it a go. Then Dad talked to Luz, and she said the kids have new guardians, and they were all getting ready to move back to Scottsbluff. But I expect you know all that."

Charles grunted and turned back to his menu, trying to find another topic. One that had nothing to do with Luz. "So how goes the job search?" Alan had been denied tenure the year before and was finishing out his contract at Denver State.

"I'm a finalist for a position at Regis."

Charles managed to ask enough questions to stretch that subject through the delivery of their food. While they ate, he talked about the Maxwell trial. The jury had taken two days to deliberate before convicting Gary Maxwell on the charges of aggravated murder, kidnapping, felonious assault, and child endangerment. Charles had been satisfied, although they'd acquitted on the charges of inducing panic and making false alarms. But those were charges more easily proven against Tami Maxwell.

"I have a huge favor to ask," Alan said, as they waited for the check.

Charles, figuring it would have something to do with the wedding, sighed inwardly, but tried not to let his reluctance show. He might be getting over Kathy, but reminders of the wedding still disturbed him.

"Dad volunteered me to go to Scottsbluff to pick up Luz and her mare and drive them to TapDancer. But something's come up. I thought maybe you'd be willing to help me out."

Charles cleared his throat. "Luz and her mare?"

"Yeah. Seems she's got a Peruvian Paso, and she talked Dad into letting her bring it along to be bred to one of our stallions. Someone needs to drive the horse trailer to Scottsbluff to pick them up."

Well it wasn't going to be him even if he did owe the Francinis big-time for making him part of their family. Besides, this whole thing felt uncomfortably like a set-up, although Alan had never done that to him before. He'd always been the one trying to set Alan up, and he surely didn't like being on the receiving end.

"Why doesn't she rent a trailer?" What Alan was asking was impossible and not because it involved eight hours of driving.

"Weren't any available."

As if Charles believed that. Definitely a set-up, and he wasn't falling for it. Luz was out of his life. And he was relieved she was. Not that he'd handled *that* with any grace. He winced at the memory of Luz stumbling through her thank you's while he'd stood aloof and silent. But graceful or awkward, it was done. He'd moved on, was moving on, although it probably would be a good idea to avoid invitations to the ranch while she was there.

"Sorry. I can't help you." Ungracious, but he had no intention of softening it.

"Guess, we'll have to figure something else out." Alan gave him an assessing look that made Charles acutely uncomfortable.

"Luz had a problem today."

Charles was back at work after his lunch with Alan, and the caller was Henry Hollis.

"She had a run-in with Martin Blair. He told her he was going to keep her from getting Mary's money."

Charles sighed. It seemed it was his day to be reminded of Luz. "She doesn't have anything to worry about. According to Ryan, the judge doesn't have a very high opinion of Martin Blair."

"That ain't what bothered Luz. Martin called Mari and Carlito mongrels."

The anger, swift and overwhelming, helped Charles

understand why men committed murder.

"Luz is real worried Martin might make trouble for Mari and Carlito. Our idea was she call Mr. Ryan, but then I thought to call you. Hoped you might give us some advice."

Yeah. Take out a contract and have Blair exterminated. Charles sucked in a deep breath, reminding himself he spent his life putting people who followed through on such impulses behind bars. "Let me give it some thought. I'll get back to you."

He hung up and waited until he calmed down, then he called Alan. "Turns out I have some business in Scottsbluff. Might as well make it a twofer and pick up Luz and her horse." So much for his determination to extract himself from Luz's life.

"Hey, terrific. This weekend?"

"Yeah. I'll have to go in on Friday, but I can drive the horse back Saturday."

But that was it. He'd help with this last bit, and then he was done with Luz.

⁊

Charles parked the horse trailer at the motel, then drove across town to meet a man he expected to dislike on sight. Hell, he already disliked Blair, sight unseen.

When he entered the Ford showroom, a young man with a toothy grin and a grease-spotted tie immediately accosted him. "Can I help you, sir?"

"I'm here to see Martin Blair."

The man's shoulders rounded in obvious disappointment as he led the way to a large office.

Blair pulled off reading glasses and put on a big smile. "Good to see you. In the market for a car or truck, are you? We have some beauties, both new and used."

As Blair spoke, Charles was aware he was being weighed, measured and his net worth calculated. He reciprocated with his own evaluation.

Blair was short and barrel-chested with the tight pink face of a man who spent a lot of time outdoors golfing and indoors drinking. His head was egg-shaped and bald except for a light fringe of colorless hair around the edges.

Blair extended a hand, and Charles took it, noting the too-tight grip of a man either uncertain of himself or oblivious that his handshake was overly hearty. From what he already knew, he'd go with the latter.

"Charles Larimore." He watched for any flair of recognition. There was none.

Blair waved him to a seat. "So what can I do for you this fine day, Mr. Larimore? A new truck? Or maybe a nice sedan for the missus?"

"There is no missus, and I'm not here to buy a vehicle." Charles spoke firmly.

The other man's eyebrows went up in a silent question.

"Understand you had something to say to Luz Montalvo recently."

Blair's joviality faded, and a calculating look came into his eyes. "Don't see why I'd have anything to say to you about that."

Charles shrugged. "You're right. Doubt there's a thing you need to say to me. But I do have something to say to you."

Blair shifted slightly, his Adam's apple bobbing, obviously working up to a good bluster.

Charles cut across it before Blair could get it launched. "This is a small town. You're well known here. Prominent. I expect you wouldn't want to find a story in the newspaper about how badly you treated your nieces and nephew after their parents were tragically killed."

"Doubt Saul would give you the time of day," Blair said, visibly relaxing.

It took Charles only a beat to figure out Saul had to be the editor of the Scottsbluff *Star-Herald*. Probably a golf buddy.

"It's a hell of a story, though. I know a reporter or two at the *Denver Post*. Expect they'd be happy to print it." He went for a thoughtful look, folding his hands together and sitting back. "You know, it's my experience, reporters are always real pleased at the chance to hear what the District Attorney has to say." And they were. Anytime Spinell had something to say, a reporter was always happy to be there to record it.

211

Charles gave Blair a sunny smile.

The other man appeared distinctly queasy, which widened Charles's smile. "Once it appeared in the *Post*, I expect it'd be damn hard for Saul to pass on it. Nice, juicy story like that. Exactly what sells lots of papers."

"What's your price."

Charles raised his eyebrows. "Well now, that sounds suspiciously like an attempt to bribe an officer of the court. It might even be a federal matter given we're dealing with two states here."

Blair moved quickly past queasy to full-blown diarrhea of the mouth. "No. No. No. That's not what I meant. Of course not. I'm a law-abiding citizen. Only want what's mine."

Charles concentrated on lounging and looking completely at ease while the other man continued to trip over his tongue. After a time, Blair fell silent, and Charles leaned in. "My price is this. You stay away from the Montalvos. You see them come into a store, you leave. They come into a restaurant and you've just been served, you leave." He paused to let it sink in. He didn't need any false anger, because plenty of the real thing fueled his next words. "And you keep your mouth shut. No more references to mongrels or attempts to overturn wills that are, by the way, perfectly legal and binding."

Blair's mouth flapped like a fish gasping for air. He was obviously trying to come up with a response. Charles waited, giving him whatever time he needed.

"Mary was *my* sister. She was nothing to that Luz person."

"She was *that Luz person's* mother." The words ground out and once again silenced Blair.

Staring at the man, at his logoed clothing and pretentious office, and remembering his focus on Mary's money, Charles realized he'd been missing an opportunity. Along with reputation, there was another driving force in Blair's life that could be used against him.

"Here's the rest of the deal. The merest hint, even a whisper from you about the Montalvos or the will, and I'll see you're sued for libel and defamation." Most people didn't know the difference, and together they sounded more menacing. "In my opinion, there's also an excellent case for charging you with fraud. And punitive damages would be completely reasonable given the way you handled the Montalvos' property." They hadn't needed the affidavit from Ross during the hearing on the wills, but it might come in handy yet.

Blair turned a puce color. He licked his lips and abruptly clenched a hand that had begun to tremble.

Pleased to see he was getting through to the man, Charles glanced around the office. "Good chance you'll have to liquidate this along with that fancy house in order to pay for it."

Blair slumped, appearing suddenly older and more wrinkled, as if he'd been puffed with the air of his own importance, and Charles had opened a valve.

Charles drove back to the motel, feeling completely satisfied, until he realized he wouldn't be able to share his rout of Blair with Luz.

The arrangement was for him to meet Henry at the farm at noon on Saturday, which meant Charles had a chunk of time to fill. Too bad he and Luz weren't on better terms, or he would call the Hollises and tell them he was in town a day early. Jean would no doubt invite him to dinner.

But that would only add another interaction with Luz, when his main goal at the moment was to avoid her, the four-hour drive to Denver notwithstanding.

To counter the temptation to call, he checked with the desk clerk for something to do. She said the Bluffs that gave the town its name were well worth a visit.

Following her directions, he drove out of town and up the winding road. At the top, he got out of the truck. A cold wind, straight off snowfields in the Rockies, ruffled his hair. Chilled, he stared at the valley below where wagon trains had passed less than a hundred and fifty years earlier.

And what would it be like in another hundred years? That vast, empty expanse, crisscrossed with ravines and gullies? Probably much the same, except he wouldn't be standing here looking at it.

And it certainly wouldn't take a hundred years before all his current pain faded away. Hell, for that matter, it shouldn't take more than a year or two before it would no longer matter that Luz was out of his life. He'd be fine. All he needed to do was find a new place to live and ask someone out. Ignore the fact the whole idea had zero appeal. Once he got going, he'd be fine.

Or if that didn't work, maybe he'd go back into training for an Ironman. That could suck up one hell of a lot of free time. Who needed free time anyway. Leisure—highly overrated. If he could just get moving, it wouldn't be so bad. Momentum, that's what he needed. This last six months? A detour. A blip. And now it was over, and he could return to regularly scheduled programming.

He and Alan had reconciled. He was okay with the upcoming nuptials. Everything was great. So why the hell did he feel as empty as the damn view?

ॐ

The next morning Charles ran before breakfast, showered, checked out of the motel, hooked up the horse trailer and drove to the farm. Henry, surprised but obviously pleased to see him instead of Alan, suggested a cup of coffee. "Real glad you're the one that come. There's something I'd like to talk to you about." Henry set a cup in front of Charles and sat across from him.

"That meeting between Luz and Martin pushed this other clean out of my mind. You see, when we cleared out the house, we found a box of photographs and letters in the attic. Everything in Spanish, so it had to be Esteban's. Anyway, we gave the box to Luz."

Henry stopped to swallow more coffee. Charles sensed Henry was also pausing to put his thoughts in order.

"The letters were written by Luz's grandma, Esteban's mother. Seems something bad happened in Chile. Maybe you can find out what. Has to be done real careful though. Luz was spooked."

"Spooked how?"

"When I suggested we look into it, she said she wasn't sure we ought to. It was the look on her face that got to me, though. Luz is a tough little lady. Don't much get to her, but that did." Henry pulled a piece of paper from his pocket and handed it to

Charles. "Here's what I know."

Charles read through the information. *Esteban Montalvo Arellano dob 9/12/50. Arrived in Scottsbluff May, 1984. Possibly owned a ranch somewhere in Chile named Estancia Arellano.* "This is awfully thin."

"It's all I have. Luz'll know more from the letters. Get her to tell you. She trusts you."

Charles wasn't at all certain that was true, but he didn't feel like debating the point with Henry. Actually, he wasn't entirely certain Luz was even talking to him, something he'd shortly be putting to the test.

They finished their coffee, and Henry rinsed the cups before going to the barn to get the mare, which he led into the trailer. Driving one of the Las Flores pickups, he led Charles to the house to get Luz.

Everyone was pleased to see Charles, except Luz. "What a surprise." Her voice wavered into a higher pitch, and she snapped her mouth shut. Then her expression smoothed, but Charles had already seen the unpleasant shock on her face at her first sight of him.

"Alan had something come up. Called in a favor." Charles stooped to lift Carlito, who had run over to him and was gripping the leg of his jeans between two small fists.

Charles swung the little boy, who squealed delightedly. Still holding the toddler, he hugged Marisol and Cora.

By the time he turned to Luz, her expression was calm with no hint of the earlier distaste. She pointed. "There's my stuff."

The garbage bags used for the Christmas visit had been replaced with a set of matched luggage. And if that wasn't the perfect metaphor for Luz's changed circumstances, he didn't know what was.

"I'll get that loaded," Henry said. "You relax for a minute."

Marisol chattered happily, telling him about Missy and her new school, and Jean offered him something to drink, which he declined, and everything was going just fine until he and Luz started to leave.

Marisol rushed over and threw her arms around Luz's waist, beginning to sob. That set Carlito off. Jean took the crying toddler from Charles and carried him over to Luz. Luz's arms stretched around both Marisol and Carlito.

"Why don't we let the womenfolk sort this out," Henry said.

Charles was more than happy to follow Henry outside.

The two of them stood next to the truck talking weather and road conditions until Luz came out by herself. She gave Henry a quick hug, and got into the truck. Charles was relieved to see she had survived her siblings' grief without giving in to it herself.

He climbed into the truck, suddenly apprehensive about being closed into this small space with Luz for four hours. But if that was the price he had to pay for the chance to put Martin Blair in his place, it was still worth it.

He glanced at Luz, and his nerves kicked into high gear. Ridiculous, of course, to be nervous around Luz. Disheartening, too, that leap of joy at seeing her. Joy that had been quickly doused by her reaction to the sight of him.

He took the turn at the end of the Hollises' street and forced himself to speak casually. "How have you been?"

From the corner of his eye, he saw her head shift toward him. "Fine. Good. How about you?"

"Busy." *Ridiculous.* His profession demanded eloquence, but at the moment he was no more able to tap into it than he could fly. If that was all they could manage to say to each other, screw it. He reached for the radio, and his hand banged into Luz's on the same errand. "Sorry."

They both withdrew their hands quickly. After a moment, Luz reached out again and turned on the radio. "What do you like to listen to?" Her tone was polite. The tone one used to make inquiries of strangers.

He could handle polite. "It doesn't matter. Whatever you'd like."

She flipped through the stations, settling on the one with the best reception. It was playing country western, not his favorite, but preferable to awkward conversation. He enjoyed driving, so he concentrated on that, although like running or cycling, it didn't take a lot of thought.

As he drove, he let his mind drift. The only problem was, it kept drifting to Luz.

He glanced over to find her staring out the side window and

swiping at her eyes with her fingers. Luz crying? Damn. Was it best to ignore it, or should he stop and try to find out what was wrong? Except, given they were on a two-lane highway with a dirt shoulder, it was probably not the best idea to pull over with a loaded horse trailer.

But he couldn't ignore her, although the reality of Luz crying made him acutely uncomfortable. "You okay?"

"Sorry," she said, with a sniff. "I'm just missing Mari and Carlito. And I'm still a bit worried about Martin."

"They'll be fine." Not the smartest or the most sensitive comment he could have made, but he could reassure her on one point. "Actually, I had a conversation with Blair on Friday. I don't think you need to worry about him anymore."

He caught the quick movement as she turned to stare at him. "Is that why you came?"

He shrugged, keeping his eyes firmly on the road. "I don't like bullies."

"Yes of course." Her words sounded oddly flat. He wasn't entirely certain what he'd hoped for, but a bit of enthusiastic gratitude would have been nice.

Luz blew her nose, sat up and put the tissue away.

Relieved she'd stopped crying, Charles decided to leave her alone. Let sleeping dogs lie and all that. He'd wait until they were closer to Denver to ask her about the letters.

With that decided, he turned his attention to the lyrics of the songs, finding some of them inane and some quite well done. He suggested a stop in Fort Morgan, but Luz said she preferred to get to TapDancer as soon as possible. He kept driving, and she put her seat back and slept.

Outside of Denver he pulled into a rest area, and Luz awakened and stretched. "Where are we?"

"Almost to Denver. I need a break. If you want to check the horse, I'll be right back." He went to the restroom and then spent a few minutes stretching until Luz came out of the restroom as well. Without speaking, they climbed back in the truck.

"Henry told me about the box of letters they gave you to read," he said, as he merged back on the highway.

He glanced over to find her staring at him with a startled

look that rapidly changed to anger. "He had no right to do that."

Feeling hurt by this obvious evidence that Henry didn't know what he was talking about when he said Luz trusted him, Charles backpedaled. "He's concerned about you. He wants to help."

Luz shook her head. "If I was supposed to know more, *Papi* would have left me more."

"He probably figured he'd have plenty of time."

"Just drop it. Please." The *please,* spoken in the same flat, angry tone as the *just drop it,* was obviously tacked on as an afterthought.

Conciliation having failed, Charles retreated. "So, what about this fall? You going back to Colorado College?"

"Actually, I might go to DSU."

He cocked his head, trying to decide if her words held anything more than the simple information they conveyed. Unfortunately, his search for more meaning showed him he hadn't made much progress on his plan to forget this young woman. "It's a good school."

"I like Denver. I didn't think I would. Well, you saw Scottsbluff. I didn't know if I could stand living in a big city."

He wanted to say he hoped she would go to DSU, and if she did, maybe they'd see each other sometime.

Nope, bad idea. Absolutely the worst. Not fair to either one of them. The shallow person who broke up with Tiffany because she wanted marriage and kids wouldn't have the staying power to wait for Luz to finish college. Besides, if he waited, she might grow up and decide she didn't like him much.

Actually, he wasn't entirely certain she liked him now. Not that he blamed her.

He tried to figure out why he wanted Luz in his life. Finally he gave up and let it be. He just did, although he had no intention of doing anything about it.

He pulled into the rest area where he and Alan had agreed to meet so Alan could take over and drive the rest of the way to the ranch. Alan was already there, with Charles's car.

Luz got out of the truck when Charles did. "Thank you."

He stopped, half-in, half-out of his car. "You're welcome."

He met her eyes for a beat, before climbing in and closing the door. In his rearview mirror, he watched her turn away.

A feeling of desolation kept him company for the remainder of the drive back to the Draper Arms.

ॐ

Spinell sat back and laced his hands over his substantial paunch. "Tami Maxwell wants to deal."

Charles stiffened with annoyance.

"It'll save the taxpayers considerable expense," Spinell continued.

"So what's the offer?" Last minute pleas like this always made Charles feel like a sucker, after he'd spent weeks, or in this case months, dealing with the intricacies of the evidence.

"Three to five years' incarceration followed by community service and extended probation."

"Not good enough."

"Figured you'd say that." Spinell gave Charles a complacent look. "Go ahead. Stick it to her. You have my blessing."

Of course, Spinell didn't mean for him to actually take it to trial. They had a strong case, though. Given Gary Maxwell's easy conviction, he could negotiate a long sentence for Tami as well and not feel too bad about the trial.

Spinell was correct about one thing. The Maxwells had already cost the Colorado taxpayer enough.

Chapter Twenty-two

In spite of Kathy's best efforts to keep everything simple, as the wedding drew nearer, there seemed to be a lot of details pushing and pulling at her.

Whenever it got to be too much, she had Alan take her to the ranch for the day. As spring advanced they occasionally had a day warm enough for a ride to the lake. On other visits, Kathy sat with Luz on the top rail of the corral to watch Alan and his dad work with the yearlings.

"How are Marisol and Carlito adjusting?" Kathy asked Luz one of those times.

"They're doing fine although it's hard being apart. Mari and I talk all the time."

"And how are you doing?"

"I miss them. Like blazes. This helps though." Luz gestured at the horses and the surrounding land. "Sure is different from the Droopy Arms."

"Droopy Arms?"

"That's what Mari called where we lived."

"It wasn't so bad."

"I guess Charles moved too."

Kathy had a sudden memory of the way Luz had gazed at Charles at Christmas, and certain Luz was hoping for news of him, she complied. "I haven't seen his new place, but Alan helped him move."

"Bet he didn't buy any brown furniture."

The thought made Kathy smile. "Bet you're right. He's been keeping busy with the Maxwell trials. Alan says he hardly has time for lunch."

"Yeah, he always seemed to work really hard."

"He sent the RSVP for the wedding this week. He's not bringing a guest. Alan said that had to be a first." Kathy glanced sideways in time to see Luz's mouth curve in a slight smile.

Alan had told her to leave it alone, but she couldn't. As she'd become better acquainted with Luz on these trips to the ranch, she was becoming convinced Luz was the woman for Charles. Equally clear, Charles wasn't going to figure that out on his own.

She didn't know if Charles had held off because he thought Luz was the mother of two, but if so, he no longer had that excuse. She felt a brief concern at the thought Charles might actually not like children, before she decided she didn't believe it, not after seeing Charles with Marisol and Carlito at Christmas.

The only other potential difficulty was Luz's age. She had to be at least ten years younger than Charles. Kathy didn't consider it a major problem given Luz's intelligence and maturity, but maybe Charles did. Men had strange ideas sometimes.

"What about college?" Kathy said. "Have you decided?"

"I've been accepted at DSU this fall."

"You're not going back to Colorado College?"

Luz shook her head. "Too many memories." Her voice thickened, and she stopped speaking to clear her throat. "Anyway. I like Denver. And if I go to DSU, I can still spend some weekends here. Rob said Salsalita can stay, and, well, it seemed better."

Colorado Springs was no further from the ranch than Denver, but Kathy thought she knew why Luz preferred one over the other. "Alan will be glad to hear that. With him starting a new job and trying to finish his second novel, it may be hard for us to spend as much time here. In fact, it took a huge weight off his mind to know you'd be here for the summer." As she spoke, the plan came to Kathy in a flash. Without debating it, she plunged in. "You know, I'd love to go shopping with you. To help you find something to wear to the wedding. If you don't have something already, that is."

Luz turned and smiled at Kathy. "I don't, and I'd like that. Very much."

"How about next Wednesday?"

"Okay, sure."

Alan and Charles had a lunch date Wednesday, and Kathy knew she'd be able to find out where they were planning to meet without Alan realizing, until it was too late, why she wanted to know.

&

Charles struggled to keep his voice steady. "She's way too young for me."

"She may be young, but she's a hell of a lot more mature than most twenty-year-olds," Alan said. "Maybe even more mature than present company."

"This is so none of your business." Charles spoke through gritted teeth, willing the damn waiter to get there to take the order.

"Consider it payback time." Although the words were light, Alan's tone wasn't. "After what you helped me through, I can't just stand here and watch you let your best chance go by without saying something."

"She's not my type."

"And let's consider what exactly that type might be. The light and easy type? The type who's not interested in anything but a good time, no strings? Yep, I'll agree, Luz isn't a bit like that. Don't notice that type's made you happy."

Charles narrowed his eyes. "You don't know that."

Steadily, Alan returned his look. "I've seen the difference."

Charles felt like Alan had punched him, and for an instant he wanted to strike back. Yes, Alan had seen him in those heady days when he'd been falling in love with Kathy, discovering for the first time what it was really like. And it was damn cruel of him to bring it up.

"At Christmas," Alan added.

What the hell was Alan talking about? Charles had behaved perfectly around Kathy, but he certainly hadn't been happy about it... Christ, Alan wasn't inferring something about Luz, was he? The possibility caught Charles under his guard with an even sharper pain.

He thought he'd covered his tracks on that one. Dammit, why wouldn't Alan leave him alone? "Look, if this is about me bringing a date to the wedding, I can do it if you want me to. I just figured I'd save you the cost of a meal." An empty threat. With his social life in suspension for the past nine months, the old date cupboard was bare.

Alan was silent, until Charles finally looked up. "I never thanked you, you know," Alan said.

"What? For being your punching bag?"

"I'm beginning to understand what you went through the past five years. With me."

"Then you should also remember it made you feel like crap and not inflict it on a friend."

"Yeah, it surely did. Worked though." Alan swiped a napkin over his mouth, looking thoughtful. "If your only concern about Luz is her age, how about asking her how she feels about it?"

"And she'll say, what? She loves me and doesn't care about college or having a career? That none of it matters if she has me?" Where the hell was the waiter? Not that he was going to be able to eat.

"I don't understand what the problem is."

"Then I spend the rest of my life worrying that maybe someday I won't be enough. And she'll regret making that choice, when she might have had so much more."

"I'm sorry. I still don't get it. Why does she **have** to choose college and a career, or you? What would **stop** her from marrying you and going to college, too?"

He was grateful Alan didn't point out he'd as good as admitted he loved Luz. Too much to shackle **her**. "It never works."

"Sure it does. A good quarter of my students are married. And they do better than the singles who are cruising the bars instead of studying."

Charles maintained a determined silence. The conversation, as far as he was concerned, was over.

"Don't make the same mistake I almost did," Alan said.

The waiter finally came to take their order, and Charles breathed a sigh of relief although he no longer had any interest in food. And that interest went lower still when he looked up to see Luz walking toward their table, accompanied by Kathy. The two women both striking but very different. Kathy, petite, her bright hair gleaming like fresh copper. Luz, tall, graceful and dark-haired.

His stomach clenched, and his heart did a queer little flip before the beat evened out.

Kathy put a finger to her lips, walked up behind Alan and leaned in to give him a kiss. "Hi," she said softly.

God, the man literally glowed. The taste of envy was bitter in Charles's mouth. He attempted to paste a smile on his face, although what he wanted to do was walk out. Luz appeared as nonplussed as he was.

"What a lovely surprise." Kathy beamed at both of them. "We've been shopping."

The waiter, who had mostly ignored them, was suddenly there setting places for Luz and Kathy. For a second, Charles suspected Alan had arranged the meeting, until he remembered Alan's surprised reaction. It had certainly seemed genuine.

Of course he had noticed immediately how good Luz was looking. No longer sallow and too thin, but bright-eyed and healthy. Not to mention sophisticated. The skirt she was wearing swirled slightly as she walked, drawing not only his glance but the waiter's to a lovely pair of legs.

Kathy and Luz glanced quickly at their menus and gave the waiter their orders. That was followed by a brief uncomfortable pause until Kathy turned to him with a bright smile. "I'm glad to see Alan managed to pry you loose for lunch."

"Yes. Well, Tami Maxwell's case is about to wrap up. Looks like she's going for a plea bargain." He picked up his glass of iced tea. This was Kathy's game, let her play it.

Although he didn't suspect Alan of collusion, Kathy obviously knew where to find them, and her "what a lovely surprise" didn't fool Charles one bit.

Kathy turned to Alan, laying a hand on his arm. "It's really lucky we ran into you. You can drive me back to work. That way Luz can head straight back to the ranch."

And Charles was willing to bet Kathy would also make sure she and Alan left first. They might not have consulted on this meeting, but they were both obviously in on the push-Charles-and-Luz-together plan.

But if he and Luz were able to avoid saying anything that counted for four hours on the trip back from Scottsbluff, they'd certainly be able to manage for the space of a lunch.

With that thought, his appetite returned, at least partially, and when his sandwich arrived, he ate it and let Kathy, Luz and Alan do the talking.

As he'd expected, Kathy maneuvered Alan out of the restaurant before Luz finished eating. "Can you keep Luz company, Charles?" She put a hand on Luz's arm. "Please, take your time. Sorry I have to scoot. I had fun this morning."

"So did I," Luz said. "Thank you."

"My pleasure." Kathy grinned at Luz, nodded at him and she and Alan left.

Charles watched them walk out the door. "Slickly done. They make a good team."

Luz was obviously having trouble eating. She'd ordered a salad, but she'd barely touched it. He hoped she wasn't now worrying about gaining too much weight. In the middle of taking a small bite, she gave him a quizzical look.

"We've been set up. By a couple of professionals."

Luz shook her head. "I don't understand."

"Well, if you don't get it, I don't think I can explain it." Nor did he want to. Sticky territory that.

"I'm really not very hungry," Luz said, putting her fork down. "And I'm sure you need to get back to work."

"I do. But if you don't eat any more than that, you're going to shrivel up and blow away."

"Stella won't let that happen." She pushed the plate away

and opened her purse to pull out a ten-dollar bill, which she laid by her plate. Her face worked for a moment as if she might say something else, but in the end she simply pushed her chair back and pulled her coat on. "It was good seeing you, Charles." With that, she turned and walked out.

He sat unseeing, angry at himself, angry at Kathy, Alan, you name it, until the waiter showed up with his bill. "Hey, man, you let a babe like that pay her own way? Umm, umm."

Charles glared at the man, who dropped the check on the table and retreated, moving faster than he had all day.

The shopping trip had been fun. They had gone to Cherry Creek, and Luz tried on about twenty dresses, modeling each one for Kathy. They picked some of the dresses because the styles made them giggle. Some were so short Luz didn't dare bend over, not to mention they had swooping fronts and no backs. Not that a swooping front was going to compromise Luz. She'd gained a few pounds, but none of them where it counted.

After trying on several dresses, she decided the ones most people would label sexy just made her look ridiculous. Kathy obviously agreed. Maybe not with the ridiculous part, but she shook her head decisively after Luz modeled the second short, low-cut dress. "That's simply not your look, Luz."

Luz went back to the dressing room to try on the next dress, and when she came out, Kathy was waiting for her, holding a dress Luz didn't remember noticing when they were going through the racks. She wouldn't have picked it. It was too, well, modest, she supposed. If she was going to attract Charles's attention, didn't she need a dress that made her look sexy and grown-up? This dress was full-length, with a high bodice. Very plain. Well, it did leave one shoulder bare and it was a lovely color. A deep turquoise.

Kathy handed her the dress. "I know it doesn't look all that promising, but I want to see it on."

The fabric at least was lovely, a smooth, heavy silk. Back in the dressing room, Luz slipped the dress on, then surprised, stood staring at her reflection.

"Let me see," Kathy said.

Luz opened the door and walked out.

Kathy grinned at her. "Oh, do you look... Oh, my. That dress was made for you, Luz. You're going to knock his eyes out."

Luz had never admitted to Kathy she cared for Charles, but she had no doubt whose eyes Kathy was talking about. "It's more than I was planning to spend."

"You can afford it though, can't you?"

Luz nodded. She had the salary the Francinis were paying her as well as the allowance from her parents' estate. So yes, she could afford it, although it did seem odd to spend as much on a dress as she'd previously spent for several weeks' worth of groceries.

She bought the dress and matching shoes, and then Kathy suggested lunch. Luz, who was driving, followed Kathy's directions to the restaurant, only to discover Charles and Alan there.

Charles. Seeing him took her breath away, but it was perfectly clear he wasn't happy to see her. She stiffened her spine, determined to see this through with her dignity intact. Then Kathy made it worse by maneuvering to leave her alone with him. Luz escaped and drove back to the ranch feeling forlorn and angry, and not sure on whom to project either emotion, although she did consider Alan the only innocent in the whole encounter.

Except, he had been the one who told Kathy he was having lunch with Charles. So maybe he wasn't completely innocent.

છ૦

"I'm sorry," Kathy said when Luz came to the phone that evening after dinner. "I blew it, big time, didn't I. Alan told me off."

Kathy sounded so contrite, Luz wanted to comfort her rather than snap at her for forcing the meeting with Charles.

"Was Charles unpleasant after we left?" Kathy asked.

"I didn't give him a chance to be. I almost beat you to the parking lot."

"Oh, I am sorry. Alan said I assumed a hell of a lot, and

when Alan swears, it means he's pretty upset."

"What were you assuming?"

"Well, you are in love with him, aren't you?"

"What makes you say that?"

"I saw you at Christmas. And...well, call it woman's intuition."

Luz felt herself blushing, and was glad Kathy wasn't there to see. "It's just hero worship. Usually I try to keep it under wraps. Actually, I don't believe he likes me."

"Are you kidding? Alan's convinced Charles is crazy about you. He just doesn't know what to do about it."

Luz's heart thudded. "Alan can't possibly be right. Charles likes Marisol and Carlito more than he likes me."

"That's the other weird thing. Alan said Charles has a rule. He never dates women who have children because he thinks kids get in the way and cause problems. Alan didn't believe his eyes at Christmas. The way Charles acted with Carlito and Marisol. That's what convinced him Charles has it bad."

Luz wanted to believe, but if she did, she was likely setting herself up for a nasty fall. Because no matter what Charles might feel, he'd obviously decided not to follow up on it. "He always acts like I'm the last person he wants to see. Well, you saw how he was today."

"Alan also said he pushed Charles to see you, and Charles said he wasn't asking you out because you have your whole life ahead of you. You need a chance to go to college and decide who you want to be without him tying you down."

Anger flared. "So what gives him the right to make all the decisions?"

"Alan tried to tell him that was ridiculous. Apparently Charles clammed up, and then we showed up."

"I doubt anyone's going to push Charles into doing something he doesn't want to do."

"You're probably right about that. You're going to have to finesse it with him."

"How do I do that?"

"We'll work on it this weekend."

ॐ

After seeing Luz at lunch, the odd story Henry Hollis told him about her fragmented history nudged at Charles. Or maybe it was because Tami Maxwell's plea bargain had been approved. With months of work completed, and in spite of the other cases awaiting his attention, he felt at loose ends.

But how the hell did one go about unearthing what might or might not have happened to someone maybe named Esteban Montalvo Arellano, fifteen or maybe sixteen years ago somewhere in Chile? All the records would be in Spanish, for one thing. Charles wouldn't know if he found something relevant or not. Not to mention he had no idea what he was looking for.

ॐ

Her face glowing, Joanna tipped the tiny pink bundle toward Charles. "Isn't she beautiful?"

Charles leaned over to inspect the baby. Damned if she didn't look more like an elderly monkey than a new human. He smiled, trying for an appreciative look, hoping it would be good enough.

"Here, would you like to hold her?" Joanna lifted the small bundle toward him, obviously expecting a *yes*.

Reluctant, but trying not to show it, Charles accepted the baby. Wrapped as she was, she was roughly the size and shape of a football. The thought made him smile. The baby opened one eye, peered at him, and her mouth curved into an *O*. In spite of his initial negative impression, Charles warmed to tiny Maria Brianna Maldonado, until Maria Brianna opened her mouth and, after a brief hiccupping sound, began to cry. In a panic, Charles practically tossed her back at her mother.

"She doesn't bite, you know." Joanna grinned at him as she settled the baby on her shoulder and patted expertly. "No teeth."

"Amigo, good to see you." Eduardo Maldonado entered the room and shook Charles's hand. "How about a beer?"

"Sure. Good." If he was holding a beer, it was unlikely Joanna would insist he try holding the baby again.

Eduardo brought the beer, and as he sat next to Joanna, his phone rang. He pulled it off his belt, said hello then continued the conversation in rapid Spanish as he walked from the room.

Joanna smiled. "Sounds like Argentina may come through."

"Argentina?"

"It's been a good year. Eduardo has developed several new markets in Chile, and next year he's expanding into Argentina."

The mention of Chile reminded Charles of the mystery surrounding Luz's family. He sipped his beer, rolling around the idea of asking for help while he exchanged shoptalk with Joanna.

By the time Eduardo finished his phone call and returned to the living room, Charles had decided to raise the issue. It might be his only chance to find out more, something he felt compelled to do, because Luz's uneasiness on the subject made him uneasy as well.

He gave Eduardo a quick outline of what he knew. "Is there a chance of being able to track down any part of that?"

Eduardo rubbed his chin. "It's all pretty vague."

"That's what I thought." And given Luz refused to discuss the issue further, vague it would likely remain.

"Maybe I can help," Joanna said.

Both Eduardo and Charles gave her questioning looks.

"It sounds like something tragic happened to the Arellano family. I've done a lot of research on South America, gathering information for Eduardo. Maybe I can find some hint of it."

"You need to be careful. Luz's dad was still in hiding over whatever it was years later. We sure don't want to stir things up."

"Not to worry."

He didn't expect much, but at least it gave Joanna something interesting to do as she adjusted to motherhood. Unfortunately, accepting her offer meant he was still maintaining a connection to Luz, but then Luz wouldn't know that, so it didn't need to interfere with his decision not to see her again.

And if Joanna found out something? He'd deal with that in the unlikely event it actually came to pass.

Chapter Twenty-three

From his place beside Alan, Charles watched the matron of honor and the two bridesmaids pace solemnly down the aisle. Then the music swelled, and Kathy and her father began their slow approach.

For a moment, memory overwhelmed him, the what-might-have-beens bringing a lump to his throat. But as Kathy drew near, her gaze fixed on Alan, he realized somewhere, sometime he'd reconciled himself to this. To her marrying Alan. He took a breath, expecting his chest to ache at the finality of his loss. When it didn't, he breathed out in relief.

A flutter of movement caught his eye. The bright turquoise of a dress worn by a woman in the pew behind the Francini family. Luz. Relief was replaced with longing, a longing he knew to be every bit as useless as his love for Kathy had been.

Afterward he had little memory of the actual ceremony, but he must have managed to do his part, because there had been no expressions of surprise or puzzlement on the faces of Alan or the priest. But during the reception he did receive one or two odd looks when he abruptly excused himself in order to move to a different part of the room, away from Luz.

When the toasts came due he stood, and as he turned to face the bride and groom, Luz caught and held his gaze from across the room, and his mind went blank. After an agonizing moment, he raised his champagne flute, sucked in a panicked breath and spoke the first words that popped into his head. "To Kathy and Alan. Proof to the rest of us happiness is indeed possible."

It wasn't what he'd planned to say. But short and sweet

was likely better than a longer tribute. Especially given it wasn't the first time he'd offered a toast to a newly-married Alan. Weddings brought too many memories. Why did people put themselves through them?

Thank God it was almost over. The only remaining hurdle was the dancing. As best man, he did his duty, dancing with Kathy's matron of honor, although the term matron sat lightly on Jade's slender shoulders. After that, he danced with Stella, and then he sat back down, wishing ardently that he was an ordinary guest who could just leave whenever he wanted without exciting comment.

"It wouldn't kill you to dance with me, you know." Luz stood in front of him, a stubborn look on her face that indicated she knew he'd been avoiding her.

He shook his head. "I'm not much of a dancer."

"*No es verdad.*" She tipped her chin, looking irritated. "You just don't want to. As long as it's with me."

"Sure. Okay. I'll dance with you." He stood, and she waited for him to come around the table and walk with her toward the small dance floor. The DJ segued from a fast to a slow song, and Luz stepped into his arms. He held her carefully, keeping his distance.

Not many women were tall enough to look him in the eye, but Luz wearing heels was. Tall enough to fit comfortably as well when he'd kissed her.

He shoved the thought away and tried to concentrate on the music.

Although she still had a coltish quality, Luz was a wonderful dancer. Another couple came swinging toward them, and he pulled her closer and twirled out of the way. He kept the tighter hold after they were out of danger, and Luz didn't try to pull away.

Without pausing, the DJ played another song, this one more up-tempo, and he kept dancing with Luz. By the middle of the second dance, he was trying complex steps to see if she was able to follow. She did, easily.

Dancing, he relaxed, setting aside, at least for the moment, the decision to keep Luz out of his life. With her in his arms, it was impossible to imagine never seeing her again. But it was what he had to do. Let her go. For her sake.

With quick decision, he maneuvered Luz toward the edge of the pocket dance floor meaning to walk her back to her table.

When she realized his intention, she gripped his arms. "How did we get to this place?"

He spoke quickly, trying to push her away with words. "I don't know about you, but I drove."

Her lips trembled. "You were so nice to me at Christmas. Now you're acting as if you don't even like me. Why?"

"I didn't realize I was."

"Of course you did."

"Well, you very often act as if you don't like me either. Like right now for instance."

"Because I don't."

They were both speaking in low, fierce voices.

Charles pulled her closer, lowered his voice further and spoke in her ear. "Then why ask me to dance?"

Her cheek rested against his, and he had to start dancing again or they'd quickly become a spectacle.

"I like to dance. And everyone else has a partner."

The tone of her voice was changing. Instead of the irritated note, it was now soft, with a husky edge to it. And she didn't remove her cheek from where it rested against his.

"You dance very well."

"I'm Latina."

They danced for a time in silence.

"You didn't answer my question," she said.

"I've forgotten what it was."

"I doubt that."

"I thought I did answer it."

"No. I'm quite certain you didn't. But I can always ask another one. What do you want to be when you grow up?"

"That question's about twelve years too late. I am grown up."

"What about marriage and a family? Are they in your plans?"

234

"Maybe."

"You have someone picked out? To marry?"

"Luz, I don't want to play this game anymore."

"Game. You think this is a game?" Her voice was a full-throttle angry whisper. "Dammit. Who made you God, and said you get to make all the rules? Because you're older and presumably wiser, I suppose. Although I have to say I'm not sure I buy that. Older sure. But definitely not wiser."

"Luz."

"Just be quiet and listen for a change. What do you think age is about? Time? I beg to differ. There are forty-year-olds who couldn't do what I did this past year. I've had experiences some people won't have if they live to be eighty. I bet I know more about who I am than you know about yourself."

"Luz, we're attracting attention."

She snapped her head away from him and saw what he'd seen—that several couples were obviously maneuvering to stay within earshot. She put her cheek back against his and spoke softly. "If you don't want them to hear what I'm saying, don't make me mad. Or, I can speak in Spanish if you prefer."

"I don't understand Spanish."

"Yeah. And you're scared spitless of horses. Honestly, Larimore, you couldn't be more wrong for me than if the matchmaker from hell brought us together."

"Luz, hush." He pulled her close and kept dancing, smiling to himself.

"Here's the deal, Larimore. I'm not a child, and I refuse to be treated like one."

"I don't treat you like a child."

"Says you. What I want to know is what you're afraid of."

"I have no idea what you're talking about."

"Hmmph. Lets start with the horses. You know what Rob said?"

She didn't wait for him to answer, but of course he did know, because Rob had said it to him as well.

"He says, you'll go out in Denver traffic on a bicycle, but you're afraid to get on a horse. As if that makes any sense."

Enough! Charles stepped away, grabbed her hand and led her off the dance floor, out of the room and into the hall.

"This isn't the time or the place for this, Luz."

"And when will that be? Never?" Her eyes were snapping, but they also looked like they might fill with tears at any moment.

He reached out and captured her hands. "I'll let you pick a time and place to talk, if you promise we'll go back in there and just dance."

She stared at him for a time, obviously trying to gauge his sincerity. He stared back, battered by the emotions swirling between them.

"Two o'clock," she said. "Tomorrow. At the ranch."

"Good, I'm glad that's settled." Although it wasn't, of course. It was barely started. "Shall we dance, Ms. Montalvo?" He raised his brows in question, and Luz nodded.

All he'd negotiated was a brief reprieve, but he ended up with more than that. Holding Luz in his arms, everything else fell away. And for a brief shining time, instead of letting her go, he held her tight and dreamed of possibilities.

Chapter Twenty-four

At TapDancer, Cormac greeted him with a flurry of barks, a jump and a quick lick. Charles ruffled the thick fur on the dog's neck and when he straightened Luz was there, leaning against the barn watching him.

He expected her to come toward him to get in the car, but she stood where she was, waiting, while he walked over to her. She was wearing her ranch uniform of jeans, tailored shirt and jacket, but he had a sudden vision of how she'd looked the day before. Beguiling and beautiful.

"So where are we going?" he asked, trying to move things along, trying to ignore how seeing her affected him.

"I need to check on the foals first." She picked up a basket of apples and carrots and led the way across the riding ring and through the fence at the far side into a pasture where a group of mares and foals was grazing. All the mares lifted their heads, and one by one they ambled over as the foals raced each other to be the first to arrive at her side.

He backed up and climbed onto the top rail of the fence, where he perched, feeling reasonably safe, until one of the mares came over to make sure he wasn't hiding any treats. She snuffled loudly and pushed at him, and panic had him scrambling to put the fence between himself and the curious mare.

Luz came over and tapped the animal on the nose. "Arista, is that any way to treat a guest? Sorry about that." She smiled at him as she stroked the mare's nose and fed her a treat.

Then she turned her back on him and continued doling out the apples and carrots. Gradually, his breathing and heart rate slowed back to normal. One of the foals came over and pushed its small muzzle through the fence against his leg. He almost jumped out of reach, but decided that would be silly given he was bigger than the foal, although his teeth weren't nearly as large. The youngster continued to push against him, until Charles found his hand reaching out to rub ears and pat a nose.

His hand slid down the bony face, until he reached the muzzle, to find it was as soft as a kid glove. Tentatively he patted, and the foal rubbed his leg, breathing in noisily. Distracted, he didn't notice Luz had walked over to join them.

"Here. The last piece. Thought you might want to feed your friend."

"The friend has big teeth."

"She won't bite. She's our biggest sweetheart. But hold it like this and she can't bite even if she tries." Luz flattened her hand to show him.

He took the apple piece and held his hand out flat. The foal lipped his hand and snorted, dancing away, before it came back to pick the treat delicately off his hand.

Luz climbed onto the fence and patted the spot next to her. Reluctantly, he climbed up and sat. The mares and foals, seeing Luz's basket was empty, drifted away.

He wiped his hand on his jeans.

"They really scare you, don't they."

"I thought the plan was to talk about what I want to be when I grow up."

"Definitely not a cowboy."

He didn't realize he'd shuddered until Luz spoke. "Are you okay?"

Of course he was okay. Except he couldn't seem to stop the tremors. It was a cool day, and he'd left his jacket in the car, but this was more than that.

"So about that talk?" The sooner he got it over with the better. Even better, if he'd never come. Not that it hadn't crossed his mind to stand her up. But with Luz working at the ranch, and the Francinis like family, ignoring her would have ramifications.

Luz dropped to the ground. "Why don't we go to the house and get you warmed up."

"I have a better idea. Let me get my jacket, and we can go for a walk." Actually, he'd prefer a run. A long, hard one. It was by far the best way to deal with difficult emotions.

"Or we can go for a ride."

"No way." It sounded abrupt, but he was rubbed too raw to soften it. He reached the car, grabbed his jacket, shrugged it on, then led the way along a trail that meandered toward the nearest foothills.

"So talk." It wasn't gracious, but he was here under duress and he wanted to make sure she knew that.

"Okay." She easily matched his rapid pace. "For starters, just how old do I have to be before you'll consider me an adult?"

He stopped walking to face her. "Kathy set you up to this, right?" It suddenly made perfect sense. Kathy playing matchmaker to ease her guilt over hurting him.

Luz appeared puzzled.

"That day in the restaurant. That was planned, too."

"No." Luz shook her head, but all the bright sass was gone.

Her eyes filled with tears, and she whirled and walked away from him, back the way they'd come. He waited a moment to see if she'd stop and turn around. She didn't.

So, Larimore. You going to stand here like an idiot and let possibly the best thing that ever happened to you walk away just because you suspect someone set you up?

Irritably he rubbed his head, then, sighing in resignation, he started after Luz. They hadn't gone far, but while he'd debated what to do, she'd reached the barn and slipped inside.

He stopped in the doorway for a moment to let his eyes adjust to the dim light, but he still didn't see Luz. He breathed slowly, listening, but there was no sound. Not even a random snort or stamp of hoof.

"Luz? Okay, you win. I'm sorry."

"This isn't about winning and losing, Larimore." Her voice came from nearby.

He turned toward the sound and found her sitting on a bale of hay, her arms clutching her knees. "You may consider me a kid, but you aren't doing so great on the maturity scale yourself, you know."

He moved nearer and leaned against a post, facing her, his arms folded. "Clearly, you could do better, then."

She cocked her head, assessing him with a thoughtful look. "Probably." She blinked rapidly. "I liked dancing with you, last night."

"Yeah. That was nice. I liked it, too."

"I'm willing to give a few points on maturity if a guy can dance."

"Is that so?" He felt oddly soothed by her quiet tone and the strange turn of the conversation.

"And I can deal with you not knowing Spanish. Likely you could learn the most important bits."

"This is a negotiation then."

"But the horses." She pursed her lips and frowned. "We're talking major road-block."

"Do I get a say?"

"Do you want one?"

"Well, I'd like to know what you're fitting me out for here."

"The horses. You said last night, you'd tell me why you're afraid of them."

The answer was an easy one, but difficult to say. Or perhaps not so difficult since he didn't remember anything about it. So why not just say it? After all, it *was* ancient history.

"One killed my father."

Luz made a small sound of distress.

A sudden knock against a stall door and a sharp whinny caused Charles's head to jerk, and as it did, a flash of memory came. A memory similar to the nightmare he occasionally had. The one he awoke from shaking and nauseated, unable to remember anything other than dust, heat and screaming.

As quickly as it came, the memory was gone. He shook his head, trying to dispel the fog, grabbing at the recollection of those nightmare screams. Could they have been an angry or frightened horse?

He turned toward the bar of light exposed by the partially

open barn door. The glare blanked the darkness of the memory, blinding him. And in the midst of the glare, a black and white movie began to play in jerky slow motion.

His father on the back of a horse. The horse heaving around a small enclosure, bucking, jumping and snorting while his dad spurred and struck the animal with a quirt. Exhausted, the horse stopped, lowered its head and stood, its sides heaving and lather flecking into the air like scraps of foam.

His dad grinned at him. "And that, son, is the way it's done." His voice was rich with satisfaction. Slowly the man dismounted, and leaving the beaten animal in the middle of the corral, sauntered toward Charles. Before he understood what his father intended, he'd been scooped up and plopped into the saddle. His father handed him the reins and, with another grin, backed off slightly. "Ride 'em cowboy," he said.

Charles's arms felt like lead, and the quivering of his body was indistinguishable from that of the animal beneath him.

"Go on, son. Kick him in the ribs. Get him moving."

But he could more easily walk on water than follow that command.

His dad's voice lost all its jollity and took on the hard edge it usually had when addressing him. "I said, get him moving."

His father retrieved the bullwhip from where it leaned against the fence. As he pulled the lash end slowly through his hand, the horse's head came up, it stopped shuddering and its muscles bunched.

The movie cut off, and he found himself leaning against the door of the TapDancer barn with no memory of how he got there. His breath, a ragged pant, was the only sound.

"Charles?"

Luz's voice made him jump.

"It's okay. You're okay." She put an arm around him and continued to speak softly, holding him tight against her side. He focused on the rhythm and cadence of her voice, not the words, but he couldn't seem to stop shaking.

He had to get out of here, before he fell apart. Before Luz saw him fall apart. He stumbled away from her touch, running, away from Luz. Running away from the memories trying to crowd their way into his mind. Moving blindly as if he was in a blizzard, putting one foot in front of the other, following the path that appeared in front of him.

He picked up his pace, and soon he was racing along a narrow trail, dodging rocks and horse apples. He focused on his breathing and the slap of his feet against the ground, pushing away the other memories waiting to sweep him away if he let his guard down.

He didn't realize Cormac had followed until the dog dodged in front of him on a curve. As the climb steepened, he pushed himself hard, ignoring the fire in his lungs and the burn in his muscles.

At the end of his endurance, he came through a stand of lodge-pole pines to find himself in a meadow. In the distance, a small lake glimmered. He slowed to a jog and then to a walk as he approached the water.

"Alan has this lake he goes to," Elaine told him once. "It seems to comfort him. Odd, don't you think? Given the way Meg died."

Maybe Alan had been running away, like he was, and the lake represented the end point of how far he could manage to get.

Charles reached the shore and bent over, his hands on his thighs, sucking in deep aching breaths. Gradually he became aware of his surroundings. The dark water, the faint click of stones as Cormac investigated along the shoreline, the buzz of insects, and the chitter of an alarmed squirrel. Two crows, in harsh voice, landed in a nearby tree and scolded him.

One for sorrow, two for joy. Or was it the other way around? And where did the words come from anyway? They sounded like the line from a lullaby, except his mother hadn't been much for lullabies.

With that thought, the dam of memory broke. Flickering and stabbing, the memories came. The harsh sound of his father's voice the day Charles had grabbed the end of the whip to stop his father from beating another horse. "Well, good to see you got some gumption, boy. Thought I was raising me a girl." And that same voice, only harder and colder saying, "You did it, Ellie. Had the brat to trap me." And his mother's shrill reply. "Yeah, and how about me? Think I wanted this? I was going to college. To college, you hear. Going to make something of myself."

He came to abruptly, to the sound of the two crows once again, or perhaps still, scolding.

A cloud covered the sun and the lake's color deepened. He sank onto a fallen tree trunk, and his eyes drifted shut. From a very long distance, the scene that had sent him running from the TapDancer barn picked up where it had left off. His dad slowly waving the whip. The sharp movements as the animal reacted, almost dislodging him. Would have dislodged him if he hadn't grabbed the saddle horn, something his father always punished him for. Then the damn horse making a high-pitched screaming sound, or maybe that was him. He held on tightly as the animal pitched and rolled beneath him, hearing, in between the screams, the solid thud of hooves hitting something other than hard-packed dirt, a sound that shook him to his bones. The animal heaved again, twitching him off its back, and everything went mercifully black.

When he'd regained consciousness, both he and his father had been in the hospital. Charles had a concussion and a broken leg. His dad had a crushed chest and hadn't lived through the night.

His leg had taken a long time to heal, and when the cast came off, the muscles were wasted, weak. It was the reason he'd become an obsessive athlete. To build up that leg...and to forget. To forget how it happened. To forget what had happened. To forget his parents hadn't wanted him.

Cormac plopped down next to him, panting, and Charles felt the soft touch of a hand on his shoulder. He turned his head to find Luz standing beside him.

"Are you okay?"

"I'm not entirely sure yet."

"What happened back there?"

He bent his head and circled his thumbs. "I remembered the day my dad died." He shrugged. "I didn't remember before."

"You said a horse killed him."

"Yeah."

"You were there?"

"Yeah." He found himself rubbing his leg. It still ached sometimes, a deep bone-ache. "He used to beat the horses. With a bull-whip." The words were out before he'd decided if it was wise to say them. But what the hell. It was the truth. And besides, the man was dead.

Luz sucked in a breath. He thought about how she would have reacted when his father raised a whip to a horse. She would likely have thrown herself at the man without stopping to think about it. It comforted him, the thought of Luz doing that. He shifted to give her room to sit beside him.

"I see why you're afraid of horses. I'm sorry I pushed at you."

"It's okay." He rubbed his head, but it didn't seem to do any good. "It's about time I remembered. Faced up to it. It's been the script that's run my life. Stupid, to give someone who's been dead over twenty years that power, don't you think?"

Luz put her arm around him and rested her head on his shoulder. He shifted slightly to hold her closer, leaning against her, breathing in her warmth.

After a time, she took his face between her hands and began to kiss him. Light hummingbird kisses across his brow, each eyelid, the tip of his nose. She rubbed her cheek gently against his and licked his ear, delicately, on the lobe.

Luz's caresses had a tentative feel. As if she'd never done this before.

He simply let her touch him. Her lips fluttered against his, briefly, before she tucked her head into the curve of his neck.

"Don't stop, now," he murmured. Gently he turned and pressed his lips against hers, delighting in her response, the sweet taste of her.

He pulled back, because he had to, and noticed the two horses ground-hitched nearby. "What's that about?"

"I thought you might like a ride home."

He hadn't realized he was shaking his head, until Luz reached up and caught it between her hands. "You don't have to. It's okay, we'll walk back."

Relief was followed by a feeling of disappointment. Disappointment in himself. What other challenges had he refused to face, without being aware of it?

He closed his eyes in pain as the answer came. The least of it was the horses. How about the inability to maintain an intimate relationship? Not to mention his attitude about children and having a family.

It was going to take time to dismantle all his screwed-up thinking, but maybe he could make a start, here and now. "Would you help me?" He looked over at the horses, one of which lifted its head and looked back. It had a mouthful of grass and a slightly comical expression that made it appear anything but frightening. Still, his pulse kicked up when Luz took his hand and walked him over to the animal.

"This is Siesta." She rubbed ears and patted a neck. Siesta finished off her grass and reached out and nudged Luz, making her giggle. "She's really a perfect lady." She handed Charles the reins. "Here, get acquainted while I adjust the stirrups."

Charles held the reins, and Siesta turned her attention to him, pushing gently against his chest. He made himself stand perfectly still, and as the mare continued her explorations, he patted her neck.

Luz came back around and pulled the cinch tight. She took the reins from him and passed them over Siesta's head, then she gave him a quiet look. "You don't have to do this."

He ignored the dread pooling in his gut. "Maybe I need to."

"Okay." She motioned for him to mount.

He did so, instinctively reaching for the saddle horn, only to discover there wasn't one. Instead the saddle had a high pommel. Holding the reins loosely, he rested his hands on it in preparation, in case Siesta made any sudden moves. Luz rechecked the stirrups.

She finished adjusting them then took hold of the bridle and began to lead the mare in a circle. "Siesta's a Paso Fino, which means she has a wonderful smooth running gait. But this first time, we'll stick to a walk. She has a real soft mouth. You don't need to pull on her at all. The slightest pressure, and she'll stop or turn or do whatever you want her to. She has lovely manners. If she backs up on you, it just means you're pulling too hard."

When the mare took her first step, he instinctively tightened the muscles in his legs, but as they continued to move, he relaxed and tried to sit straight, like Luz did. Siesta wasn't all that tall. If he fell off, it wouldn't be very far.

But once you were on the ground, you were at the mercy of their hooves.

His leg twinged in visceral memory, and he forced his focus back to the placid movements of the animal beneath him. Luz led them over to the second horse and let go of Siesta's bridle. That caused him a quick flash of nerves, but Siesta stood quietly, as if she might actually be living up to her name and taking a nap, and he once again relaxed.

Luz tightened the saddle on the second horse, mounted and turned the animal to face him. "Are you okay?"

"I think so." He blew out a breath. "Yeah. Fine. Let's do it."

"Don't worry. We'll take it slow." She continued to assess him as she spoke, and looking at her, he forgot for a moment he was sitting on a horse. Instead, he remembered kissing her.

It had been amazing. What he'd wanted to do since New Year's. And now he had. Even more amazing, she'd initiated it. His jeans tightened around his erection, and he shifted slightly to ease the pressure.

It was a relief in a way. To have that discomfort to focus on instead of obsessing about being on a horse, for despite Siesta's obvious gentleness, he still worried she was simply waiting for the right moment to unseat him.

Then he reminded himself that the horse that killed his father had been pushed over the edge into rage by mistreatment and pain. None of the Francinis' horses had ever been mistreated. None of them would have any reason to turn on the humans who fed and cared for them and obviously loved them. That was the rational thought.

But the feeling still persisted as Luz led the way across the meadow and onto the narrow trail leading back to the ranch. He ignored it, and gradually his fear trickled away. The sun warmed him, and in the aftermath of all the emotion and the physical exhaustion from his flight, he began to drowse.

He came to with a start to discover he'd actually dozed off, and he had no idea for how long. He tried to figure out where they were, but it didn't matter, because he was riding a horse, and he'd been able to actually fall asleep. He grinned at the astonishment of it.

But close on the heels of that pleasure came a wave of

exhaustion, and he knew when they got back to the barn, he needed to get away in order to examine more thoroughly this new terrain in which he found himself.

જી

It shocked Luz to discover Charles was vulnerable. From the moment she'd met him, she'd thought of him as sure of himself and sure of his place in the world. Strong both physically and emotionally.

And although she'd been angry with him for treating her like a kid, she still thought him one of the most together people she'd ever met, not counting *Mami* and *Papi*, of course.

Hard to believe the calm, sure man she knew Charles to be had an abusive father. Maybe it explained his stance on children, although Kathy might be completely mistaken about that, of course. After all, look at how well he got along with Marisol and Carlito.

And at least he'd faced some of his past and ridden Siesta. That had to be a good thing, although he'd obviously been fearful. Maybe it took more courage to overcome an irrational fear than a rational one.

After they got back to the barn and unsaddled, they led the horses to the pasture.

"I need to go, Luz." Charles turned to face her, his hands in his pockets. His face had a neutral expression, and the tone of his voice was neutral as well.

Disappointment flared. She'd thought everything between them had changed, but apparently it hadn't. "Will I see you again?"

"Of course." He spoke quickly, then he turned and walked toward his car.

She followed, feeling uncertain and irrelevant.

At the car, he turned briefly. "I'm sorry, Luz. I...I really have to go." He opened the door and got in.

She stood with her arms hanging uselessly at her sides as he drove away without lifting a hand in farewell. As if she was no more worthy of a goodbye than the mailbox or a fencepost.

She'd taken her best shot, and it hadn't been enough.

She turned and walked quickly to the barn, not waiting to watch him drive out of sight.

Chapter Twenty-five

When he reached the highway, Charles turned south toward Colorado Springs instead of north to Denver. Sheer impulse, the decision to visit his mother. He hadn't seen her in months. Actually, anymore, he barely kept up the pretense of having a relationship with her. It was down to birthday and Christmas gifts and the occasional phone call.

But now he understood part of the reason for that.

How long had it taken him to forget? Days, months, years? But after his dad died, why hadn't he and his mom been able to comfort each other, heal?

He tried to picture his childhood, but only vague fragments came to mind. Nothing had the clarity and immediacy of what he'd remembered this afternoon. And yet he was able to recall the details of every course he'd taken in college and law school, every case he'd tried.

The traffic on this stretch of highway between Denver and the Springs was always heavy and required attention, but part of his mind continued to drift from the here and now, away from the vagueness of his childhood, to Luz. And not only Luz, but Marisol and Carlito.

Before they'd found the new wills, he'd begun to think about what it might be like to step in to permanently help Luz raise Marisol and Carlito. It had still bothered him she was younger than he was, but it had no longer bothered him she would be a package deal.

Now everything had changed. Luz didn't need him to help with Marisol and Carlito. If she needed him at all, it was for herself. And he was pretty sure, given the way she acted this afternoon, she might think she was in love with him. A schoolgirl crush.

He didn't want to be the object of youthful passion. He wanted what he wasn't certain Luz was yet prepared to give. Eyes wide open, grown-up love.

At least one thing was true. She was his intellectual equal. And if he was honest about why most of his relationships had failed, he'd have to admit that after the newness of lust wore off, most of the women bored him. Not one of them would have been interested in his puzzles, let alone been able to solve one.

When he reached Pueblo, he drove the familiar route to his mother's house, but although he'd lived here from right after the accident until he was eighteen, it still didn't seem like home.

He rang the doorbell, and his mother opened the door, looking startled. "My. What a surprise."

She gave him her usual perfunctory hug then stood back with a baffled look. Clearly, she was wondering why he was there. Not that he didn't wonder that himself.

"Sorry. I should have called first." He gave her a wry smile. "A sudden decision."

"I was about to fix dinner. Why don't you keep me company? You'll stay for dinner, won't you?"

She sounded so hopeful and so uncertain, it made his heart twist. But they were always tentative with each other.

"For the night, actually. If that's okay." He was too physically and emotionally exhausted to drive back to Denver right away.

"Of course it's okay. This is your home." She smiled brightly, but she still seemed uncomfortable.

"I wanted to talk to you about something. Maybe ask you something."

She gave him a searching look before leading the way to the kitchen. "We can talk while I fix dinner."

She handed him a beer and some nuts, then bustled around the kitchen, putting together a salad and grilling a couple of chicken breasts. "It's nothing fancy. I've been trying to lose weight."

"You're looking good."

She really was. Nearly as tall as he was, with blonde hair pulled into a thick braid. Her skin was still mostly unlined and her eyes the same blue-gray his were. Anyone seeing them together would know they were related.

She looked sideways at him. "You look good, too. Tired maybe. Still doing all that running?"

He nodded.

"Lord, I remember one time you made me drive all around the neighborhood in order to calculate how many blocks equaled a mile."

He'd forgotten that.

"All the neighbors used to tell me if you didn't stop running you were going to waste away. My word, you were a skinny kid."

He sat back sipping his beer, listening to her, wondering if she always talked like this when he visited, and he'd simply ignored her. He decided to test it, see how much she'd tell him.

"You know, I never understood why we came here after I left the hospital."

"Oh." Her look was pained. "It was simple, really. With your dad gone, I couldn't handle the ranch. I sold it."

"And the horses?"

"A guy came along, needed some good buckers for a rodeo. Took the whole lot."

"What about the one..." His throat closed on the question.

She gave him a sharp look. "You mean the horse that killed him?"

"Yeah."

"I shot it."

Of course. And he could picture it clearly. His mother running out to see what was happening, perhaps standing frozen until it all made appalling sense. Then rushing to grab the shotgun his father kept in a rack in the back of the pick-up. It had likely been real quiet after the blast of the gun, except for the ringing in her ears.

He wondered what she'd done next. Rushed back to the house to call emergency services, or run to check on them?

She tipped her head looking worried. "Why all the questions? Now, after all these years?"

He shook his head, feeling as uncertain as she appeared. "I'd forgotten. All of it. Then today, I...remembered."

"Did something happen?"

"Not really. I just remembered. Some of it. That's all. And I wondered...it didn't seem like we were happy."

His mother snorted. "Your dad was a one for running his mouth. Maybe I was, too. We got awful aggravated with each other sometimes."

"Did it bother you he beat the horses?"

"Did he?" She shrugged. "I stayed away when he was breaking a horse."

Breaking. It was the perfect word for what his father had done.

"I thought you were both dead." She raised bleak eyes to him. "Think I would have died myself, if you hadn't been okay."

He stared at her, trying to process the words and the emotion they encompassed. She turned away.

He swallowed and spoke carefully. "I remember this one time. Dad was yelling at you, about how you had a kid to trap him, and you yelled back that you were trapped, too. That you'd meant to go to college. Be someone."

She turned and stared at him, then shook her head. "Oh, Charles. He didn't mean it. And neither did I. Likely we were angry with each other. Is that what you thought? That we didn't love you?"

Her lips trembled, and her eyes filled. "I wasn't much of a mother. Especially after your dad...I was all froze inside. And you were so...I don't know. Complete, I guess. Pushed me away. I figured, give him space. He needs time to get over what happened, too." She swiped at her eyes. "Never seemed like you needed me. Always running or studying. Never gave me a whit of trouble, you know that? Never had to worry you'd do something stupid. It was like you were already all grown up."

He sat paralyzed, listening.

"I was—I *am* so proud of you. The man you've become." Her mouth lifted into a hesitant smile. "Just sometimes, I wish...that you and I—I wish we were friends."

She turned away and fussed with the salad greens.

He took a breath and stood up, carefully. Moving slowly, as if in a dream, he walked over and put his arms around her. She didn't turn around. Just stood quietly.

"I'm an idiot." He spoke softly. "Never occurred to me to ask you to explain."

"Why would it? You were the child, Charles. I should have known. Wasn't natural. I should have forced you to talk to me." She placed her hands over his where they circled her waist. "Now I'd know better. I'd get you help. But then I kept thinking maybe it was better not to stir it all up. I'm so sorry."

He continued to hug her, trying not to think about what they'd both lost.

"Hey, I better check that chicken," she said.

He eased away from her and took a breath. "Do you think...maybe you can come visit me sometime. I'd like to show you around Denver."

"I'd like that. A lot."

While they ate, he talked about the Maxwells' cases, and she told him about the classes she was taking. Her goal was to have her baccalaureate degree by the time she was fifty-five, she said.

After dinner, she pulled out an old photo album. He sat beside her, and she talked about the pictures.

There was a wedding photograph on the first page. It surprised him to discover his father was a head shorter than his mother and appeared considerably older.

So what had he inherited from the man? Certainly not his dark coloring and short stature, and thankfully not his temper.

"He was something." His mother's voice was soft. She stared at the picture, her eyes bright with unshed tears. "Not perfect by any means. But smart as a whip." She humphed. "Guess that isn't the best way to put it, given what happened and all. But he was. Like you."

Considering what he'd managed to remember about his father, Charles tried to decide if this was good news. "He looks a lot older than you."

"Only a few years was all. He had a hard life, maybe that's why. Sometimes it was like I was working to tame him, same as he did the horses." She lifted her shoulders in a quick motion. "He wasn't much good at showing affection, since he never got any himself growing up. But you shoulda heard him bragging about you."

All Charles remembered was his dad yelling at him, so what his mother was saying seemed completely unbelievable. A rewriting of history. "I remember one day I grabbed the whip to stop him from hitting a horse, and he told me he was glad to see I had some gumption. He'd begun to worry he was raising a girl."

"Oh, honey. He didn't mean it. I remember...I don't know if it was then or some other time. You stood up to him. He told me he didn't dare let you know how proud he was of you, because it might spoil you."

Charles struggled to reshape his memories around what his mother was telling him. Decided finally he'd never manage it. He'd just have to accept that like anybody, his dad would have had both good and bad points and would have been viewed differently by different people. And perhaps his view was the least valid since he'd judged his father from a child's perspective.

For the first time, he wished he'd had a chance to know the man.

His mother continued to turn pages and talk about his life. The boy in the photos was a skinny towhead, and he felt no sense of recognition until they reached the pictures from high school.

In a second book his mother showed him dozens of newspaper articles mentioning him. She must have combed obsessively through her *Denver Posts* to have collected all these obscure references.

If he hadn't already figured out he was wrong in believing she didn't care about him, that collection of newsprint would have convinced him.

By the time they turned the last page, he could barely keep his eyes open. He kissed her on the cheek, telling her goodnight, and she gave him a luminous smile.

"I need to leave early. I'll try not to wake you."

"If you think I'm letting you take off without a fresh cup of coffee, you can just forget it." She tried to sound stern, but her eyes were moist again.

"I'd appreciate it." Neither one of them was talking about coffee. "I need to be on the road by six."

She nodded, and he took himself off to the small room that had been his when he was growing up. He was more exhausted than after an Ironman competition, but he felt more peaceful than he had in years.

ॐ

Over the next two weeks, Charles worked long hours on his case du jour, and only his ingrained professionalism ensured that he did decent job. Like a distant hum, the memories he'd denied were always with him. He found himself staring out the window, seeing not the bustle of the city, but a dusty corral, with the heat of a summer sun burning his neck and harsh dust drying his throat.

Gradually, the memories expanded. He remembered his dad sitting hunched over accounts in the evenings, while his mom sat in the corner with a lamp shining over her shoulder, reading. The man stood, stretched, and walked over to the woman and placed a hand on her head. She looked up and smiled. He tried to decide if that was a real memory or wishful thinking, but perhaps it no longer mattered.

Once his latest trial ended, he called his mother. "I'm taking a few days off. I thought you might come for that visit we talked about."

"Why, I—why, yes. I'd like that."

She arrived at his apartment at ten on a Friday morning. She stepped in, looking around with interest. "It's real nice, Charles. You always were the neatest kid." Her lips wobbled, and he pulled her into a hug. She hugged him back, holding on tight. "Missed you," she whispered. Then she stepped away and rubbed her eyes. "Well just look at me. What a silly."

"I have tickets for the ball game. That is, if you'd like to go.

If you're not too tired."

She straightened her shoulders and nodded. "That sounds like fun."

The tightness in his neck and shoulders gradually eased as they ate hot dogs, drank beer, teased each other and cheered the Rockies, who went down to ignominious defeat anyway.

He took her to see his office and the courthouse, and then to dinner. Through it all they talked, getting to know each other in bits and starts, catching up on all the lost years, his mother's reminiscences extending the ends of his truncated memories. He felt as if all the nicks, craters and deeper crannies of his psyche were being filled in and smoothed out.

Clear at last, the fact he'd been sleepwalking through his life. In his refusal to remember the past, he'd given up the chance to understand the present, the true reasons for his choices. Choices he'd always been careful about—the women he dated, the places he lived, career, friends.

All so he wouldn't be like his father.

"Don't be too hard on yourself, Charles," his mother said, as she was leaving. "I think what happens to us is less important than how we deal with it."

Her words stayed with him. Gradually, he was able to set aside the burden of expectation he only now realized he'd carried. Such an enormous relief to at last be his own man.

He returned to work, feeling for the first time in years as if a break had actually done him some good.

Joanna called several days later. "I have something for you."

"About?"

"The Montalvo Arellano family. Why don't you come for dinner, and I'll fill you in."

Chapter Twenty-six

"Charles called," Stella told Luz when she came in at noon. "He wants you to call him back. Number's by the phone."

Luz's heart began to gallop, but she tried to act nonchalant. "I'll call him after lunch." She'd been hungry, but now she found it a struggle to swallow.

A month. A whole month since the day Charles came to the ranch after the wedding. For the first week, she'd jumped every time the phone rang. But anymore, she worked hard not to think about him.

She dialed Charles's number, expecting a secretary to answer, but he answered himself.

"Hi." It was the only word she managed, but it was enough, because he obviously recognized either her voice or the number.

"Luz, I was wondering. Have you ever been to Pike's Peak?"

Was he asking her out? "Actually. I always meant to go. But no. I haven't, actually." She realized she sounded idiotic and clamped her mouth shut.

"Would you like to go? With me, that is?" He sounded as hesitant as she felt.

She gulped and squeezed out a yes.

"How about Saturday? We can make a day of it. If you can take the time off."

Relief made her limp. "I'd like that. Very much. Do you want me to pack a picnic?"

"Nope. You don't have to do a thing." His voice had firmed and was sounding more confident. "Just be ready by about...oh, ten work for you?"

"That would work perfectly." Luz hung up and hugged herself in delight. Charles had asked her out. On a real date. Not like New Year's when he'd just wanted to ask her questions about her family.

She floated out of the house and back to the barn, unable to stop smiling.

ॐ

"I've been worried about you," Luz told him as they drove away from the ranch. The simple statement held a question.

"I'm sorry I didn't call," Charles said. "I...well, it's just that I've been really busy." And if that wasn't the weakest apology he'd heard in a while, it was damn close.

"It's all right."

No it wasn't. He suddenly saw how selfish he'd been. Going on a search for his past, thinking only of himself, setting aside Luz, the most important person in his present, as if she were inanimate. Leaving her completely in the dark about his intentions, until *he* was ready.

Abruptly he pulled the car to the side of the road, stopped and turned to face her. She looked steadily back.

"I owe you a better apology." He'd been hoping to ease into it, sometime during the day. Not right away like this and not cramped in a small car parked on the side of a country road. "You see, the reason I didn't call you was because I..." He shifted his shoulders and stretched his neck. "Actually, it's a long story."

Luz laid a hand on his arm. "You did ask me if I could spend the day with you."

"Yeah. I did, didn't I."

"We could leave the long story for later, if you like."

"That might work."

Her lips curved. "And just so you know, I'm not letting you off the hook." Her expression abruptly sobered. "There is one thing I'd like to clear up before we go any further, though."

"What's that?"

"This is a date, right?"

"What else could it be?"

"Oh, I don't know. Maybe a wrap-up meeting on the Blair-Montalvo case. Tie up all those loose ends. Make sure all the t's are dotted, the i's crossed."

"Don't you mean the t's crossed and the i's dotted?"

"Good, you're paying attention." The words might be teasing, but Luz's expression was still serious.

He shifted, feeling just a little dishonest. "As far as I know, that wrap-up was done weeks ago."

"You do realize I'm only a month older."

"Yep."

"And?" she prodded.

"I've decided to overlook it." And more. He'd decided to accept her argument—that depth of experience trumped actual time spent on the planet.

"So this is a date."

To hell with ambiguity. "Yes."

"Good." She leaned over and kissed his cheek, then she resettled herself and adjusted the seatbelt.

Smiling to himself, he pulled back on the road.

As he drove, they talked easily and comfortably about Cora, Marisol and Carlito. About his cases and what was next for him and her college plans for the fall. That held them until they reached his favorite overlook right below the summit of Pike's Peak.

Although the day promised to be hot, the air on the mountain was cool. He led the way to the viewpoint where the side of the mountain swooped down to the plain below, and stood behind Luz, blocking the wind, letting her look. It was one of the things he liked about her. That although at times she chattered like a magpie, she could also be quiet and reflective.

She leaned back, and it felt completely natural to put his arms around her. In simple happiness, he stood holding Luz, willing to spend the rest of the day doing just that.

Eventually they drove on to the summit, where they checked the view from every angle—the plains to the east and the peaks ranged in every other direction.

By the time they watched the cog railcar arrive, they were both chilled. He suggested they go to the gift shop for cups of hot chocolate and two of the fresh donuts whose fragrance scented the air.

Sitting across from Luz at one of the wooden tables and watching her enjoying her donut, licking at the sugar and cinnamon, what he most wanted to do was lean across the table and kiss her, not on the cheek, but on those lovely lips.

Luz smiled at him, and he caught his breath. He'd been such an idiot. To have walked away from her, denying both desire and good sense, all because he'd been following the script of a man over twenty years in his grave. An unbelievable, not to mention almost irreversible mistake. The only thing giving him hope it wasn't irreversible was the way Luz was now looking at him.

"About that long story," he said. "Maybe I could get part of it out of the way now. If that's okay?"

"Certainly," she said, licking her fingers.

"The last time I saw you...afterwards I went to see my mom." He lowered his eyes to his hands, clenched together on the rough tabletop. "I hadn't seen her for a while. You see, after my dad was killed, she and I, well, she...I heard them arguing one time, and I got the idea she didn't love me. Because of that, we drifted apart."

Luz drew in a sharp breath and then leaned toward him, cupping her hands over his.

"I found out that day it wasn't true. That a lot of things I'd thought were true, weren't. It made me realize I was wrong about other things as well. Like saying you were too young, and...anyway it took awhile to work through all of it."

He glanced up to find Luz blinking rapidly.

"That's it. That's why I...I just needed time to figure it all out."

"And have you?" Luz spoke softly, but she hadn't pulled back from him, and her hands still rested on his.

"I'm just hoping...I didn't leave it too late." He looked across at her, a question on his face.

Luz met his gaze, but before she could respond, the quiet between them was filled by the loud talk of three teenage boys taking seats nearby.

It had probably been a good thing they'd been interrupted. Luz wasn't entirely certain what Charles was asking, but if he meant what he seemed to mean, she wanted time to savor it.

His story about his mother and what had happened with his father...she ached for the child he'd been. No one should grow up thinking they weren't loved. For that matter, she didn't think anyone at any age could thrive without love. Still, she didn't know if he was quite ready for her to declare she loved him.

She finally gave up worrying it and simply enjoyed considering the possibilities as they drove back down the mountain, window-shopped in Manitou Springs and had lunch in a café that smelled of fresh-baked bread.

She sat back, while Charles paid the bill, making no attempt to stifle the thrum of excitement that was making the day much more than one of simple sightseeing.

"What do you think about a visit to the Garden of the Gods?" he asked.

"Would you believe? I haven't been there either. "

He shook his head. "Luz Cristina, you can't possibly have studied all the time."

"Pretty much." And it no longer mattered in the least that she'd been almost completely dateless at Colorado College. Not if that was the price for this day with Charles.

At the Garden of the Gods, she climbed out of the car and looked at the scattering of huge red rocks. "Oh, my. I had no idea."

He gave her a bemused looked. "I used to train here. The scenery's a good distraction. I always managed a couple of miles more than I thought I could."

As if it was the most natural thing in the world, he took her hand and led the way along the paved walkway. They passed walkers, joggers and clusters of tourists taking photos. Charles pulled on her hand to lead her onto a steep side trail away from all the other visitors. They climbed a short distance to where the view of the valley and mountains opened up.

"I don't know why, but nobody seems to come up here," he

said.

They found a flat rock where they could sit side by side facing the mountains, and he put his arm around her.

She leaned against him, smiling happily to herself. Letting herself begin to believe.

"There's something I need to discuss with you," he said. "It's about those letters Henry and Jean found."

His words jerked her from her happy dream. So this day was about business after all. But what did she expect? Of course, Charles Larimore couldn't possibly be *interested* in her. That moment of connection on the top of Pike's Peak had been an illusion. Brought on by sugar and thin air. She pulled away from the shelter of his arm. "What about them?" The words came out stiff and angry, but really, she felt like weeping.

"It worried me. I have a colleague who's a whiz with computers. She offered to help."

"You had no right to do that without asking me." She struggled to hold back tears of anger and betrayal, struggled even harder not to beat her fists against his chest since that would simply reinforce his view she was too young for him.

"You're right. I should have asked. I'm sorry, Luz." He picked up one of her hands and rubbed his thumb on her wrist. "You have the silkiest skin. I love touching you."

Was he trying to distract her? Well it wasn't going to work. She jerked her hand away.

"I said I was sorry, Luz, and I am. Do you want to know what she found out?" His tone had turned brisk.

"This really isn't a date, is it. You're just finishing up my case." The thought hurt so much, she wanted to jump up and run away, except there was no place for her to run to.

He turned slightly and put his hands on her shoulders, keeping them in place even when she tried to squirm away. "I'm really blowing this, big time, aren't I. I did want to see you, to tell you what I found out. But that's not what this is about. Not by a long shot. I missed you. I really wanted to see you, but...well, I guess I needed an excuse."

She stared at his chin. "That's really lame, Larimore." He was not getting around her with pretty words. He had to prove he meant it. She raised her eyes to his and stilled. He had that look he'd had on top of the mountain. Or maybe that was simply a case of her wishful thinking getting totally out of hand.

"Yeah. I agree. Pretty amazing. Seems you've reduced me to jello. And that doesn't happen very often." His lips twitched, and then in the next moment he was smiling.

"Lime or raspberry?" Her words, without permission, skittered along the edge of laughter.

"Lime for my lovely Luz." His expression sobered, and he rubbed his thumb against her cheek.

Her breath caught.

"I really am sorry, Luz."

"It's bad, isn't it."

"It's not good."

"Maybe we better get it over with then."

He shifted and put an arm around her. Giving up, she let him hold her. From the look on his face, she was going to need that comfort.

"Joanna did a genealogy search. Your mother was Luisa Bachelet Fischer. She and your father, Esteban Montalvo Arellano, married in nineteen seventy-four. They had a son, Julio, in seventy-five and a daughter, you, in seventy-eight." He paused taking a deep breath, his arm pulling her tighter against his side. "Your mother and Julio died in nineteen eighty-three."

It still hurt. Although she'd already known, having him say it made it more real."Joanna also traced Esteban's and Luisa's parents, your grandparents. Luisa's parents died in an accident in nineteen seventy-one, Esteban's father, Guillermo, died in nineteen ninety-seven and his mother, your grandmother, Magdalena, last year. Your father has a younger brother, Roberto. As far as Joanna could tell, he must still be alive."

With the news of Magdalena's death, Luz realized she'd had hopes. In spite of her fear, she'd thought she'd have time to figure out how to safely contact her grandmother. But now Magdalena was gone as well. There was no one left but Roberto, whom she had no intention of contacting.

"I knew some of that." Her voice wobbled. She took a breath, trying to steady it. "That my mother, brother and grandfather were dead."

She sniffed, and Charles rubbed her back then rested a hand gently on her neck.

"Did...did your friend find out how my mother and brother died?"

Charles shook his head.

She thought about the fragmented story in the letters. It might not have made complete sense but it had been full of menace. "I think something bad happened. *Papi* was afraid to go home, and he wouldn't let his parents tell his brother where he was. One letter mentioned a man. *Papi's* mother called him S. She said as long as he lived in the district, it wasn't safe for *Papi* to return. But it was all just bits and pieces of information."

His hand on her neck tightened. "Maybe you'd let my friend see the letters. She might be able to discover more."

"*Papi* was a strong person. For him to be careful for so long, it had to be really bad. I don't know. Maybe it's better if we don't try to find out."

"Sometimes it's better to know your enemy. To know if there's a chance he might still be out there. So you can take evasive action."

"I think it's better to leave it be."

"If that's your decision, I think I'd better double-check with the Scottsbluff police on your parents' accident."

"You don't think..." The panic was swift, overwhelming.

"There are a few too many people dying before their time here." He took her hands in his, giving her an earnest look. "I don't want to lose you, Luz. Not when I've only just found you."

She blinked, but he was still there, looking at her the way he'd looked in her dreams. The way he'd looked at her on top of the mountain. Under the strength of that look, her fear, worry and uncertainty dissipated like wisps of cloud in a strong wind.

Without consciously deciding, she leaned toward him, and her lips grazed against his. He made a slight adjustment to increase the pressure, and delight flowed through her sparkling and fizzing, warming and soothing. Charles's arms, a strong banding, a perfect refuge. She settled against him. This was her place. As if she were the last piece of a puzzle that hadn't looked like it could possibly fit until someone placed it into the remaining gap.

"You take my breath away, you know that?" he said.

"I certainly hope so."

He leaned back and lifted her glasses off. She blinked at him in surprise. "There," he said, removing his own as well, "we don't need any distractions."

Her eyes widened then closed in bliss as his lips once again sought hers. The feel of him, the good tastes. Mmm.

He pulled away, sucking in a breath and cupped her face between his hands. "You haven't had much experience."

"Does it matter?" And how could he tell, anyway?

"Yeah. It matters. God, I want you." His voice was hoarse and his breath ragged.

She looked at him and began to smile. *Gracias a Dios.* "It's okay." She nuzzled against his neck, chuckling. "I want you, too."

He pulled back again. "No. Not yet." He took a deep breath. "I don't...Oh hell, I don't know how to say this, without it coming out sounding wrong." He stopped, and her heart thumped with sudden panic. "I don't want to mess this up. I want..." He stopped to breathe. "I know it sounds weird, but I think...maybe we have a chance... Oh hell."

He stumbled to a halt, giving her an agonized look. She didn't know all that much about men, but she had no doubt Charles had enjoyed kissing her and that he wanted to do much more than that. It made her feel powerful, and tender.

"It's going to be hell to wait." He closed his eyes briefly. "I don't even know if I can do it very long. But I want to try. I want us to take this slow, Luz, enjoy every minute."

She could do that. She touched his lips with a finger, because she didn't dare kiss him again. "It's going to be hard for me, too. I may even try to make you change your mind."

"Think you can?" His voice was hoarse.

"Oh, yes. I know I can. But I won't." She laid her cheek against his. Maybe it was too soon for her to say it, but this man had already spent far too long not hearing that someone loved him. "Dearest Charles, do you know how much I love you?"

His arms tightened around her, then he leaned back, and his eyes met hers and his lips curved in a wide smile. "*Te amo, Luz Cristina.*"

She snuggled against him, chuckling softly, her world transformed.

ꝏ

Kathy entered the apartment and walked back to the second bedroom where Alan would be working. He looked up with a distracted expression that meant he was just emerging from the nineteenth century.

Seeing her, he smiled and stood to give her a hug.

"Good day?" she asked, leaning back in his arms. But she knew since nothing was cooking it had been. If Alan hit a slow spot during the afternoon, he started dinner.

"Umm. It just got better."

Would it ever get old? This feeling of simple happiness whenever she saw him after they'd been apart.

Coming home. It meant something completely different than it had just six months ago.

She sighed with happiness as Alan kissed her. Then, as frequently seemed to happen, kissing led to something more, and it was awhile before either of them thought about dinner.

"We can order in pizza," Alan said.

Kathy stretched and ran a hand down his leg. "That's what we did last night."

"Or, if you don't mind leftovers, there just may be some Tandoori chicken in the fridge."

Kathy stilled. "Does that mean what I think it does?"

"What do you think it means?"

"There wasn't any Tandoori chicken in there this morning, so you must have gone out for lunch. With Charles?" If so, it would be the first time since the wedding, a lack she'd been worrying about.

Alan nodded.

"How is he?"

"Actually..."

"What?" Odd. She could swear Alan had a twinkle in his eye, something usually missing when the subject of Charles came up.

"His mother came for a visit."

Kathy shook her head in confusion. "So?"

"So. He and his mother have barely spoken for as long as I've known him." Alan stopped to run a hand meditatively up and down Kathy's back, making her tremble with pleasure. "And that's not all."

"I swear, Alan, if you don't spit it out right now, I'm going to—"

"What, my love? Deny me my marital rights?"

He was definitely twinkling.

"Of course not. That would be cutting off my nose to spite my face."

"Glad to hear I married a reasonable woman."

He leaned in to kiss her, and she let him before she pulled back. "About Charles."

"Ah, yes. Charles. I wonder if Luz will be as remarkably reasonable as you are?"

"Luz? And Charles?"

"Yep."

"Oh, that's fabulous news. Why didn't you tell me immediately?" Kathy felt like both laughing and strangling her husband.

"Didn't want to distract you until I'd had my way with you."

She leaned against Alan's chest, laughing. "You are so bad."

"But you love me anyway, right?"

"Oh, I most certainly do. Now, I want to know everything about Charles and Luz."

"Why don't we just go out to the ranch this weekend, and you can pump Luz for all the details. It would be simpler."

Men. "At least tell me what Charles said."

"He told me I was right about Luz not being too young for him."

"And?"

"That's it."

"You've got to be kidding." Kathy glared at Alan who gave her a bland look.

"Cross my heart."

"A man of few words, huh?"

"That's Charles."

"Like someone else I could name." She leaned in and nibbled on Alan's neck. "Well, you just earned yourself a visit to the ranch this weekend."

Chapter Twenty-seven

"I can't wait much longer, Luz." Charles took her face between his hands and gently rubbed his nose against hers. He'd brought Luz to his apartment for dinner, but they'd gotten sidetracked by the couch.

"Me either." She turned her head, her mouth seeking and finding his.

"I mean it," he said, pulling back and blowing out a breath.

"Yeah. I got that." Laughter shimmered in her eyes. Then her expression changed to that wise, fey look he loved. "Dearest, Charles, I love you so much. And I can't think of a single reason we need to wait another minute."

But there was one reason. A biggie. And it wasn't the dinner left warming in the oven. "Luz, listen." He placed his hands on her upper arms, holding her slightly away. Far enough that he could look her in the eye and manage his own desire, at least partially. "I want you to have it all. A career if you choose, and...children." He hated that he'd hesitated on that last word. But he was, after all, a work in progress, and over the past month, Luz had seemed to understand that, better perhaps even than he did. "I just don't want it to happen too soon. Before either one of us is ready for it."

Luz matched his serious look and, as he stumbled to a stop, she frowned. "You do want children, though. Don't you?"

It was what he'd been afraid of. That she would think his wanting to delay their arrival meant he never wanted children. He met her gaze head on, without trying to hide anything from her. "Yes. I want them. But I want to make sure it's a choice we've made, eyes wide open. Not something that happens because we, well, we got carried away." And he was very much in danger of that every time he kissed her.

"Okay. What are you suggesting?" She was still frowning slightly, but the look in her eyes told him she was concentrating on what he had to say.

"Just that we need to make sure you won't get pregnant before we're ready. I don't want to short-circuit any of your dreams."

She cupped his cheek with her hand. "As long as you love me, my dreams will be just fine. No matter what happens."

"But you do understand?"

Her lips curved into a smile. "Dear Charles, of course I do. Besides, I want you all to myself, at least for a while. So I went to a doctor. The pill takes a week to be safe, and I've been on it for two and a half weeks."

He blinked at her in surprise. "You—you're on the pill?" It was the most fantastic news he'd ever heard. And a blessed relief as well. He pulled her close and, chuckling, she settled against him.

He kissed her, letting desire build. Luz was the one who pulled back, but when he saw it was only to remove her shirt, he laughed with the sheer joy of it and shed his own.

After several minutes of trying to fit together on the couch, he lifted her in his arms, carried her to his bedroom and laid her on the bed. Lying next to her, he traced a finger over her ribs. "You know, the first time I saw you, I bet if you'd taken off your shirt, I would have been able to count every one of these." His fingers did a delicate dance down her breastbone and circled her belly button.

"Are you trying to tell me I'm fat?" Luz, mirroring his movements, was doing her own explorations.

"Nope. You're just right." He curved his hand around one of her breasts. It fit perfectly in his hand. "See, look at you. How beautiful you are."

Luz's expression abruptly sobered, and she bit her lip. "I'm not really, you know."

He shook his head, his gaze locked on hers. "Oh yes, you are. My lovely, lovely Luz."

After a brief hesitation during which her eyes continued to

question him, her hand drifted down and touched his erection. "You're beautiful, too. And I want to see you. All of you."

Meeting her look, he dispensed with the remainder of his clothing, kicking it off the bed.

Luz's gaze left his face, and he watched her as, eyes wide, she looked her fill. She reached out a finger and slid it down his length, and he shuddered, almost coming right then. She touched him again, more firmly, her mouth curving in a smile. "It's so soft."

He couldn't help it, it made him laugh. "I don't think that's quite the adjective you're looking for, my love."

"*Sedoso*, then."

"What's that?"

"If you look it up, you'll remember it." There was a prim note in her voice, but she was grinning.

"I think it's time we see whether you're *sedoso*, too." His voice trailed off as she began to wriggle out of her jeans.

She freed herself from her clothing, then raised her eyes to his face. No longer did she look uncertain. But there was a question there.

He left the question to simmer as he in turn let his eyes drift down, taking in the long elegant lines of her before he reached out to slide a hand over her hip and down into her soft, her *sedoso* place.

She pushed against him, her eyes widening further.

"Help me out, here, love," he said. Her hand firmed around him, guiding him as he eased into her. She was tight. So tight, he knew pushing harder would hurt. He pulled back while he still could.

There was a quick flash of worry in her eyes. "Is something wrong?"

"Nope. You're just really tight is all. I don't want to hurt you."

"It only hurts the first time, right?"

"That's what I've been told."

"So maybe we could just get that over with."

Once again she surprised a laugh out of him. Laughter and lovemaking. An odd pairing, but one he was thoroughly

271

enjoying. With the possible exception of one not-so-minor detail. "You're not the only one it might hurt, my love." His laughter faded as his own discomfort became acute, something he tried to hide from her.

But she was watching him too closely. "I think I know what the problem is. But you may have to help me." She circled him with her hand and began to stroke.

He made a grab to stop her, but he was too late.

Afterward, Luz used the hand that had held him to trace his eyebrows and mouth. "That felt really good, right?"

Oh my God, yes.

"And you can make me feel that way?" At the trust in her eyes, his chest tightened.

"It may take a little longer for you. And you have to promise not to do that again while we work on it." He leaned his forehead against hers, catching his breath. "Are you ready to try?"

"Oh, yes, please," she said.

&

The day Luz moved her things to his apartment in anticipation of their wedding, Charles saw the portrait of her parents in its large, old-fashioned frame for the first time. He recognized Esteban from the photograph that had accompanied his obit, and the woman resembled Luz.

He held up the picture. "These are your parents?"

Luz looked over from the clothes she was transferring to the dresser and nodded. "It was in the box with the letters."

The letters she had yet to show him. As he set the picture down, he noticed the backing was torn, and sticking out was the edge of a piece of paper.

"Looks like there's something behind the picture." He set the portrait face down on the table and went to the kitchen for a knife. He returned to find Luz with an odd look on her face, her finger tracing the back of the picture.

She took a deep breath. "Now I know how Pandora felt."

"We don't have to look." Although he thought it might kill him if they didn't.

"No. Go ahead."

She stepped away, and he touched her shoulder before using the knife to pry away the back from the frame. There were several pieces of paper lying against the picture.

Luz picked up the pages and looked through them. "It's addressed to me. From *Papi.*"

Walking over and sinking down on the couch, she began to read. She finished the first page and passed it to Charles.

He sat beside her, accepted the paper and started to read. "It's in Spanish, Luz." He might be making progress, but his vocabulary was still too limited for something like this.

Luz glanced up, obviously distracted. "Oh. Sorry." She took the page back from him and read it aloud, speaking slowly and occasionally stumbling over the translation of a word or phrase.

> *My Dearest Luz,*
>
> *I leave it to fate to determine if you should know this story of your family. Perhaps if you are reading this, I am dead. And if that is so, I pray my death was not in any way mysterious.*

Hearing that, Charles was glad he'd made a point of speaking to the officer who had been first at the scene of the Montalvos' accident. They had been killed, the officer reported, in a head-on collision with a car full of drunk teenagers. The only mystery associated with their deaths was why young people continued to drink and drive.

> *But I am confusing you. I am sure you are reading this with that little crease of worry between your eyes. When you were little, you would look at me with that question mark on your forehead, and I did my best to reassure you, but not to answer.*
>
> *Eventually you stopped asking questions, so perhaps you remember very little from before.*

> *That is probably best.*
>
> *Still, I have decided to write this and put it in a place you will be unlikely to find it, trusting in the Blessed Virgin and the Holy Saints to lead you to it, should that be necessary.*
>
> *If you are reading this, my Lucita, I want you to accept this as a story, and not to act on it, except as may be needed to protect yourself. I hope and pray that is not the reason you have been shown these words.*
>
> *You must be careful with this knowledge, my daughter.*

Luz's voice had begun to shake. She stopped translating and looked at him. "I don't know what to do, Charles."

What he wanted to do was take the pages from her and give them to Joanna to translate. Then he would read the translation and figure out what to do. But as Luz had reminded him on more than one occasion, it was her right to solve her own problems.

"Why don't we put it away until after the wedding? Then we'll sit together, and you'll read it to me. And we'll discuss it."

Luz shook her head. "I think I need to read it now, so I can put it out of my mind."

But that might be impossible. A simple mystery was one thing. An appalling story of ongoing danger, which the preamble seemed to be promising, was something else. Still, if Luz decided to read the pages now, he would help her through it.

He moved closer and circled his arm around her. He loved holding her, touching her. Loved even more her responsiveness. At first she'd been uncertain and tentative in her caresses, but her delight and the fact she made no secret she adored him, had made it seem as if he, too, were discovering lovemaking for the first time.

Perhaps in a way, he was.

Luz shifted until she was snugged in tight against him and continued to read.

There once was a family. A mother, a father and two sons. They lived on a huge ranch in a country with lush pastures. They had fat cows and many beautiful horses.

The sons were raised to love and care for the land and the animals because one day it would be theirs.

Unfortunately, the younger son, knowing his brother would receive the better portion—the best rooms in the house and the lushest part of the property—began to envy his brother. It didn't seem to matter that even a lesser portion would be more than adequate to meet younger brother's needs and give him a comfortable life.

Younger brother's envy made the relationship between the brothers tense and often unhappy.

The brothers grew up, and older brother married a woman whom younger brother also fancied. The woman had a son, and younger brother's heart was consumed with anger and envy at the happiness of his older brother, an anger and envy he expressed with harsh words and tantrums.

His anger brought younger brother to the attention of an evil but powerful man in the district. At that man's word, people disappeared.

The evil man took younger brother under his wing and taught him his ways, and younger brother was well satisfied. Except he still wanted everything his older brother had.

Over the next six years, younger brother became more and more angry and sullen, and the evil man more powerful. Meanwhile, older brother had a second child. A girl.

One night, older brother and his daughter were up late, assisting at the birth of a litter of kittens when older brother smelled smoke. He took his daughter and the cats outside and hid them.

Older brother didn't yet know what was happening, but he knew of other families who had been burned out, and he feared his family might be in danger from more than a fire.

He rushed back into the house to get his wife and son. He discovered wet straw on the floors of the bedroom wing. The wet straw created thick smoke, and it and flames blocked his entrance to his son's and his wife's rooms. In despair, he called to them, but received no reply. And he knew. It was too late for them, but it was not yet too late for him to save his daughter.

Before he returned to where he'd hidden her, he circled the house and saw younger brother getting a hose in order to put out the fire. Older brother almost made the mistake of showing himself. But he remembered how sullen and angry his brother had become over the years, and a terrible suspicion entered his heart. He hid from his brother, to wait and see what would happen.

The evil man arrived. He questioned younger brother about survivors, and younger brother said he had been watching, and no one had come out. Older brother knew then he must flee. He had only a few hours before it would be known he hadn't died in the fire.

He waited for an opportunity, and it came when neighbors arrived to help. He hid his daughter in the ranch's truck, and in the confusion, he was able to drive away without being noticed.

After the escape, older brother and his daughter fashioned a new life in a new country, waiting for the day they could return. But then he learned younger brother had accused him of setting the fire, and the authorities were searching for him. And so for the sake of his daughter, older brother put away the dream of going home, and built a new life.

In order to keep you safe, my daughter, I

chose never to return to my home and to maintain only minimal contact with my parents. If my brother could set a fire, hoping to kill four people, I knew nothing would stop him from trying again to get rid of me, and of you, my Lucita. It is better to have lived in peace in Scottsbluff and let go of all that has come before.

Be wise, my daughter, and do likewise.

Love, Papi

Luz dropped the papers into her lap.

Charles waited for her to speak.

"It's h-horrible."

"Yes. It is."

She turned in his arms and laid her head on his shoulder. "*Papi* had dreadful scars on his hands and arms, and when I asked him about them, he said they happened when he was a boy. But they didn't."

From the dampness of his shirt, he knew she was crying. Silent tears. An outpouring of sorrow for all her losses. A mother and brother she didn't remember and a father she remembered too well.

She took a deep shuddery breath. "Do you believe *Papi*'s right? That we should do nothing?"

He chose his words carefully. "No court would convict his brother based on what your father has given us."

"The ranch was *Papi*'s. That means it should be ours. Marisol, Carlito and me. We can take it away from *Papi*'s brother."

"Is that what you want to do?" Charles hoped not, but the question had to be faced.

He held her and waited.

She sighed. "I'm glad I know what happened. It's hard, but it's good to know. But *Papi*'s right. I can't take a chance of putting Marisol and Carlito at risk."

Charles was relieved Mari and Carlito provided Luz the perfect excuse not to follow up on any of this. He loved them all too much to risk losing them over mere acres of land, fat cattle and beautiful horses.

Luz stirred in his arms. "Thank you, Charles." Her voice was soft.

"For what, my love?"

"For letting me make my own decision."

"Even an old guy like me can learn new things on occasion."

"*Gracias a Dios.*" Luz leaned away and gave him her fey look. "Do you have any idea how much I love you?"

He shook his head, matching her solemnity.

"*Con todo mi corazón.*"

A whole-hearted love. It was what he'd almost lost hope of ever finding. The words soothed him like water falling onto a parched land and briefly sparkling in the sunlight before disappearing into the heart of the earth. Proof that beyond death and grief and the loss of hope, dreams persist.

"*Te amo*, Luz Cristina. *Con todo mi corazón.*"

"You'd better show me," Luz said.

And so he did.

Epilogue

From *Bobby and Brad* by Kathleen Hope Jamison-Francini:

Sky color shimmering like visible laughter
Snowflakes and sunsets and leaves falling down
Rainbows and bells
Waterfalls and light
Books, pictures, memories, tears, stars, and time
An enchantment of comfort for those left behind

ॐ

Old enchantments broken. New, blessed ones, cast.

About the Author

As a former professor of toxicology, Ann helped solve medical mysteries. Now, as an author, she explores the mysteries of the human heart.

To learn more about Ann or to send her an email, please visit www.annwarner.net.

Breaking his heart may be the only way to save his life.

Where Dreams Are Made
© 2008 Anne Hope

A woman running from the past...

Jenny Logan is alone, penniless, and indebted to a ruthless man who will stop at nothing to own her. All she wants is a chance to pursue her dreams and make a fresh start, but the past refuses to release her.

A man hiding from the future...

Daniel Frost, a scarred, reclusive toymaker, is trying to escape his memories. Burdened by guilt over a violent car accident that destroyed his family, he believes loneliness is the only way to atone for his sins.

Sometimes, today is all that matters...

One magical Christmas, Daniel's meddlesome grandfather secretly hires Jenny to act as his grandson's assistant, starting them both on the road to recovery. On a remote island where miles of sea meet miles of sky, two lonely people learn that love can heal even the deepest scars—but it comes at a price.

Warning: This title contains violence, sex, emotional intensity that may cause your mascara to run, and a dark, sexy hero who'll make you want to believe in Santa all over again.

Available now in ebook and print from Samhain Publishing.

Enjoy the following excerpt from Where Dreams Are Made...

"It looks like a painting." Jenny gazed at the lighthouse perched on a shelf of ultramarine blue and burnt umber rocks, as they circled San Juan heading for the harbor.

"That's Lime Kiln Lighthouse."

Kelp and driftwood floated at the foot of the bluff, framing the shoreline. The cool saltwater breeze kissed her face, left a salty taste on her lips. "It's so beautiful, and so lonely."

The tall, solitary structure, set against gray mountains and encompassed by blue sky and water, reminded her of Daniel— solid, quiet, admired from a distance. How sad that something so enthralling should be so isolated.

"We'll reach Friday Harbor soon." Daniel steered the boat, his back turned to her, his expression vacant.

She was happy he'd let her come with him, even if he *had* only invited her because he'd felt sorry for her. What an enigma he was. Yesterday when they'd danced she'd sensed a connection between them. There was nothing indifferent about the way he'd held her, the way his fingers had stroked her back, the way his hand had clasped hers. But today miles separated them. She might as well have been alone on this boat.

She absorbed the sight of him. His features seemed chiseled in stone. She longed for the gentleness of the man who'd comforted her late at night when the nightmares had risen to ensnare her, the man who'd helped her decorate a Christmas tree and who'd held her in his arms so tight she hadn't known where her heartbeat ended and his began.

"Do you come here often?" she asked above the deafening whoosh of the waves.

"Once a week," he replied.

A gust of wind whipped his hair, raising it from his face. Briefly, she caught a glimpse of the scars he went to great lengths to conceal. White grooves dug into his flesh, crisscrossing his cheek. Her fingers itched to trace them, to heal them with the loving care of a tender touch. But she couldn't. Daniel didn't want her looking at him, let alone touching him.

As they rounded the island they drew nearer to Friday

Harbor, where a line of fishing boats and pleasure yachts floated patiently. Seagulls screeched overhead, flapping their wings as they spiraled above the bustling port. A brilliant procession of boats, decorated in shimmering Christmas lights chugged around the harbor. Jenny leaned over the bow, impressed by the sight.

Her face must have reflected her enchantment, for Daniel said, "It's the annual Parade of Lights."

The whole town—what she could see of it—twinkled with a rainbow of Christmas lights. "It must look incredible at night." She felt as if she'd stepped into one of those gleaming villages people placed under their Christmas trees.

They finally managed to dock. Daniel secured his boat, and Jenny followed him to an old red brick building facing the waterfront. A short, plump man with round glasses and prominent cheeks came to greet them.

"Daniel, you're late." The man slapped him amicably on the arm. "In the years we've worked together you've been like clockwork. I can usually time your arrival to the minute."

"Sorry, Saul. We got stalled by the parade."

"Ah, they hit the water earlier this year." Saul's gaze settled on Jenny. Surprise spread across his round face.

Daniel's stoical expression faltered. "This is Jenny, my assistant."

"Is that what they're calling 'em these days?" Saul cackled at his own remark.

Heat suffused Jenny's cheeks, perspiration pearling in her joints. This Saul had taken one look at her and known what she was. Not an assistant, but a hired companion.

He can't know, she reassured herself. Only she and Sam Leland were aware of their deal. Guilt sank like a bucket of rocks to settle at the pit of her stomach.

"The shipment's in my boat. Can you send a couple of guys to help me unload?"

Thank God Daniel had steered the conversation away from her. Even though the pragmatic side of her brain told her she was overreacting, her crushing conscience made her foolishly paranoid.

"Sure, I'll send them right out." Saul smiled at Jenny. "You come back again soon."

"That's up to Daniel." Stealing a glimpse of him, she noted the firm clasp of his hands, the darkness cloaking his eyes. He had no intention of bringing her back, unless it was to escort her to the ferry that would carry her out of his life.

Jenny had never much believed in prophecies, but that moment she had a vision. She saw herself standing on the deck of an open ferry, staring at the fading silhouette of a dark-haired man, feeling her heart break with each new wave that crashed against the hull as she floated further and further away. Floated back to Prospect Valley, to Leo, to self-effacement. If she went back there, the glitter inside her that made her the person she was would dim and die. She'd become a robot wearing human flesh, a programmed machine, with all emotion banned from her life.

Perhaps she would have been able to live that way before, but not now. Not after tasting peace, security. Not after savoring the warmth of Daniel's kindness. She'd never thought a man's presence could be so comforting. Before Daniel, Jenny had believed men inspired only fear, submission. But Daniel made her feel protected, cared for. He gave her hope, and she hadn't had that in a very long time.

As they stepped outside, she eyed the numerous restaurants and cafés dotting the waterfront, all outfitted with glimmering lights. Although the small town wasn't crowded, the sight of bikers and pedestrians filling the quaint streets was a welcome change from Daniel's secluded cottage. "Can we stay and walk around town?"

"No." Daniel's reply was curt and dry, almost frantic. He seemed out of his element here amidst society—tense, uneasy. "We have a deadline to meet."

Jenny understood. She caught the real reason in the way he averted his eyes. He wore the unworthiness he felt the same way he wore his scars. As much as he tried to conceal it, it was a part of him and it refused to stay hidden.

In a few minutes they'd boarded his boat and pulled away from the dock, Daniel skillfully bypassing the parade. Jenny leaned back against the railing. He seemed anxious to get away, eager to drift onto the wide, flowing ocean.

"Why are you staring at me?" He hadn't as much as slanted

a glance her way and yet he'd sensed her gaze.

"Just wondering why you feel so uncomfortable around people."

He looked at her then, taken aback. "I don't. I told you we have work to do."

She placed her hand on his shoulder. "You don't have to pretend with me. I understand how you feel. I just don't understand why."

He stared at the rippling water, his expression unreadable. "Please don't touch me." His voice was gruff, strained.

"Why not? Don't you like being touched?" Boldly, she ran the back of her index finger across his right cheek. He jerked away as if she'd grazed him with a burning flame.

Compassion squeezed her heart. "What happened to you, Daniel?"

A light drizzle began to fall, but the sun continued to shine. Up ahead on the distant horizon a rainbow glowed. She'd never seen anything so magnificent—a prism of sparkling color diving into the boiling waves.

"Maybe you should go below deck."

She shook her head. "No, I don't mind the rain. I don't get to see a view like this everyday. Isn't it incredible? How two total opposites can form something so breathtaking?"

Daniel didn't reply. He just continued staring blankly ahead. Moving to his left, she did something terribly brazen. She touched the hair that veiled his cheek, brushing it aside. In an instant his fingers clenched hers. "What the hell are you doing?" Panic flared in his voice.

"I just—I wanted to see your face."

Realizing how tightly he clasped her hand, he loosened his grip, releasing her. "Don't ever do that again." His clipped, non-negotiable tone delivered the message loud and clear.

In the past, Jenny would have backed off, retreated into silence, but not now. "Why not? What are you so afraid of?" she asked. Then, unable to stop herself, she added, "You're the most beautiful person I've ever met."

Her words touched him; she could tell. His taciturn expression vanished, and for a brief instant before doubt set in, she sensed he almost believed her. "Beautiful? Have you looked at me?"

"More than you know."

Something blazed in his eyes that made her gut clench and heat stir in her belly. To her delighted surprise, he raised his hand, tenderly cupping her face.

He was going to kiss her.

The ground beneath her feet moved at the thought. Or maybe it was just the boat hopping along the waves, but right now she didn't want to think about that. She just wanted to think about the way his thumb trailed up her cheek to settle at the corner of her mouth, stroking it. Something deep and primitive told her Daniel's kiss would be as magical as everything else about him. She closed her eyes, leaned into his wide, rough palm...

GREAT cheap FUN

Discover eBooks!

THE FASTEST WAY TO GET THE HOTTEST NAMES

Get your favorite authors on your favorite reader, long before they're out in print! Ebooks from Samhain go wherever you go, and work with whatever you carry—Palm, PDF, Mobi, and more.

Samhain Publishing Ltd

WWW.SAMHAINPUBLISHING.COM